# Ocean so Wide

Other works by

*Nichole Giles*

*Descendant*
*Birthright*
*Legacy*

*Sea so Blue*
*Water so Deep*

NICHOLE GILES

*For all the survivors.*

# Chapter One

## James

**March 17**
*22 days since departure*

A THICK LETTER FROM ORANGE Coast College glared at James from the kitchen counter. He wasn't sure when his father had left the house and made the fifty-yard journey to the mailbox, or why a college was sending him recruitment packets two months before graduation. It felt wrong that any school might want him when he'd deserted his team during playoffs.

By some miracle, he'd maintained a league shot record for the season, and though he'd all but dropped his pursuit of scholarship offers, a handful of recruiters continued to reach out to him.

A label pasted on the slim brown envelope hinted that the package was more than simply junk mail, especially since said label—slightly askew—appeared to have been placed by hand. His stomach jumped with nervous anticipation as he turned away, ignoring the mail. He didn't have time for college. Awaiting his high school diploma had become little more than obligational torture, since every morning he forced himself to class—mainly to keep the promise that he wouldn't waste his life while hoping for a miracle.

Though she'd begged him not to, he continued to wait for Emma's return. Every day, for however long he could manage, he trekked to the private cove and planted himself in the sand, where he shared the details of his life. He imagined the wind spiriting his love across the mighty expanse, reminding her of all she'd left behind, and inspiring her to find her way home. Though he knew his words couldn't reach her, giving voice to the tumbling thunder of emotions provided a method of therapy.

But as his grades crashed, his bank account drained, and his social life died a silent, empty demise, awareness plunged him deeper. Promise aside, he couldn't keep this up forever. Not if he wanted to build a life, a future.

Desperation clawed at the torn halves of his soul.

Though she hadn't materialized in his presence, he knew with every fiber of himself that Emma had visited the cove at least once, maybe more. Her sense of timing must be off from living fathoms below the deep, dark blue. He couldn't guess how the Mer measured time, but on one particularly tough day, only weeks after she'd left, he'd arrived to find a tiny, white pearl sitting on the ledge where she used to leave her cell phone. That pearl had become the seed of hope that kept him afloat.

His motorcycle key chimed as he twirled it around his finger, grabbing a water bottle on his way out the door. As he stepped onto the porch, curiosity turned him around and marched him back to the kitchen to shove the letter in his pocket. He'd left his earring on the ledge in place of Emma's pearl, and though over a week had passed, it hadn't been moved. He hoped she would return soon. Even if only for a moment, seeing her could bolster his courage, giving him the strength to survive a while longer. More than anything, he needed her to know that he hadn't given up.

On school.

On basketball.

On life.

Or on her.

Even if the letter was junk, she would know that he still had options. His father had collected a stack of college correspondence, all addressed to James. Maybe it was time to open some.

The idea of college still felt like a pipe dream. He wasn't sure there was still a scenario in which he would magically be handed a scholarship, but though he'd never considered them before, he realized that there were other ways to pay for his education. Financial aid, grants, government programs—and probably more if he invested time to research.

He strapped on his helmet and straddled Lola—the name he'd given his bike. After Emma vanished, loneliness had threatened to crush him. He'd spent hours, even days, riding to everywhere and nowhere, but always on Lola. She'd become his go-to, the only thing left in life over which he had control. The engine rumbled as he balanced her weight between his thighs and accelerated down the driveway, setting his sights on the cove.

After Emma's sudden disappearance, the police had kept him on their radar. From what he could tell, he wasn't under *constant* surveillance, but it wouldn't have mattered. Paranoia followed wherever he went, as though walls and roads and trees had eyes that unpeeled his skin, layer by layer, until they'd revealed each secret James kept buried. To safeguard Emma's private sanctuary, he'd developed a habit of taking a different route every day, including multiple detours that led inland and across town.

At a strip-mall intersection, a young man sold flowers out of a bucket, holding a sign that read:

*Don't wait until it's too late.*

The sentiment flooded James with nostalgia. He'd never had a chance to bring Emma flowers, or take her on dates, or buy her gifts—and there was a part of him that desperately needed that opportunity. He waved the man over and offered some bills in exchange for a single aqua rose, wrapped in cellophane. He tucked the flower inside his jacket, zipping it close to his heart to protect it from the wind's harsh battery.

If only he'd been able to protect Emma the same way, keeping her next to his heart, where she would be safe from everything and everyone.

Since the police knew his motorcycle, rather than park along the curb, he pulled into the thick vegetation growing at the top of the cliff and rolled Lola into a shrub that curved into a "C" just above the top of his handlebars, creating a canopy of vines that stretched back toward the dirt. He dropped his helmet on the seat and navigated the narrow, twisted path, using the sheer cliff-face as a handhold to steady him. Far below, aqua waves lunged at the rocky shoals, foam-tipped giants that rose, shrunk, and then swirled back out across the wide expanse of ocean.

Once he reached sea-level, James leaped over rocky ledges, across tide-pools, and around wild plants bursting with colorful blooms, until he reached the furthest point, and then he swung around the threshold and into the privacy of the hidden cove. Her cove.

Honey-gold sun blazed against sand and rocks, reflecting off the surface of the water and sending warmth into the shaded cave, at the same time illuminating the crystal depth for hundreds of feet below. James stood at the edge of the water, absorbing what he could from the gusty breeze, while he projected his love across the vastness, hoping that somehow Emma would feel it.

He unzipped his jacket and laid it on the ledge, along with the flower, then dropped into the sand, waving the letter like a fan while he built up the courage to open it. "Looks like college is still possible. Maybe." She couldn't hear, of course, but he spoke to her anyway. He tore open the top and unfolded the single page inside.

*Dear Mr. Phelps,*

*Thank you for sending us a letter of interest, along with the digital reel showcasing your basketball skills. We would like to schedule a meeting to go over some options for your potential attendance at our school, along with a tour of the campus and sports facilities, and an introduction to the coaches who oversee the basketball program. Please call the administrative secretary, Lisa, to set up a time and day that is convenient for you.*

*Sincerely,*
*Arnold Bronson*
*Dean of students, Orange Coast College*

Triumph thundered, more powerful than the surf that crashed around him. "Yes!" he screamed, and then crowed the victory of predatory bird, startling a seagull that swooped toward him into flailing for another location.

Standing to pace, James re-read the letter, crinkling the paper in his hand as he debated about how best to share the news with Emma. He settled on leaving the envelope with a note scribbled on the back—even though leaving a note would require trekking up the hill to retrieve a pen from Lola's cargo hold.

Not in any hurry to make the hike a second time, he lingered, drawing hearts in the sand while he spoke as if Emma could actually hear him. He told her about working for his uncle, and expressed relief about his father's recent attempt to seek treatment for depression. He discussed school, how he was down to weeks before the end of the torture, and how torn he felt about potentially attending college.

After over an hour of gazing across the broad slash of water, he stood and brushed off his backside, and then trudged across the tide pools and uneven ground to climb the hill to the hidden grove. His new parking spot proved harder to reach, but it kept Lola out of sight, and would hopefully alleviate suspicion if the police happened by.

He dug out a pen and braced the envelope on the seat so he could write . . . something. What should he say? How could he explain the storm of emotions that had deluged him since she'd surged into his life and then floated away again?

*I love you* seemed . . . too small. And *I miss you* didn't come close to defining the aching hole she'd left in his life. There was only so much space on the envelope. Frustrated with his lack of romantic poetry, he settled on:

*I'm still here.*

*~J*

He folded the envelope in half and replaced the pen, startling when a twig snapped nearby, and bushes rustled, stirring the scent of damp earth to mix with the salty brine of the sea breeze. Coming across another person—either friend or stranger—was not in his best interest, so James progressed silently across the vine-covered ground until he reached the trail, where he squatted below the edge and waited for several long minutes. When no other sound followed, he stood and, breathing a sigh of relief, crunched down the precarious hill to the treacherous ground below.

He swung into the cove, heart thudding with anxiety, and muscles bunching with frustration. This was no way to live his life. The sensation of being followed was not new or unusual to him, but hearing noises to substantiate the fear was a first. Breath tightening his chest, he listened at the thin, cave wall, and by the time his breathing evened out, decided he was being paranoid. He'd seen both birds and squirrels, along with the occasional stray neighborhood pet skulking around before.

James crossed to the ledge and secured the envelope under a heavy rock, next to the flower. Should he have written her a true love letter? He had zero experience in wooing a woman he couldn't pursue in person, although, he also had zero experience being in love. "Pretty words aren't necessary, right?" he asked the empty cave. "You already know, don't you?"

"I do."

James whirled, hope leaping into his throat, and then melting into panic at the sight of Emma's best friend, Heather, standing barefooted on the sand. On Emma's sand. In Emma's cove. "You do what?" James croaked.

Her hands fisted at her side, and her face twisted into a vicious scowl. "I know you did something to Emma. You're the reason she's gone."

James pressed his fingers to his eyes, shaking his head in a jumble of fear and anger. "We've been through this already. I love Emma. I would never do anything to hurt her. I miss her as badly as you do." Worse, he was sure.

She stepped closer, inches shorter than him, but the fierce anger in her eyes sharp enough to cut down a ten-foot giant. "You were the last person to see her, to talk to her, and no one has seen her since. No trace of her has been found, except what you brought back with you. How can you have no explanation for where she's gone if you weren't part of her disappearance?"

"Because I don't know!" he shouted. "Don't you think if I knew I would be there too? Don't you think if I knew, she'd be here right now?"

Another step toward him. "If she was still alive, Emma would be with her family. She would never let *anything* keep her from her brother."

He swallowed a lump of pain lodged in his throat. "I know. I agree. You're absolutely right. Still doesn't make me guilty of anything. I would *never* try to keep her from Keith."

Heather drilled a finger into James' chest. "Tell me the truth. You killed my friend, didn't you?"

"No, I didn't." James swatted away the offending finger. "Of course I didn't. I could never hurt her. Not ever." He stumbled backward, leaning his elbow on the ledge as the weight of his entire life teetered on his shoulders. "Besides, if Emma were dead, we would have found her body by now. The reason we haven't is because she's not dead."

Unconvinced, Heather dug her toes into the sand, spitting with every word that spewed from between her lips. "Not if you were good at hiding bodies. For all we know, you could be a serial killer with a stash of corpses in your secret lair."

Annoyed to have Heather invade the place that James considered so sacred, so secret, he slid his arms into his jacket, determined to get her out too. "Yep," he sneered. "That's me. Hiding a stash of stiffs in a shallow cave I can barely get into by myself without the risk of tumbling into the ocean."

Heather stormed around him and snatched up the note. "What's this? A note to your accomplice? Should I have brought a bodyguard? Are you going to kill me, too?"

James plucked the note from her fingers. "I might. It would probably be wise for you to leave now. Go home and never come back here."

"Oh, I'll go home. And I'll sleep well, tonight too. You, on the other hand, should get used to sleeping in a tiny cement box, because that's where I hope you spend the rest of your life." She tried to tuck the note into her pocket, but James wrestled it away from her, inadvertently ripping the envelope in half. She crowed in triumph, stuffing her half into her pocket and eyeing the flower. "That looks like a memorial to me." She turned her back on James and teetered around the ledge. "Interesting, considering you've told the police over and over again that you have don't know what happened to Emma."

"I don't." It wasn't a lie—he had the name of a place, but no location, means of contact, or real communication. "But I'm going to find her, Heather. And bring her back. Then you'll see, you'll know."

She spit on the ground at his feet. "The only thing I see, the only thing I know is that I will not rest until you're behind bars, charged with my best friend's murder."

# Chapter Two

## Emma

EMMA LAY LISTLESS IN A seaweed hammock within the walls of her palace prison, staring at the glowing blue plankton swimming around inside the clear, ice ceiling. It was a nice room, especially when compared to others she'd seen throughout the strange building. Coral walls had been decorated with a pattern of shiny abalone and smooth, white shells that swept like a wave from corner to corner.

Upon her arrival, she'd received a wardrobe of exquisite accessories, as well as access to gold trading chips—which may have been created from broken pirate doubloons—for purchasing things at the market she'd seen when she first passed through the city.

She'd yet to make use of either, since she hadn't been allowed to leave the palace, and had spent the majority of her time moping in her room. She didn't want to see more of the underwater city, or learn to appreciate the educational opportunity to understand her new culture. Homesickness had dampened any curiosity about her second heritage.

The soft sand flooring didn't bother her, since she rarely walked on it, preferring instead to swim. She was officially full mermaid now—this according to Merrick—and had thought her legs might fuse into a full-fledged fin, like some of the others she'd seen, but like Merrick, Emma's legs remained separated, exhibiting the human portion of her genes.

Every so often, she'd dangle her legs over the edge of the hammock and drag her toes along the silt, digging them in as she reminded herself that unlike the other mermaids, she was lucky. She still had toes.

The glowing azure plankton pulsed with the change of current, soothing and hypnotic. She hadn't left her hammock bed in over a week. During her first days here, she'd hoped to find an exit around which she could build an escape plan, so she'd humored the Sea King and attended his court, his meals—but that was all, and most days was more than she should have done.

She'd accepted her grandfather's *offer* to live in the palace, and pleaded for time to adjust before a forced joining with Merrick. When her grandfather acquiesced, she tried to be a dutiful Princess, but as time wore on, the pining to go home matured, sucking away her energy and submerging her into a deep depression she was unable to combat.

Her chambermaid, Maia, knocked on the doorframe, since the only privacy screen was a traditional Atlantian beaded curtain. "Princess Emmalina? I've brought your mid-tide meal."

"Enter." She dug her toes into the sand, still a tad embarrassed about her lack of an actual fin.

Maia glided in, her delicate frame expertly balancing a tray filled with a variety of raw, half-wiggling fish and a side of seaweed. "On today's menu, we have unopened clams and a baby swordfish, but I can bring you something else if you don't like those choices."

Emma bowed away from the disgusting spectacle, longing for a simple can of store-bought tuna, or a salad with creamy dressing. She knew she'd become dangerously thin, but persisted the struggle over eating a steady diet of raw fish, no matter how she worked to persuade herself that raw wasn't disgusting, or unhealthy. "Leave it with the others."

Maia drifted around and noticed Emma's tear-stained face, and sat the tray on the table next to Emma's swinging bed. "You must eat sometime. You feel better with nourishment."

Emma wiped away her tears, lacking the will to argue. "Only if it has the power to send me home."

A stream of bubbles floated from Maia's gills as she let out a sigh. "Eat. Tangaroa has summoned you before the council. You'll need your strength to pretend you are happy, as you do each mealtime."

Emma rolled listlessly again so her fingers trailed into the bowl of raw clams. She picked one out, then dropped it again, shuddering. "I miss cooked food."

"What is cooked?" Curiosity piqued, Maia snapped to attention. "I will get you some of this thing you desire."

Emma used her hands, attempting to demonstrate fire, and then a stove—neither of which Maia understood. "Cooked is when you use fire to change the taste and texture of the fish."

"What is fire? How does it change a fish?" Maia planted herself on a stool near Emma's dressing table, riveted by details of another way of life. "Will you tell me all about the land? Tell me where you've come from and the ways of human people, and I will show you where you belong and the ways of the Mer."

Thoughts of James and her family engulfed Emma, stealing her ability to talk, and move, and exist underwater. Everything here was different, even language. The Mer would never understand what she'd lost, because they didn't understand emotions the way she did, and some feelings couldn't be explained. But maybe if she told someone, unloaded some of the burden, she would at least find the strength to go on.

She rolled onto her side and faced Maia over the edge of her hammock. "Fire is like holding captive a slice of the sun."

"But the sun is dangerous, my Princess, as is the air."

Emma remembered the warmth on her shoulders, the brightness in her eyes and the breeze in her hair as she drove her convertible up the coast. How it felt to breathe, to recognize scents and feel the difference in altitude whenever she went anywhere far. The sweltering heat of dry sand beneath her feet, grass under her fingers, the cool, rough stones in her cove that lacked formations and moss. She remembered the fear of her past, the pain of fists connecting with her face and body, the stabbing wounds inflicted every time judging eyes trailed her in the halls at school, and finally understood that what had happened then was part of another lifetime.

That was before. Before James had come into her life and forced her to feel again. Made her proud to be who she was, regardless of what that meant. Her past had no bearing on her future, and only as little or as much meaning to her true self as she allowed.

"The sun is a wonder, Maia." She rose from her hammock and used the mini-spear—intended for opening clams—to draw a round sun on the sandy floor. "Glorious and warm. A bright orange ball in the sky that forces people outside, urges plants to grow, and heats the surface of land."

A memory James flashed in her mind—the fervor in his eyes, the security of his embrace, and the ferocity with which he'd defended her and Keith, despite her initial resistance to his advances. "The sun and its fire can transform water into air. It burns with the zap of an eel, and squeezes as the tentacles of an octopus around your middle. It can turn white skin red, and then make it fall off, leaving behind pale, new layers."

Maia shifted, but her attention remained riveted on the circular pattern Emma carved into the sand. "I don't believe I would like fire."

"Fire dwells inside me," Emma told her, entranced by her own hypnotic drawing. "Fire. Not water. I have to find a way to go home."

"You are home, Princess." Maia's fin swished, compelling her toward the entrance as if to block Emma from an inevitable departure. In that moment, Emma realized that the only way for her to escape the prying eyes of those around her was to create an inner circle of people she could trust, people who wouldn't raise suspicion. People who had something to gain. "Of course. Of course, I'm home. I only meant that I can't explain land to you here. If you really want to understand, I will have to show you."

Maia bobbed in the heavy water. "We cannot leave the palace. The Sea King . . ."

"Is my grandfather. And he doesn't decide what I get to do or not do." She picked up one of the gold pieces. "He has even given me money to visit the market."

Maia's lips twisted in doubt. "But you do not wish to visit the market."

"No. We're going somewhere else. Somewhere lovely and peaceful and smiled upon by the golden sun." When Maia didn't respond, Emma insisted, "No one will ever know." Her mind scrambled for a solid, strong reason that would convince Maia to join her in visiting the cove. She had only been allowed to go back once since her arrival, and she felt certain that Merrick had taken her in secret, with hopes of winning her over. She also recognized that Merrick continued to use the place as a segue between earth and sea. The knowledge gave her hope that maybe James still visited too.

"I can show you my world, the fire of the sun, and return in time for the council meeting. We'll bring the King a gift, and he'll be happy."

"What kind of gift?" she asked.

"Something no one else has given him." Emma thought of the feathers she'd once collected along the beach with Gran, and that she sometimes found in her cove. Seagull, pelican, crane—all manner of fowl hunted the shoreline, leaving behind treasures from the air. Treasures no one else who lived in the sea could give him. Treasures that people collected on land, though humans were free to see birds often and regularly. Surely the Sea King would be happy to receive such an exclusive and unique gift. "You'll see how wonderful it is."

Maia frowned, crossing her arms as she continued to watch Emma with suspicion.

Energy surged through Emma, her brain racing. Maybe James would be there. Maybe she could breathe air, for however long her shrunken lungs would allow. At the very least, she could feel the warmth of the sun on her face again and inhale the salty scent given off in the place where ocean and sky collided.

Not wanting to come across as suspicious, she searched a wardrobe of mermaid accessories and found a cloth of woven seaweed that had been embedded with tiny pearls, and tied it around her bright red hair. "Come with me. I promise, we'll be back in time. We won't get in trouble."

The idea of swimming to the surface sent blood rushing through her body—so much that she felt ill-equipped to deal with the extra energy.

When Maia continued to block the doorway, Emma shoved past and continued toward the back galley. "Please come," she said. "I'll show you the sky. I promise, we'll be back."

Emma peeked around the corner, sizing up the guards at the mouth of the tunnel through which they would access the city gate, and from there, the open sea.

"Princess, I am not sure this is a good idea." Maia twisted her hands together, crossing her arms as if doing so would keep her heart from beating out of her brightly decorated chest.

"Nonsense." Emma waved off Maia's growing concerns. "The Sea King is going to love the gift we bring for him."

A well-built, young merman who wore a guard's sash exited the tunnel, conveniently providing a distraction by collapsing the moment he arrived. While the guards focused on the injured merman, Emma and Maia made their unobtrusive escape by slipping into the tunnel.

"Of course, I wish to please the Sea King." Keeping pace with Emma, Maia continued to peek behind them at the shrinking blue light that marked the city entrance. "But *displeasing* him leaves me fearful."

"How will gifting him an extraordinary treasure displease the Sea King?" The question was rhetorical, and meant as a distraction to prevent thoughts of turning back. She didn't necessarily *need* Maia to accompany her to the cove, but Emma hoped that having her present for the journey would soften the blow when her grandfather found out she'd left the city unguarded.

"It's not the gift I'm worried about," Maia muttered. "But the means with which we must find it. I do not wish to be known as the maid who directed the mighty Tangaroa's granddaughter—his only remaining heir—into danger."

"All the finest gifts involve a degree of risk. Besides, I'm no stranger to land. You don't need to worry—we'll be fine." Emma quickened her stroke until she'd cast herself into the draw of the shoreline current—a movement of tide that would draw them up and out. As she ascended from the most frigid depth, the constant pressure holding tight around her insides loosened its hold, warming her muscles and allowing further mobility. The mermaids reached the end of the channel and burst into the open sea, rising beneath the pillars of rock from which Merrick usually guarded.

When they reached the shallows, excitement burned in Emma's chest and sent her speeding ahead. Would he be there? What he would say to her? Did he still miss her, or had he moved on? She wondered how her family was adjusting, if James had received his scholarship, and if so, to which school? Eagerness shot her forward, until she narrowly avoided colliding into the ground level cliff. She lifted herself out of the water, her body weight heavier than she remembered after the almost weightless sensation of wheeling in the buoyant ocean.

Sadly, she found the cave empty. By the time Maia caught up, Emma had planted herself on the sand, soaking up sunshine in the spot where she'd once sat with James. In the bright light, her pale skin contained traces of blue that hadn't existed before. Merrick had explained multiple times that her body would soon adapt to her new home, but she hoped this change wasn't permanent. Not only did she enjoy standing out from the other mermaids, but those differences served as a continual reminder of her goal to remain human. Distinctions in her appearance allowed Emma a layer of insulation that kept her one step removed from the culture of Mer. She wouldn't become attached, which would help her to remain whole when she left again.

Maia bobbed nearby, refusing to depart the safety of the water, but watching—fascinated—as Emma stood on her feet, stretched, and shook out her wet hair. "This is my place," she explained. "Where I used to come to swim while the change occurred." As she twirled in a circle, a flash of blue drew her toward the ledge shelf, where she used to keep her cell phone and car keys.

A flower, wrapped in cellophane. Emma brought it to her nose to breathe in the sweet, floral perfume, so specific to land. James and Gran were the only two humans who knew that this was her place—the one place she would come if ever she could. Since Gran was physically unable to visit, the gift must have come from James. Recently enough that the silky petals had not yet begun to wilt.

He'd been here recently. Maybe only hours ago. Sadness cast a shadow over her excitement of finding the flower. *I missed him. Probably by minutes.*

A light breeze swirled into the cave, flowing around her like eddying water and rustling a paper beneath the flower. She tried to make sense of what was only— apparently—half a note. She read and re-read the crumpled page, unable to make sense of the words. What was missing, and why?

How much time had passed since she'd been forced to Atlantis? She studied the sky, deliberating the amount of brine in the scented air, the warmth of the sun, the clear, blue expanse dotted with only tiny wisps of clouds. Had the seasons changed? Had she missed graduation? Would James spend his life pining? Waiting in this cove for her to return? She yearned to know if he missed her as badly as she missed him. And yet, if she somehow failed to return, she hoped James would move on and find happiness, and perhaps love again.

"Princess Emmalina." At the sound of Maia's gasp, Emma spun, crumpling the note into her fist.

Merrick dragged himself from the water, glaring with red-hot anger as he waited for his fin to dry so he could stand. "Visiting this place is dangerous for you, Emmalina. And for your handmaid. You have been warned of this, more than once."

"Leave Maia out of it." Emma clasped the paper tighter. "I was only showing her the shore. I needed to get out of that dungeon, Merrick. I've barely even left my room since I arrived, and that's completely unlike me."

Merrick glowered at Maia anyway. "You know better than to allow her to leave. The Sea King gave orders."

Maia cowered under Merrick's hot stare, her shoulders sinking deeper into the surf as if the waves could somehow hide her. "I could no sooner have stopped her visiting this place than stopped you from following. And the Sea King will be pleased when we bring him a land-gift."

Merrick blinked. "Gift?"

"I'm looking for something." Emma's eyes skimmed the ground near the mouth of the cave, biting her lip when she found no feathers. "To bring back to my grandfather."

"Not another human, I hope."

Merrick had never been one to joke, and that he had done so now startled a giggle out of Emma. "We both know that would be a bad idea, on every level."

The set of Merrick's shoulders relaxed in a way Emma had never seen before. "As was visiting this place."

Sighing through her mouth, rather than her gills, Emma set her flower aside. "I've come to retrieve a gift as an offering to the Sea King. Let me locate it, and then we can go." Already feeling the tightening in her chest, the way her shrunken lungs contracted and her heart raced, Emma scooted along the cliff and around the edge of the cove. At the rocky tide pools, she plucked a flower from a nearby hibiscus shrub. "This will do." She offered the bloom to Maia. "Don't crush it."

As she stood again, Merrick's hand clamped Emma's wrist. She tried to yank it away, but though her muscle strength had built, she was no match for Merrick. "Let go of me. I'm not going to run away."

"Not until we see the Sea King." Dragging Emma with him, Merrick dove, returning them to the water, and then to Atlantis. As they departed, Emma dropped the flower James had left, dipping its silky petals into the sand, where it shriveled in the briny air.

# Chapter Three

## James

HIS DAY CONTINUED TO GO downhill when James showed up at work, only to find a new guy hauling the stone—a job that should have been left for James. "Who are you?" He asked.

The guy lifted another box of tile and continued into the job site. "Name's Matthew. I started yesterday."

"James," he muttered, not offering his hand to shake, since Matthew had his arms full. "Where's Ryan?"

Matthew jutted his chin toward the supply truck. "Unloading."

James stalked to the truck and up the ramp to where his uncle carted an ungodly amount of weight in ceramic tile. "Did you replace me?"

"I got another assistant." Methodically, Ryan set his stack at the top of the ramp and dusted his hands off. "I have deadlines, James. And you keep showing up late, or, more often, not at all, which puts me in a bind, because for every hour that you aren't here, I have to work two to catch up."

Guilt niggled at James' conscience. He hadn't meant to put his uncle in that positon. "I'm sorry. I just have a lot on my mind, and . . ."

"Oh, I know," Ryan said, sarcasm dripping into his voice. "Your teenage life struggles are so overwhelmingly important that any grown-up commitments can, and should, be set aside."

"Not *more* important than everything else," James insisted, his hackles raised. "But overwhelming is a good word."

Ryan bent to pick up his stack and lugged it down the ramp. "Join the club. We all have lives to live, and jobs to do. You're no different from the rest of us, except that responsible adults actually show up for work every day—on time—regardless of whatever else is happening. That's what grownup responsibility is."

"I'm sorry," James started, following Ryan inside. "I swear I would never intentionally make your job harder, I—"

"Don't apologize," Ryan snapped. "Be a man. Show up. If you have depression, admit it and get treatment. Don't let life turn you into your father—who, by the way, at least goes to work."

The dart to his heart struck true. James' father—for all that he spent his home-time lazy, lonely, and at an all-time low—continued to show up at his job. No one could claim he enjoyed it, or found a single ounce of fulfillment, but he hadn't missed a day since James' mother had left. They might be broke, but their rent was paid, their utilities mostly stayed connected, and when James contributed, they usually had a few groceries in the fridge.

"Ryan." James took the box from his uncle and set it next to the room where they'd start. "I'm so sorry. Let me make it up to you. I need this job."

"Don't apologize. Fix the problem." Ryan pivoted, heading back to the truck for the next box. "In the meantime, I'm cutting your hours to cover a second assistant, because if I don't, I have to fire you and find a replacement. I don't want to do that, because I like to tell myself that I'm taking care of you, keeping you out of trouble. That's another part of my grownup responsibility."

Heather's threat reared up. From the way she talked, *trouble* was coming for James, whether he was prepared or not. Following Ryan's lead, he hoisted a box of tile and carried it into the house where they were working. "Do you still need my help today then?"

Ryan eyeballed the massive great room, sporting over a thousand feet of sub-flooring. "More hands make faster work. But James, I mean it. Just because you're my sister's kid doesn't mean I'm honor bound to let you take advantage of me. Either you start communicating, or you find another job." With that, he stalked off, leaving James to ask the new guy for his assignment.

His uncle had never expressed such frustration at him. James had officially hit an all-time low.

When he arrived home that night and found a police cruiser parked in front of his house, James realized he'd lost the ability to be surprised. Fear snaked up his spine as he stowed his motorcycle under the carport and removed his helmet, shaking the dust out of his hair, and then smoothing a nervous hand down his too-long locks. He couldn't remember the last time he'd had a haircut. Or a shave. The stubble he'd once worn so proudly had grown into an unruly, shabby mess. To top it off, tile dust covered his work clothes and skin, leaving streaks of brown where sweat had cut through. No clean-cut working-boy impression to be made here.

Mustering his courage, James entered the house to greet his father, along with Detective Peters, the officer who had helped him and Emma when Keith went missing. James held out a hand of greeting. "Detective. I'd like to say it's good to see you, but when the cops show up at your house unannounced, it's usually not good news."

The man shook James's offered hand. "True story."

Once the courtesy greetings were dispensed, and James sat awkwardly on the couch, a mere two feet of distance between him and the detective, Peters began. "I suspect you know why I'm here."

"Heather." James had to fight to keep from rolling his eyes. "Look, I've given you statements three times already. My story hasn't changed."

Peters sighed. "Right. I know that. The problem is that we still don't have a body. Keith can remember nothing except that you were there, and last time he saw Emma, she was talking to you. Both of your cell phones pinged off the same tower that night, putting you with Emma the night she disappeared. Now Heather's thrown in some *serious* accusations. I don't think Emma's family suspects you of foul play, but they believe she's still alive, which is common in cases investigated without the presence of a body. Once they get past that belief, the Harris family will sing to a different tune." He paused for the final delivery. "No matter how this plays out, it looks extremely bad for you."

James stiffened. "She *is* still alive somewhere. I know you think I made her disappear, but I didn't. I couldn't do anything to hurt her—not ever. *No one* wants her back more than I do, I swear."

The detective tapped his fingers on his knee, choosing his words with care. "You were the last person to see her. You returned with her brother, her car, her clothes and her cell phone—but not her. Other than Keith, you have no witnesses, and I have to be honest, James, if you were on trial and I was a member of the jury, you'd be looking at a conviction."

Desperation clawed at his throat. "But the video—"

"Coercion. Editing skills. Bad lighting, a good actress with a similar look—that video is not enough when the rest of the evidence points directly at you."

James' heart thundered in his chest. "I didn't hurt Emma."

Peters stood. "Then help us find her. Look, I know there's something you're not telling me. Now's the time for you to share whatever information you're holding back, otherwise, you'll be answering for more serious charges than outing a secret."

James pinned his focus on the wall behind the detective, too stunned to move. His father stood, grunting with the effort, and pointed at James. "That's enough. Don't say another word." He directed his next words at the detective. "My son is done talking to cops without a lawyer."

Peters raised his brows, but didn't seem all that surprised. "Does that mean you're finished cooperating with the case?"

"It means." Richard's commanding tone was a voice James hadn't heard in years. "The next time you have questions, make an appointment."

"Okay then." Detective Peters flipped his notebook closed and slid it into his jacket pocket. "Guess that will do for now." He stood, offering a friendly hand, which neither of the other men accepted. Peters let his arm drop to his side and started for the door. "James, we're considering you a person of interest in Emma's disappearance. It would be best for everyone involved—especially you—if you don't leave the state."

He nodded in acknowledgement, numbness flowing into his limbs as his father ushered the detective out and locked the door behind him. Then Richard returned to his James, draping his arm across James' shoulders in a show of support. "Don't worry, Son. We'll get this sorted out."

James embraced his father, trying not to think about how awkward the practice had become since the man had almost doubled in size over the last few years. "I don't know, Pops. From the way he talks, I wonder if the only way to get me out of this mess would be to find Emma and bring her back."

"So let's do that, then." Richard released James, wheezing with effort as he returned to his chair.

James scrubbed his hands into his dusty hair, causing white tile powder to rain on his eyelashes. "It's not that easy."

Richard dropped into his recliner, clearly relieved to be sitting again. "I'm only going to ask this once, and I promise I'll believe you, as long as I can see that you're telling the truth." He leaned a thick elbow on the arm of his chair, tipping the entire frame to one side. "Did you do something to that girl? Do you know where she is?"

James fell back against the couch cushions, shaking his head in despair. "No, and yes. I mean, I didn't do anything except hold her while she cried, and kiss her when she didn't. I don't know where she is, exactly, but I do know . . . she's alive somewhere. Somewhere the rest of us can't go, because if we could, I'd have rescued her long before now."

"Okay." Richard sighed, reclining his chair. "I hate to say this, especially at such a critical point in your young life. But . . . if you feel a need to leave the country, I'll sell my car to come up with some cash."

"I wouldn't know what to do with it." Warmth spread in James' chest. His father hadn't offered him money in years—not even reimbursement for groceries when he'd picked up specifically requested items. "Besides, I've been instructed not to leave, remember?"

His father hummed, ignoring the reminder, but the idea of selling things for cash planted an idea in James' mind. He'd considered learning to scuba dive, but had discovered that scuba wasn't a cheap venture. If he were to sell his motorcycle, maybe he could afford lessons and equipment.

"I hear Mexico's nice this time of year. Seems to be a hot ticket for petty thieves and lawbreakers, even your age." The offhanded remark suggested how much faith his father had—in the legal system, and also James' ability to get out of this mess on his own.

Taking his cue to exit, James headed for the bathroom, where he hoped a hot shower would clear his head. "Thanks Dad. I'll keep that in mind."

# Chapter Four

## Emma

FOREBODING STRUCK EMMA AS MERRICK towed her into the palace—governing in the same way he'd transported her the first time she visited the city. A tremor reverberated from the bottoms of her webbed feet to the bluing tips of her hair.

Her stately grandfather held court from the dais, while behind him, remains of the ice-walled box slowly melted, blending with the surrounding water and leaving no trace of the cold chips of ice. It had deteriorated so rapidly, that it now stood only half of its original size, its structural walls thin and brittle. Now that she lived here, Emma recognized that the thaw was caused by a minor rise in water temperature as summer weather advanced on land. The esteemed, rainbow-haired Sea King spun away from his aid, halting speech mid-sentence when the trio—Emma, Merrick, and Maia—appeared.

"Ah, and here she is. We were just discussing you, Emmalina. My granddaughter, offspring of my fallen son."

"Were you? And what, might I ask, were you discussing?" Emma leveled her backbone, hoping to appear as regal and elegant as the aging Sea King. Since timid behavior was an expected norm in her grandfather's court, she determined to behave exactly the opposite of that expectation. With thousands of Mer living in the city, she had the most to prove, the most to lose, and potentially, the biggest payoff to gain. She only required one thing: The medicinal necklace she'd so carelessly given to Merrick. That necklace would allow her more time ashore—time enough to find James and talk to him, hold him. Time to visit her family. It wouldn't be enough, and she knew that even as she thought it, but if they couldn't find another, more permanent solution, at least they could all gain closure from one last visit.

Tangaroa rose from his throne, leaning his weight on a worn-out, oxidizing trident, compelling himself nearer to his granddaughter. "The return of my only living heir is a regular subject with the Mer-council. You are the future of Atlantis, after all."

"Oh." Though it took some effort, she willed her traitor face to form an expression of light happiness. She'd learned the bulk of information about her new culture by listening more often than she spoke, and by now an evolution of strategy swirled inside her. If she could recover her necklace, she might be able to breathe on land again—however temporary. At least long enough to travel far away, before she was forced to swim again. Life in another city of Mer would be nothing like the life she'd had on land, but at least her future would be hers to choose, rather than dictated by virtual strangers claiming to care. And then, once free to live as she chose, she would study how the pendant had kept her breathing on land, and attempt to duplicate the process.

A strand of Emma's hair floated toward Tangaroa, and he caught it, rubbing it between his fingers as if developing an unusual fondness for her. "Emmalina, you are of age. I recognize that you continue to adjust to your new life, but the time has come for you to take a mate." His attention landed on Merrick, then on Emma, and the foreboding morphed into a tremor of panic.

Words tumbled from her mouth before she could stop them. "I'm not ready. I'm too young. I don't want to join with Merrick."

Tangaroa let the hair slither through is fingers as the current shifted, urging it to float away. "You are a

Princess of Atlantis, and of prime age to reproduce. Merrick has awaited your joining since you were a youngling. He was transported to our city for this purpose, acting as guardian of the gate, and of you, while he awaited your change. He has constructed a dwelling for your comfort, complete with the air pockets you so enjoy."

Maia fluttered, and Emma warned her and Merrick both with the flash of a single, piercing glance. She would not allow them to tattle about how she'd just visited the surface, which happened to be the biggest air pocket in existence. "Grandfather, you know my feelings about this. Merrick kidnapped my brother and forced my transformation months before it should have completed. I won't become his mate. I refuse."

Merrick shifted with discomfort, his blue skin purpling with the humiliation of rejection, but Emma refused to validate his actions by regretting the harsh response. As much as her grandfather had vowed to allow her a period of adjustment, she could only stall for so long before being forced into the joining. The idea left a dry, chalky taste in her mouth that reminded her of eating sand as a toddler.

The Sea King returned to his throne, easing himself into it with a pained groan, as if he'd aged by decades since Emma's arrival. "Twelve tide cycles. In that time, you will present to me an alternative mate. He must be loyal, fair, and capable of ruling at your side. I will allow this experiment because you are my heir, and in royal circles, a smart match is vital, even if that match is not my initial selection."

Relief poured over Emma. "Thank you, Grandfather. I—"

Tangaroa cut off her response. "If you do not find a merman who can be deemed equal to or more suitable than Merrick, the palace staff will begin preparations. One way or another, the city of Atlantis will celebrate a joining on the thirteenth tide."

Relief warped into distress, subduing the water that filtered into her gills. Emma gasped for air—true air, the kind she would never find at this depth—and choked on a mouthful of water. "Grandfather, please. I'm not ready. I've yet to visit the market by myself. I can't be expected to rule a city."

"More reason for you to be joined to someone who can." The Sea King adjusted in his throne, leaving Emma wondering how tall and intimidating he would be if he were to stand on human feet. Certainly basketball height, at least. "Emmalina, you must accept your fate in this society. Until that happens, Atlantis must have a ruler who understands the civilization of Mer."

Defiance fluttered her fin-like feet as she crossed her arms over her chest, attempting to swallow the bulk of her anger. "What if that never happens? What if I never figure out how to be a mermaid? I was raised as a human. I *am* half-human. What if I belong on land?"

"Time," the Sea King stated. "Everything can be learned with time."

Stunned, Emma stared at her grandfather, eyes burning with frustration. She would lose this battle between her logic and his, no matter how she entreated him to feel her agony. He could not feel something he couldn't understand. The details of her life here had been decided during her infant years, and Atlantis was a culture of little change.

Maia nudged the newly forming scales on Emma's arm, prompting her to produce the flower she'd held, crumpled in the safety of her palm. If her grandfather could see, if he could comprehend a fraction of her love for surface life, maybe he would find some compassion and give her more time. From her earliest memories, a certain persuasive pout had worked wonders on her human father, and she employed this same façade by widening her eyes until they glistened with sadness and pressing her lips together until the top threatened to hide behind the bottom. "Please, Grandfather." Her free hand covered the fisted one in front of her, pleading. "Twelve tides? I'm new here. I haven't had time to explore the palace, let alone the city. Allow me thirty, at least." She opened her fist and offered him the withering bloom.

"Perhaps twenty-seven tides then." Tangaroa's frown deepened, creases forming in his forehead as the thin petals flapped with the movement of the water. "What is this?"

"I brought you a gift from my former life. A gift that can't be acquired in Atlantis."

The Sea King's cheeks turned an angry shade of red as his gaze cut to Merrick. "You allowed her to visit the surface? After I forbade it?"

"No, sir." Merrick's chin jutted out, permitting him to stare down his nose at her. "The Sea Princess escaped alone. I followed in secret, concerned for her safety, and transported her back without predatory incident."

*At least he had the decency to leave Maia out of it.* Closing the flower in her fist again, Emma let her arm drop to her side, mind scrambling for an explanation that would not further anger the Sea King. Maia retreated to cower behind the merman guards, and Emma sent her a short nod of approval. She couldn't afford to lose her one and only friend.

Tangaroa, face twisted with anger, rose again from his golden throne, leveling his trident at Emma's chest. "Emmalina, you are not permitted to depart the city boundaries, under any circumstances. This was a rule set forth when you first arrived."

Heart galloping in her chest, Emma wrestled with her reflex to cower. In the moment, she envied Maia's ability to hide. Instead, she stiffened her body, hoping to appear more confident than she could ever feel when facing the angry Sea King. "It's just that . . . I wanted to find this gift for you. I went to the surface, hoping to bring you joy."

"The sea has plenty of treasures." His unrelenting glare pierced Emma's façade without mercy. "We do not need such tokens from a world where we are not welcomed."

*I'm welcome there,* Emma thought, but didn't say the words. It would not help to further remind the Sea King about her home—the one she intended to visit again, soon.

"You are no longer human." Tangaroa's voice shook with fury, fist tightening on the trident as he rammed its staff into the ground and leaned heavily on it. "You no longer breathe air, as you once could. If you are to return, you will wither and die in the manner of your father, Prince Caspian."

Nerves clustered in Emma's chest, hindering her ability to speak. "If . . . If my necklace was returned to me—"

"Even if you still possessed it, Caspian's treasure can no longer save you. You now belong to Atlantis, as it belongs to you." Sagging against the trident that he now used in place of a cane, Tangaroa signaled his aide. "Glan, lock her in the dungeon."

Emma and Maia both objected.

"What? No."

"Not the dungeon."

But it was Merrick's words that moved the aging Sea King. "Your Majesty, how is Emmalina to find a mate in the dungeon? I am promised a joining on the twenty-seventh tide. My life has long awaited this joining, as has yours. You grow weary of your position. Please do not cause additional delay to its end."

Sense and rationality returned as Tangaroa sorted his thoughts. After an extended silence, he drilled a gnarled finger in Emma's direction. "Twenty-seven tide cycles. If you do not produce another worthy and acceptable mate, you will join with Merrick on the twenty-eighth tide." He urged Emma's fisted hand open so he could swat the delicate flower aside, leaving it to drift to the sand. "One more attempt to visit the surface, and Glan will lock you away until the joining ceremony can be arranged."

He skewered Maia with demands. "Prepare the Princess for her joining. Twenty-eight tides from now, this kingdom will have a suitable heir who is fit to lead the Mer of Atlantis, be it through blood or joining."

Maia bowed, fiddling with a scale on her thigh as she accepted Tangaroa's rattled instructions, never once raising her eyes from the sand.

Though she got the distinct impression that Maia withheld a secret entirely separate from their visit to land, Emma couldn't dedicate the brainpower to wonder what that might be. She had bigger problems to digest. Her plan to find the necklace and save herself had just been given a timeline, which meant she had no time to waste. She would begin the moment the Sea King allowed her to leave the throne room.

If only she knew where or how to begin.

# Chapter Five

## James

**March 18**
*23 days since departure*

HARD AS HE TRIED, IGNORING Heather's accusations became impossible. James couldn't simply move forward with his life as if everything was normal and okay. It wasn't, on any level, and that knowledge cast an additional shadow over everything he attempted to do. As if he wasn't already stressed enough.

At work the next day, he wasted five pieces of expensive marble attempting to cut one notch, and barely avoided chopping off his thumb with the tile saw. His workout went south within the first ten minutes, when he wrenched his shoulder during his second set of reps on the bench press. Then, since it was his assigned cooking night (as opposed to his father's grab takeout nights) he over-boiled the pasta, leaving a mess of burned water on the stovetop, a layer of soggy pasta at the bottom of the pot, and setting off the fire alarm in the house.

"I give up." No longer hungry, James dumped the entire mess into the trash and stomped out to his bike, determined to be productive with the remainder of his evening. He straddled the machine and snapped on his helmet. The engine's steady rumble soothed his nerves like nothing else. He needed to see Emma, needed to visit the cove, but as he rounded the bend into the neighborhood where he usually parked, a ribbon of yellow caught his eye.

He parked against the curb, ignoring the ominous premonition that bubbled in his gut as he freed his head from the helmet and shook out his long, dark hair. A wide strip of yellow police tape rippled in the breeze, tied to a branch of the arching shrub in which he'd recently been concealing Lola. A string of swearing looped through his head, but salt from the briny air coated the inside of his mouth, leaving it too dry to speak. Lieutenant Peters stepped out of the lush greenery, a role of crime scene tape hanging from his forearm.

Peters paused mid-step when he spotted James. "Mr. Phelps."

"Lieutenant." While his instincts screamed at him to run, logic insisted that he hadn't done anything wrong—he had a right to be here. Though a warm spring breeze dried beads of sweat on his forehead, James hung his helmet with cold fingers, fumbling to secure it on Lola's handlebar. "What's going on?"

"We received a tip." Peters closed the distance between them, positioning himself between James and the trail with the same squared stance James had first noticed on the night Emma's front window was shattered with a brick. "The informant believes that we'll find evidence here that could potentially break this case open." His eyes said what his mouth did not. He talked to Heather, and they were looking for a body.

James' heart froze, then hammered like a rabbit on steroids, the resulting rush of blood causing his ears to buzz with pressure. The cove—Emma's cove—would no longer be a safe place for him. If Emma ever came, he wouldn't be there to see her. They couldn't exchange messages when they missed each other. Worse, the police would find everything he'd left in the cave, including Emma's clothes, and any correspondence she could have left since the last time he was here. "And have you? Found evidence."

Peters toyed with the roll on his arm, electing to slide it off and fold his arms across his chest. "I'm not at liberty to say. This is an open investigation."

James' ribcage squeezed around his rioting heart, numbing his extremities. *They're going to arrest me,* he thought. *I haven't done anything, but I have no alibi, no proof. And they have Emma's things. With my fingerprints all over everything.* He imitated Peters and folded his arms, desperate to keep his heart in place until he could wake up from the nightmare that had become his life. "You don't seem surprised to find me here."

The lieutenant's attention shifted to Lola-the-bike, then refocused on James. "Look, Phelps, I don't want to scare you, but I'm going to be honest. When Emma's brother went missing, I saw how protective you were of her, and I pegged you as a stand-up dude. The kind of young man I might let my daughters date someday. Now, I want to believe that you're truly that guy. I don't like questioning my own bullshit meter. In my line of work, I can't afford a malfunction." He waved his arm in the direction of the cave. "This looks bad for you. Very bad. Heather," he coughed. "The *informant* told us you'd come, and here you are. The alleged scene of a crime, where we've recovered more evidence than my detectives have found in weeks, and you—our only lead, our only witness, *and* our only potential suspect."

Words tumbled from his mouth before he could stop them. "I didn't hurt Emma. I would never—"

"So you've said," Peters agreed. "But the evidence is stacked against you."

James clutched his keys until they bit into his palm, forcing his brain to slow its spinning. "Am I under arrest?"

"Not yet." Behind Peters, two uniformed officers scoured the foliage, twigs breaking and leaves crunching as they tramped through the underbrush. "But if I were you, I'd find a good lawyer, because I suspect you're going to need one. Sooner than later."

"Suggestion noted." Like he could afford a lawyer. Like he could afford anything. Legs shaking, James backed up a step, wishing he had wings that would pick him up and fly him far away. "Am I free to go?"

Peters relaxed his stance and waved James away. "For now. But like I said the other day, don't go far."

James swallowed his response and mounted Lola, revved the engine, and took off from the curb so fast his tires squealed. The wind stung his eyes and face, shirt whipping against the bare skin of his back. When he'd lost Emma, he'd believed his life was over, that he had nothing left. But now, faced with the real possibility that he could go on trial for her murder—a murder that never happened—desolation threatened to swallow him whole.

Even if he wanted to move on, his relationship with Emma would haunt him, and regardless of the final outcome of a trial, the details would follow him for the rest of his life. The Irony of his current situation came in the form of predictions made by his basketball teammates only weeks ago. Exactly as he'd been warned, loving Emma turned his life upside down.

Without a destination, he drove aimlessly, begging his mind to calm, his heart to slow. Long after dark, he found himself at the beach where he and Emma had shared their first kiss in the moonlight, feet submerged in water and waves threatening to hurl them into the sand, together. Memories came alive, her lips on his, her small, slender body pressed against him, delicate hands clasped around his neck, gentle fingers in his hair—he'd lost his heart from her very first touch.

Setting aside the mermaid thing, Emma was unlike any other woman James had met, any other woman on the planet. From the way her skin transitioned from smooth to rough, to the way her fiery hair tumbled around her shoulders. From the cloudy confusion in her eyes first thing in the morning, to the way she reigned in her anxiety to protect Keith from his own. Even as she experienced PTSD from a past relationship, she'd offered James—at the time a virtual stranger—a ride home. He'd only just begun to peel back her layers, and already understood that Emma was irreplaceable, and he'd known it from—well, maybe the first time he'd seen her.

He couldn't bring himself to regret her, regardless of what it meant for his future.

Desperate to find that lost connection between them, he left his shoes on Lola's seat and trudged barefooted to the water. "What do I do?" The waves replied with a gurgle and a hiss. "I need you to tell me what comes next, because I've got nothing."

On the distant horizon, lightning flashed, followed by rumbling thunder—the commencement of a pre-summer storm. James let the surf wash his feet, then waded up to his ankles, the way they had that first night. This time, the enchantment of the silver moon gilding the edges of inky, foam-tipped waves only fired his frustration. He wanted to scream at the sea, at the unchangeable fate that had taken Emma away and destroyed his future.

Instead, he chased every piece of coral, every shell or sea stone the surf carried to him, and lobbed them back with every ounce of strength he had left. When the sky opened and dumped a torrent over his head, James endured, submerged to his knees, hands full of jagged rocks that he continued to chuck into the ocean until his sore shoulder shrieked in protest.

He needed to go home and warn his father. Needed to find a lawyer. And then he needed to decide if he should take his father's advice and leave the country.

Shoulders slumped in misery, James sloshed out of the waves. Lightning rent the black sky, trailed by a roar of thunder, so when a neon business sign flickered to life, his eyes drew immediately toward it.

*Last-Chance Scuba*
*Become fully certified in three short weeks.*
*Register today for a glimpse at the fascinating underwater world.*

Goosebumps speckled his skin. James blinked, reading the sign again. He'd begun to question fate's plan, but the eerie timing of this couldn't be coincidence, could it? Unless the universe *enjoyed* dumping on him. Desperate to believe that fate wasn't *that* cruel, he crossed the street and took shelter under the awning long enough to wring out his sopping shirt before entering the shop.

Once inside, he absorbed the saline fragrance of a giant fish tank, which dominated the wall to his right. Displays of scuba equipment peppered the remainder of the shop: masks, snorkels, fins, booties, wetsuits of different sizes, brands, and colors. The overwhelming selection would spark interest in anyone, but James found it exhilarating, because this was the equipment that would bring him closer to Emma.

An L-shaped desk in the corner housed a cash register and a glass display of specialty items, while the wall behind it, papered with vivid underwater photos, showcased clusters of divers interacting with sea life. Dolphins, turtles, eels, fish, lobsters. James longed for a photo of his own—but not one he would ever dare put on display.

After several moments of standing at the desk with no sign of a shop employee, James checked the posted store hours, and then his watch, before calling out. "Hello?"

Metal clamored nearby, and a slender man with deep-brown skin hobbled into the shop, wrinkled arms laden with palm-sized devices connected to the ends of long, black tubes. "Sorry. Just finished a lesson. I'll be with you in five minutes. Is that okay?"

"Sure." The deluge outside persisted, unrelenting until the water-logged street became a river. James was in no hurry to drive in it. "I'm here to talk about getting scuba certified, fast, like it says on your sign."

"Fantastic." The man shifted his equipment until he'd freed a hand with which to greet his new client. "My name's Tony. I run the place. And teach the lessons, and set up the dives. Pretty much everything around here, actually."

"A man of many talents." James shook Tony's hand. "So, three weeks. Is that really possible?"

"It is." Tony arranged his burden on the counter, unaffected when the dripping tubes formed a puddle on the glass. "Not the ideal way to learn, but candidates who are athletic, strong, book smart, and who can dedicate several hours a day to the program, have the potential to get it done in that timeframe."

"I'm all those things," James assured Tony. "I'd love to accelerate, certify faster, if that's plausible."

Tony soaked up the puddle with a thick towel, cleaning off each device by hand. "Not really. We try to leave twenty-four hours between each of your certifying dives. It's partly about pool availability, but also beginning divers need time for their bodies to offload the nitrogen mixed into the tanks." He tapped a single tank on the floor near his feet. "This is not hospital grade oxygen. Takes a bit of getting used to." Tony cleaned every device, hanging each tube on a drying hook, and then wiped the counter a second time. "When you dive for the first time, you'll understand what I mean. One of many topics we go over in the text."

"Fantastic." Maybe learning to dive wouldn't help him find Emma. Maybe it would. At least he could feel like he was doing *something*. "When can I start?"

Tony flipped through a binder of release forms and cross-checked an old-school calendar, covered in scribbles. "I can squeeze you in tomorrow, if you get here by five."

"Deal." For the first time in months, James grasped a hint of fulfillment. Learning to dive would provide him with both purpose, and a potential means of returning to the cove, even if he had to be sneakier about how he got there. "What do I need to do to prepare?"

Tony set a heavy instruction manual, complete with DVD, on the counter. "Read the first six chapters, and watch all the DVD's. Read, don't skim, because tomorrow, you'll show up and take a quiz. The next day will be a repeat—until we get all the way through that book. You'll have a short exam after each section. Any failing grades will set you back a day, two—however long it takes. Once you've passed the final, the fun begins. We'll get you suited up and out back to our pool to pass off the first round of skills. As long as you master them, we'll do a second day of the same, with an off day in between. After that, we move onto open water dives, supervised by me and an assistant. Usually we do two, possibly three of those. Assuming all these things go as planned, you'll receive your diver's card on the last day. It can be used anywhere in the world."

"Perfect." With each day since Emma left, the weight James carried had compounded until he worried his back would break from the pressure, but leaning against the counter in Tony's dive shop, a splinter of that weight broke off and sloughed away. "Last question, then I'll leave you to your work. How much is this going to cost, and what equipment do I buy or rent?"

Tony rattled off a number that was more than James' last two paychecks, combined. The news jolted him like a hook to the stomach. "But," Tony continued, his bright voice adding a positive spin, "that includes a mask, snorkel, booties, and fins, all of which you're going to need. Everything else, I provide for class purposes."

James swallowed any objections. These lessons were not a choice, but a necessity. He would find the money, however he could.

Outside, lightning flashed again, drawing an outline around his precious Lola, the bike he'd once believed he loved more than life. A bulge crawled into his throat, but fate had spoken. He'd learned the hard way to never ignore destiny's demands. He could always buy another motorcycle—but this might be his only chance to take control of his future. He took out his wallet and handed Tony his warped and faded debit card. "It won't go through for the full amount. This is a spur-of-the moment decision, so I'm not prepared to pay the total tonight. If I manage a partial deposit, could I borrow the course materials and pay the rest tomorrow? I can give you my contact information if that helps."

"Absolutely." Tony stared at the well-used card, but didn't run it. He stacked the materials and thrust them into a plastic sleeve, presenting them, along with the debit card, to James. "I don't normally give this stuff away. It's not a smart way to run a business. But something tells me that you're not the typical no-show candidate. I sense a determination in you that I haven't encountered in a long time. Take all this and get to work. Don't worry about the deposit tonight, just promise you'll show up tomorrow. We can square up then."

James left the shop, informational materials tucked under his arm, glowing because he'd found his next step. One way or another, he'd track down Emma and bring her back—there was too much riding on him to accept anything less. He only hoped he could find her before the police showed up to arrest him.

# Chapter Six

## Emma

EMMA CLOSED THE SEAWEED DRAPE that acted as a privacy curtain for her bedroom. It wasn't a soundproof door, but even the illusion of privacy was better than nothing, especially while she was confined to her room. In the entire palace, she'd seen only one room appointed with an actual door—and decorated with a lovely and intricate design of shells and jewels, she assumed that one belonged to the Sea King. In town, she'd seen real doors. Made from wood or stone, and a few from ice—though those would likely melt, and offered little privacy through the opaque sheets.

Not having the privilege of a door grated on her ego. She might not be the Sea King, but the Princess of

Atlantis should be protected by a much stronger security measure. *At least it's not noisy to open,* she thought, reminding herself that the curtain would make it infinitely easier for her to sneak out during the sleep tide.

She and Maia waited several long minutes in silence, but as soon as the escorting guards were out of earshot, she rounded on the younger mermaid. "What are you hiding? What do you know?"

Maia's words spilled out fast, heightening Emma's suspicions. "I am not hiding nothing, Princess. I know nothing."

Frustrated beyond measure, Emma scowled at her handmaid. Sarcasm wasn't common here, any more than intrigue, which baffled Emma more than she liked to admit. If this was true, Merrick's deception must be a cultural anomaly compared to the city Mer. Most of the Mer spoke in painfully honest phrases, often coming across child-like or naïve. Maia must be facing serious consequences to remain buttoned up so tightly. "I saw how your gaze dropped to the sand, how you twisted your hands together. Those are signs of secrets. There's something you're not telling me."

Maia's focus cowered beneath Emma's wrath. "Princess Emmalina, please do not ask this of me. I could be banished from the city."

Emma cornered her chambermaid, disallowing the potential for Maia to escape Emma's questions. "Don't ask what of you?"

Maia's nervous habit of wringing her hands risked tangling her webbed fingers together and tearing the fragile tissue between each knuckle. "Do not make me tell you things I am sworn to hold in secret."

They'd threatened to banish her. Of course. Whatever the secret, it must be huge. "All right," she conceded. "I won't make you talk. Not today. But if you ever feel compelled to tell me voluntarily, your secret information might save my life."

Maia remained in place, her spine straighter than Emma had ever seen. "Or destroy it."

Though her patience wore thin, Emma knew that pushing Maia right now would do more harm than good. "I guess I need to meet some bachelor mermen. Where would I go to do that? And how would I go about it? I know literally nothing about Mer courting practices."

"Bachelor?" Maia retreated to Emma's dressing table to straighten things that didn't necessarily need straightening.

"Um, single mermen in want of a mate." Emma slid aside the drape in the corner to peruse the baubles and coverings that her grandfather had provided.

A satisfied smile tugged at the corners of Maia's mouth when she joined Emma at the Mer version of a closet. "I do not know, Princess. Most Mer become betrothed soon after hatching. Our parents choose our mates."

Emma withdrew a heavy cloth that had been torn into strips and decorated. If she were to tie it around her waist, the strands would dance around her legs and hide her lack of a single fin. *Salvaged shipwreck curtains?* "When you say, *most of us,* I guess that includes mermen?

Maia frowned as Emma tied the skirt around her tiny waist, but didn't offer help. "Yes. Once a match has been negotiated, we spend our guppy years as playmates, our adolescence hating each other, and when we become of age, are happily joined to the mate with whom we have spent our youth."

The more she learned about the Mer, the stronger grasp she gained on the difficulty of the tasks she faced. No wonder the Sea King allowed her to try and replace Merrick. All suitable young mermen were probably taken. "Is there a way to locate a merman who isn't promised? Do any exist?"

"Of course." Maia moved to the trunk of jewels and threw open the lid, her face illuminating with delight. "A merman might lose his mate to death, or choose to frolic with another, or his parents are unable to bargain for a suitable match. These are the Mer who gather in the market, hoping to negotiate for unmated younglings, or maids who have lost their mates, and are still of an age to reproduce."

*Of an age to reproduce? Oh dear.* "Are there a lot of unmated youth?" While Maia rifled through the trunk, Emma continued scrutinizing the closet's contents, searching for adornments or coverings that would hide her surface-made bikini, and attract the eyes of the eligible Mer. She settled on a cloth made of tiny shells, and tied together with seagrass. She knotted it around her neck, and then again around her ribs, effectively covering her bikini.

Maia selected a long strand of pearls, and wound it around Emma's neck numerous times so that each layer fell to her hips. Next, she selected a shorter, abalone strand that shimmered in the soothing blue light, followed by a braid of tarnished silver, and two chains of delicate pink shells. The last, she looped into Emma's hair, leaving it heavy and controlled, the wild tips brushing her shoulders and back, instead of floating around her face.

With Emma's hair secure, Maia produced a seashell filled with inky brown liquid. "The dye from a cuttlefish," she explained. "This will mark your skin until the water washes it away." She dipped the fine tip of a swordfish blade into the ink and proceeded to draw a lavish design across Emma's stomach, and then continued it around to her back.

"It's temporary?" Emma asked, fascinated by this very human-like custom of decorating one's self.

"Usually," Maia muttered, inspecting her work. "Should dissolve in two or three tide cycles."

"What do the markings mean?"

Maia prodded Emma's side, her webbed finger beginning at the apex of the intricate scrolling. "Royalty, the king's favor." She tilted her head, pausing to add another flourish to the markings. "This one was Caspian's. He designed the pattern just before leaving Atlantis, where he encountered his human love. It has never been worn, until you."

A bubble of pride gurgled inside her. She had not given the Mer credit as a society of clever, industrious artists. Atlantis had a unique, and interesting culture— and whether she wanted to be here or not, this place was part of her. Would always be a part of her.

"Is this a traditional courting practice?"

"No, Princess." Maia continued to draw, her steady hand adding finer details. "These are the symbols of royalty. By displaying them, you invite available mermen to seek your permission to court. It should not be a difficult task. You are Atlantis's most high maid."

Emma jerked away from Maia's creative fingers. "Wait. You want me to wear symbols that declare my status, because it will help me *catch* a merman?"

Maia froze, face crumpled with confusion as Emma seized handfuls of sand—the best scrubbing agent in the sea—and attempted to work the ink off her skin faster than it had been applied. "No offense, but after Merrick and his stalker-ish extremes, I prefer to discuss my position in person, *after* I've met a possible date. No tattoos necessary."

"I am sorry, Princess. I assumed that you would expect to be looked upon as the Sea King's heir. Such a position demands respect, while gathering attention." Flushing with embarrassment, Maia joined the scrubbing until a majority of the ink was either absorbed or removed, and only faint lines remained.

"Maia, if a merman is unable to treat me with respect before knowing who I am, he is not a merman I want to pursue."

"Yes, Princess." Maia returned to the trunk and swung the heavy lid closed, but as she did, Emma glimpsed a familiar lustrous shimmer.

"My necklace!" She hastened to the trunk, pulling out each item one by one, frantically searching for the necklace she knew—deep down—would not be found inside this trunk.

Maia held the lid to prevent it slamming down on Emma's head and forearms. "You've chosen the best adornments, Princess. But you may wear as many as you like. Such excess is common in Atlantian culture."

Emma's hope dwindled with each piece she flung aside. "There's only one that I truly need. A gift left by my father before he passed. A solitary memento from the man I met only once, as an infant. It was misplaced when I arrived here, and I'm desperate to find it."

"Misplaced?" Maia retrieved the pieces Emma discarded, and piled them on the dressing table.

Explaining the truth to a handmaid she hardly knew could turn into a slippery slope, and Emma refused to take that chance. She tried another word. "Lost?"

Maia's lips bowed into the kind of smile that was surely the cause of so many misguided mermaid legends. "I will help to locate your father's treasure," she declared. "And also a mate."

Emma worried about the quickness with which Maia had agreed to help. Once again, something about her too-bright smile seemed . . . off. "And in return?"

"I am to be joined in sixty tides." Her eyes darted to the floor, webbed hands twisting together. "As with you, I do not wish to join with my chosen mate. He is not a good merman. I desire to beg the Sea King for my freedom, that I might choose a mate who is not so easily angered."

Appalled, Emma gave up her search. "Easily angered? Maia, does he hurt you?"

More hand twisting, told Emma all she needed to know. If all mermen behaved like Merrick, the Atlantian culture was not as innocent and unassuming as Emma had believed. She couldn't allow such a timid young maid to be forced into a union with a monster.

Not if she had the influence to help. "I don't know if the Sea King will hear a request from me, but I can try—"

"No." Maia clutched Emma's arm, her blue skin hinting on transparent as fear radiated from her eyes. "We can tell no one. Not yet. I accepted this assignment as your handmaid, because Duke Merrick has connection with the family of my intended, and I wished to request his assistance first."

*Oh dear. This just got complicated.* "Maia, I'm not sure Merrick is the right guy to ask."

"Duke Merrick is of royal descent, and favored by the Sea King. If I am to convince anyone, he will be the merman who listens."

Blinking with disbelief, Emma coached her face into a phony smile, unwilling to argue over Merrick with a mermaid who clearly knew very little of Emma's current intended. *I will do everything I can to put a stop to your joining. No one should be forced into an abusive marriage.* "I'll see what I can arrange."

Maia's relief brought the color back into her violet-blue skin, and sent a stream of bubbles from her gills. "Thank you, Princess."

Emma watched the bubbles float away, fascinated by the difference in breathing in her two homes. So many legends told of mermaids coming ashore to abandon their younglings into the arms of humans. They couldn't all have had to use Emma's necklace. There must be something else, something forgotten or forbidden or—overlooked from years of disuse. But something. "Maia, do we keep of historical records or stories shared from the Mer who settled our city?"

"Of course." Maia animated as if Emma had offered to take her shopping. "We must begin in the chamber of palace history."

Interest piqued, Emma nudged Maia through the seaweed curtain. "The market full of mermen can wait. I've got to see this."

# Chapter Seven

## James

**March 19**
*24 days since departure*

JAMES GRITTED HIS TEETH, CONSCIOUSLY suppressing his fist from hammering the slimy salesman's face. "Four thousand dollars? That's it? I paid twice that, just last summer, when it had only half an engine, a shredded seat, and peeling paint. This bike runs like new now. She's worth a lot more than four grand. Eight. At the very least."

The man's smile flashed, showing off green and black bits of food in his teeth. "That's my offer. Take it or leave it."

He really didn't have the ability to say no, but accepting so little of Lola's value revolted him worse than the idea of selling her had. It would be like giving away free money—his money—to a con-artist. This wasn't a good time for throwing around money, especially thousands of dollars, while his family scrambled to find an affordable lawyer who wasn't the public defender.

But he had to come up with the payment for his scuba class tonight, and the balance of his bank account wasn't even close to enough. He suspected that the dealer could smell his desperation. He had to calm down, think this through. "I don't know." He turned his back on the salesman, and ran his hand over Lola's shiny fender. "I'm having a tough time parting with her, as it is. I'm going to make some phone calls, see if a drive to San Diego might be worth my time." He pulled out his phone and dialed a number, walking away from the dealer, and praying that the man didn't call his bluff. He couldn't get to San Diego today, and if he did, transportation home would cost more than the trip was worth. Steadman's Recreational was the only local dealership that James knew would pay cash on the spot.

The salesman shoved his hands in the pockets of his cheap slacks and rocked back on his heels. "Offer's only good for thirty minutes. You wanna go somewhere else, that's fine. But when you come back, my number drops."

James swallowed the expletives that crammed into his brain, and put the phone to his ear, ambling onto the sales lot. Under any other circumstances, he would have called his Uncle Ryan for advice, but Ryan was past the simmering point after James called out of work today. His uncle would explode when he discovered that James had sold his bike after all the effort they'd put in to finally get it running.

His friend and former basketball teammate, Cameron, answered. "Guess a phone call means you're alive. That's something, at least."

"Ha. Yeah." James laughed, but the sound echoed in his ears. "Remember a few months ago, when you told me to call you if I ever decided to sell my motorcycle?" Future James would later be embarrassed by the desperation most certainly evident in the way the conversation unfolded. Ultimately, Cameron, having only been finished with basketball for a week, didn't have a job, nor did he have five thousand dollars to spend, and James knew that before he'd pressed call. Still, he had to explore every possible avenue, and so commenced the dance between friends who hadn't spoken in weeks, and who had never been all that close in the first place. Maybe the salesman would consider increasing his offer if he thought another buyer was interested.

As he chatted with Cameron, James wandered, running his fingers over all-terrain vehicles, taking an interested gander at camping trailers and motorhomes, and getting his daydream on by wishing he could afford any of the adrenaline-building machines currently for sale in the lot. The conversation came to an abrupt halt when he rounded the side of the building and happened upon a vehicle that completely altered his train of thought.

An older model, center console, salt-water fishing boat, marked at what appeared to be a bargain price of three-thousand dollars. The white paint had yellowed in the sun, and what remained of the decorative silver stripes was chipped and peeling from neglect. But the propeller appeared unbent and free of nicks or dents, and while the motor casing was banged up, it didn't seem to be terribly damaged. James ended the call with a gruff thanks to his friend, and shoved the phone in his pocket. Yes, he needed a lawyer. But no lawyer could save him the way Emma's return would.

He lowered the ladder and climbed aboard, prying open the top of the outboard motor and finding it much cleaner than he expected. The slick deck had yellowed more deeply than the outer hull, and two narrow cracks ran under the back bench, but didn't shift when he bounced on them. The upholstery needed major repairs, and though the tower console rattled when he shook it, that was easily fixed with a few turns of a wrench. Surprisingly, the bright blue sunshade maintained its color—he assumed that was new. But most importantly, his inspection of the hull proved it a sturdy, floatable craft, and James was thorough.

He stood at the helm, imagining the breeze in his hair and the salt on his face as he sped toward the arch, where he'd last seen Emma. Then he planted himself on the driver's bench, eyes glazing over as they glowered through the grimy glass at the salesman coming his way. How hard could it be to drive this baby?

The salesman braced his foot on the bottom rung of the ladder, chin raised and chest puffed, but made no other move to board. "Pretty, isn't it? Considering taking on a new sport?"

James stood, rubbing the faded wheel. "I don't know. I mean, I'd love a boat, but don't have anywhere to store one. Or a vehicle to pull it with."

Threading his arm through the ladder, the salesman poised on that single rung, his eyes just high enough to survey James' every move. "Happy to sell you a truck to pull it, and the boat trailer's included in the price." When James didn't respond, he continued. "Most marinas offer storage, and a lot of private docks rent out slips."

Owning a boat involved variables that James wasn't confident he could manage, no matter how his instincts compelled him. Discouragement threatened to crush him, so he swiped his hand across the dash and disembarked the craft. "Not today."

Nonplussed, the salesman continued, his entire body involved in the pitch. "I can practically *give* her to you. In fact, I'll trade you straight across for that piece of junk you're looking to sell."

James' eyebrows shot up, blood boiling as it pulsed in his neck. "That *piece of junk* is a Harley, in pristine condition, and worth four times the sticker price on this boat. You offered me more than that just ten minutes ago, and even that was less than half what my Lola's worth."

The salesman straightened his tie and puffed out his chest, finally dropping all pretenses. "I know desperation when I see it. Kids your age don't often show up on newly restored machines asking for same-day cash. That tells me either the motorcycle's stolen, or you've got a major debt to pay. Now, here at Steadman's Recreational, we believe that where a vehicle comes from is none of our business, so long as the seller produces a valid title. But buying any as-is vehicle is a risk. By policy, we never offer more than one-third of book value."

"It's not stolen." Again, James gritted his teeth, patting the title folded neatly inside his pocket. "And I don't owe anyone money." Yet.

The salesman hooted with laughter, his large, round belly shaking his entire body. "I see. Funding a new habit? Drugs will never get you anywhere, kid."

James swore, the last threads of his patience snapping. "You know what? You don't need to know the reason I'm selling. Either you want my motorcycle or you don't. My friend just offered me five grand to hold onto it for a month. I'm considering it."

That belly kept jiggling, despite the salesman's attempts to internalize his amusement. "If that was true, you'd be gone already." He knocked on the boat's hull. "How bad do you want this baby?"

*Worse by the minute.* "Not enough to trade away my favorite toy for a fraction of its value." James pivoted and marched away from the overzealous, overconfident sales-slime. He checked his watch, the timeline shrinking by the minute. Maybe he could borrow some money to pay for the class, and try to sell Lola online?

"Wait!" The slime-man hollered across the lot, huffing as his stubby legs scurried to overtake James' athletic pace. "I'm a reasonable guy, but you have to understand, I'm only authorized to pay wholesale value for any vehicle. But listen. Since your little beauty's been restored, and is obviously in great running condition, I might be approved to go as high as forty-five hundred. That's the ceiling. My boss would never approve a higher pay-out. But if you end up finding somewhere to put a boat, I can promise to work you a killer deal."

*You mean soak me for more money,* James thought. But since he didn't have months to find another buyer, accepting this offer was his only option. "I can't buy the boat. Not today. But if you'll give me a lift to the coast, I'll take the forty-five hundred, cash."

The glee reflected in sales-slime's smile struck James as wolfish, and did nothing to relieve the squirming in his stomach when he signed the papers and said goodbye to his beloved Lola.

He could now afford scuba lessons, but the chances of finding Emma in that huge, wide ocean were about one in ten-billion, probably worse. And unless his father and uncle could magically scrape together the tens-of thousands of dollars required to retain a high-powered attorney, he'd be stuck with the public defender.

*You wanted to take control of your life, and that was indeed a controlled choice. Hope you didn't just screw up everything worse.* He chewed the insides of his cheeks all the way to the beach, but when the salesman's car crested the hill and the ocean sprawled out before them, the hope James had been desperate to find returned to him.

The logic made no sense whatsoever, and explaining to his family would be next to impossible, but, somehow, he knew he'd done the right thing.

He stumbled into the shop, ten minutes late for class, and mouthed an apology to Tony, who nodded at him and pointed out an empty chair. Similar to a school classroom set-up, long tables lined either side of the room, accompanied by folding chairs, with a walkway in between. Seven other students were seated at the provided tables, the same course materials that Tony loaned to James spread out in front of them.

James unloaded his backpack and opened his workbook, praying to remember everything he'd studied last night. Losing a single important detail could extend his classroom time, as if he didn't have enough pressure in his life. Luckily, Tony's easy-going style of teaching helped, along with his use of visual aids.

Two hours later, James—along with the rest of his accelerated class—had taken and passed four quizzes. On his way out, he stopped by Tony's register to pay up. Tony grinned at James, clearly pleased that he had shown up, as promised. "What'd you think?"

"I haven't failed a quiz yet, so I guess that's good." James unzipped the hidden pocket in his backpack and, curving toward the wall for discretion, unfolded the bills he'd carefully counted at the dealership.

"Thanks for letting me borrow the study guides yesterday. I can pay my fee now."

"Great." Tony directed James to a section of equipment. "You'll need a mask, snorkel, booties, and fins. The rest can be rented, but those four things are personal. You'll be glad to have your own." He showed James the basics—included in his package—and suggested a couple of upgraded pieces, meant for deeper, more intensive dives.

James made his choices, adding an upgraded mask and snorkel to his total, and feeling grateful that he now had money for the more dependable essentials. "I'm excited to get in the water and apply the skills I've learned so far."

Tony counted out the change, adding a bottle of defogger to James' sack. "You've got more classroom work to complete first, but if you keep up, we'll have you in the pool by next weekend."

"And after that, open water."

Considering that he didn't appear to carry an ounce of body fat, Tony's full-belly laugh looked nothing like that of the salesman at Steadman's. Maybe it was the difference in professions, or background, or the way each man was raised, but unlike the sales-slime who practically stole Lola, Tony was the real deal, a genuine, good guy. Someday, James hoped to be that guy for someone else. Someone like himself. "I've never met anyone so anxious about that part. Most beginners start out nervous, even claustrophobic."

Nothing could make James more claustrophobic than the idea of being confined in a cell.

Tony followed James to the door, brow creasing as he peered through the glass storefront to the empty street. "What happened to that gorgeous motorcycle you had yesterday?"

Dark clouds churned in his chest, the beginning of a massive storm. The last month had been an endless lesson on learning how to let go. "It's not mine anymore."

As if sensing that he'd hit a nerve, Tony shifted his attention to the fish tank, where he sprinkled food flakes into the water. "You have a ride home?"

James slung his backpack and equipment bag over his shoulder. "The bus."

"How far away do you live?"

Embarrassment tickled the back of James' neck as he jostled the door open. "Not too far."

Tony followed James outside, squinting at the dimly lit bus stop down the street. Above it, a street light flickered, casting ominous shadows onto the sidewalk. "If you can wait ten minutes, I'll give you a lift after I close up."

Shame won out over temptation. Even with the extra wait, having a ride would get him home thirty minutes faster. That was thirty minutes James could use studying—for scuba, and his impending school finals. "Thanks, but I hate to inconvenience you. I'll be okay."

"I'm not a serial killer, I promise. Look, James, I know what it's like to feel lost. If I can help you find your way—that's just me, paying it forward, as someone did for me when I was around your age. Please let me." Tony nudged James back into the shop, steering him to the desk, and arming him with a feather duster. "This will go faster if you'll dust the fixtures while I close the till."

# Chapter Eight

## Emma

THE CHAMBER OF PALACE HISTORY was not what she expected. When Maia confirmed the existence of historical records, Emma envisioned a great library, stacked floor to ceiling with . . . she wasn't sure. Though she'd never seen a hint of paper in Atlantis, understood that no such thing could exist in her current environment, books were still the picture her mind conjured. One more of many things she missed about home.

They left the palace behind, turned away from the market and the population of the city, traveled toward the outskirts of town, while maintaining a quick, steady pace. Soon, they encountered a glorious building, nearly as large as the palace. Built from a substance Emma didn't recognize, the exterior resembled bricks, or maybe iron. Something new, that glimmered like nothing she'd ever seen before. Mesmerizing and lovely, the building itself created a distraction that might have held her captive for tides, until an exquisite melody floated from the inner sanctum, drawing them in the way the guardian mermaids had first drawn Emma into Atlantis.

Hallway after narrow hallway displayed sculptures, drawings, exhibits. And shelves, stacked with pages and pages of . . . not paper. Everything but paper. Stone tablets, leather-like parchment, etched metals. None of the writings made sense to Emma, not a single symbol read the way letters form words, but the stories they told were obviously important, as they warranted the creation of shrine after shrine—not to mention the gigantic edifice in which they were housed.

Entire works of art stood as idols to the gods of earth, sea, and sky. And each statue told a story, the carvings so intricate, so detailed, as to make text unnecessary. One figure—that of a human woman, draped in the remains of a dress—bore the same shocked expression that Emma imagined she, herself, had worn the first time she'd been pulled beneath a rip-tide and discovered she could breathe underwater.

Next to the first sculpture stood a second, and a third, and on for rows and rows. Each carving depicted another evolutionary stage of a people who appeared to have begun as humans. Maia urged her past the monuments and through an archway to a chamber, where they found more rows of shelves holding more tablets, each stack slightly different from the rest, made from slate, sandstone, metal, shells, skins. Some even appeared to have been sculpted from clay, and all were etched with writing.

Maia chose a specific shelf. "We shall try here first." She hoisted a stone tablet into her arms, then added two others, beckoning for Emma to do the same. They stacked both loads on a table, and Maia laid the first two side-by-side, settling in for what appeared to be a tedious process of deciphering.

While Maia read, Emma returned to the hall of sculptures, allowing her fingers to trace the curves of each statue, occasionally catching on one of the many elaborate details. She began in front, at the sculpture that had originally caught her eye, and then moved on to the next one, a funnel-like wave, surrounded by broken structures and expressing how a great tragedy had plunged the thriving metropolis into the sea.

Next, a smaller, longer display indicated that hundreds of humans were left grieving at the edge of the broken shore, another statue demonstrated the effects of that grief—unrest, hostility, warfare. And then another, a mass divergence that drove half of the survivors further ashore, and sent the other half wading into the sea in search of their lost city.

A sculpture of transformation depicted the hand of the Sea God—Poseidon—touching the necks of those who chose the sea, causing their human lungs to collapse and be replaced by gills, and their skin to develop scales. Eventually, their legs fused together and formed a fin, and webbing grew between their fingers for quick, efficient swimming.

"Princess Emma," Maia called. "Please come. I have found something."

The face of the next statue embodied a peace more complete than any she'd experienced since her arrival in this city. An angel, or—maybe a human woman, since this sculpture still had feet—whose face looked so familiar, as if peering into a mirror. The strong, narrow jaw, chiseled cheek bones, wide, expressive eyes. Of all the pieces she'd seen, this figure confused Emma the most. Why did it feel so familiar?

"Emmalina?" Maia's second prompt broke the trance that held Emma frozen, allowing her to return to her handmaid's side. Maia floated above the table, reading from a tablet on her lap. "This is the story of Atlantis, Oceania, and the origin of Mer."

She summoned Emma closer, and Emma complied, narrowing her eyes at the cryptic text. "Oceania?"

"It is another city of Mer."

Stunned, Emma snatched the tablet, screwing her face up as if doing so would magically allow her to read the ancient language. "There's another city? Outside of Atlantis?"

A laugh bubbled from Maia's gills as she uncurled Emma's fingers from the tablet and returned it to her lap. "There are many cities of Mer. The ocean is a wide and vast expanse."

Emma's muscles contracted with excitement, while her mind struggled to process this new information. If she was unable to reclaim the pendant, forcing her to live in the confines of the sea, if her grandfather insisted on her joining with Merrick—maybe she had options outside of Atlantis. But the sculptures . . . "I don't understand how this is possible."

Maia tapped the plate with her finger as she translated, like a parent teaching her child to read. "Tangaroa and Tangaloa are brothers, born of the God of Sea and the Goddess of Earth. Twin brothers of the variety that never got along. It's been said that they were born fighting, competing, and have not stopped since."

She continued, "Centuries ago, Old Tangaloa, God of Sky, lived with his children in the heavens above earth. One of his sons, Young Tangaloa, was a builder. All of his creations eventually became lands and colonies. Sometimes, he was known to tip his wood chips into the sea, where his uncle, Tangaroa, ruled—

and those chips formed new underwater cities. When Old Tangaloa discovered that his son had betrayed him by populating the sea at the same time as the land, he became angry, and sent another son, Maui, to fish the islands from the water using a giant hook. But Old Tangaroa loved his people, and fought with his brother to keep the colonies under his rule, below the depths of the sea.

The next time Maui fished a colony from the bottom and created an island, Tangaroa waited at the ready, and a battle ensued. Tangaroa cut Maui's fishing line, leaving half of the colony below the surface, while the other half broke apart and formed tiny islands.

The unrest among the gods—and the war that waged for many years—forced the newly evolved sea-people to choose between land and sea, air and water, Tangaroa and Tangaloa. This caused much hostility among those remaining below, eventually driving entire families to make their homes elsewhere in the sea.

After a time, the Mer world regained a balance, and Old Tangaroa sent his son, Young Tangaroa, to rule the colony of Atlantis." Finally, Maia set the tablet on a shelf, and picked up another.

"I guess the other colony is Oceania." Emma thought aloud. Though if there was hostility, it was likely that those who left Atlantis had not all gone the same direction, or settled in the same place. By now, there were probably hundreds of Mer colonies, or thousands.

"Correct." Maia's finger began on the next document. "There's more here. Legends of Maui. One calls him Maui the Sky-Raiser, giving him credit for pushing the sky up to allow room for the land-people to breathe. Another refers to him as Maui the Sun-Snarer, because when the sun tried to escape, he caught it and tethered it to the earth. Maui the Fire-Bearer, because after visiting the underworld, he brought fire to the surface so that people in his new lands could use it to cook their food and warm their homes, as you once explained to me." She smiled brightly at Emma. "I should like to see fire one day."

Homesickness swelled, filling the empty place in Emma's chest that continued to grow with each day she was unable to visit her family. "I'd love to show it to you."

Maia chose another tablet, setting her others on the table. "Oh! Maui had a son, Young Maui. When Old Maui next visited his brother, Tangaroa, he realized that the sea spanned more of the Earth than land. Believing that this permitted his brother more power than him, Old Maui sent Young Maui below, instructing him to *assist* Tangaroa in ruling the Mer. When Young Maui refused, Old Maui touched his son's neck, causing his lungs to shrivel and gills to form—forcing Young Maui into the sea, forever.

Rejected by his father, and devastated at the loss of his family, Young Maui journeyed to Atlantis, begging his uncle, Tangaroa, to take him in. But Tangaroa, believing Young Maui had come to raise mischief in the ways of his father, sent his nephew away."

Emma blinked, incensed for the demi-god who was betrayed on every side, every level. "What did my grandfather expect him to do? He couldn't return to land, could he?"

"It doesn't say. These records are kept by historians of Atlantis—not Oceania or any other city." Maia pressed her lips together, continuing to read, and then nodded. "But Maui did return to Atlantis, in the time of Caspian, your father."

Hearing her father's name, Emma attempted, again, to read the symbols on Maia's tablet, and then, frustrated, she folded her arms, hugging tightly as her thoughts spun in crazy circles. "Maui wanted to go home. And at some point, my father became involved—that must be how he arose to land. They must have discovered a way to use their lungs again." Her insides lit up, as though a lamp flared to life after years of darkness. Maui and her father found a way to return to land, and she could too.

And then another clue slid into place. "Maui is the name of an island!" Thoughts working into a frenzy, Emma pointed her entire arm in the direction she assumed to be west. "In this very ocean. Far away, certainly, but not across the globe."

Maia clutched the tablet to her breast, wild, blue hair floating around her face. "If there is an island named for Maui, it must be the place where he can be found."

"If he can be found at all." Emma swallowed, thinking of her father, and wishing she had a better understanding of how he died. Something must have gone wrong.

Excited with what they'd found, Maia returned to the table, where she examined plate after plate. When she ran out of those, she sent Emma to bring her more. Helpless to do more, and too worked up to return to the sculpture displays, Emma picked up a small, smooth shell, rubbing it between her fingers while she paced.

Eventually, Maia sang with triumph. "Young Maui the Freedom-Fighter. This describes him as a trickster, who fought against all rules set out by his father and uncle, and who liberated the city of Oceania, offering inhabitants the ability to choose between land and sea."

Emma dropped the shell, pulse thumping. "Choose? What do you think that means?" Could it be possible to have the best of both worlds?

"I've heard stories of Oceania, but they are legends, only. I cannot verify that any is truth. My grandfather once told me that Oceania is a glorious place, where younglings are gifted with a fin to swim, as well as legs to walk, and that, upon coming of age, those younglings must choose one—legs or fin. It is a permanent choice."

That didn't sound right to Emma. Her Gran would have told her if such a thing was possible. She'd done tons of research trying to help Emma find a way to stay with the family. Although, every legend began with a single grain of truth. This grain might be worth digging for.

The current moved, indicating a disturbance. Maia set her tablet aside and grasped Emma's arm. "Someone is coming. We must leave this place."

Unwilling to risk being tossed in the dungeon, Emma shadowed the servant girl through another doorway and into a narrow corridor that led them to a ceiling access hatch, and a tube so slim that they had to swim through one at a time—and Emma's shoulders rubbed the sides just before being spit out and away from the roof.

They continued into the heart of the city, past large, spacious buildings, through the market, where Emma feared all eyes were drawn to the strange mermaid with the underdeveloped fin and pale, ivory skin. She'd worn adornments around her neck and torso, hoping to blend in, but as Maia led her through the crowded marketplace, Emma found herself jostled and bumped, shoved, and butted until her neck adornment snapped—the pearls and shells tinkling on the stones that lined the swim paths below.

Maia stuck close to her side, but before long, a crowd of market Mer gathered, circling like vultures around a dead carcass. They communicated in titters and snickers, using hand signals. Emma's chest squeezed, sending her heart into a throat that felt recently coated with dry sand.

One merman yanked a handful of her hair, threading it through his fingers as if he'd never touched anything so interesting before. "Leave her!" Maia attempted to swing to the rescue, but her command only aggravated the market Mer, who propelled her away until Emma could no longer see her.

A hefty merman rubbed a meaty hand over Emma's shoulder, catching her wrist with a firm grip, and dragging her down an alley between two market structures. "This way."

She strained to fight free, only to have her other arm captured by a wiry, chiseled merman whose inked markings obscured his entire face, and who jerked her in the opposite direction. "I say she's going this way."

Panic stole her breath, replaced by the instinct to breathe through her nose and mouth, rather than her gills. She gasped, a scream gurgling in her throat that then filled again with water, reigniting the desire to breathe. Her brain registered the difference of environment that made air-breathing impossible, but the craving persisted, demanding that she try.

Terror jolted her body as she kicked hard, hoping to twist her arms free. But the mermen only held tighter, tugged harder. *They'll tear me in two*, she thought, spots blinking in her vision. *If I don't suffocate first.*

"What is the meaning of this?" The imperious voice echoed, rising above all other noise, and bringing the mermen's tug-of-war to an abrupt stop. "Why do merchants lay fins on my betrothed?"

Merrick.

She'd been avoiding him since the confrontation with her grandfather, but in this moment of distress, no other merman in the sea could have caused Emma such relief.

The hefty merman released his hold as if his palm had been burned. More reluctant, the wiry merman kept a strong grip until Merrick parted the crowd like Moses and the Red Sea, after which the remaining merman fled.

"My mate." Genuine concern flooded Merrick's voice and colored his pale skin deep purple as he encompassed a quivering Emma in the safety of his arms. "Have they harmed you?"

Too horrified to speak, Emma shook her head, lips pressed together to hold in a sob.

Merrick's gaze swept the crowd, finding and skewering Maia. "Why would you bring her here? You understand the dangers of the market, especially for a Sea Princess."

Maia's eyes dropped in shame, cheeks flaming indigo. "The Sea King has granted twenty-seven moon cycles for Emmalina to seek a suitable mate. We . . . came in search of body adornments appropriate for courting, and as well as a joining ceremony."

"Body adornments?" Merrick drew Emma away, webbed hands caressing her shoulders. His brow furrowed as if his brain struggled to process such information. "Is this what you desire?"

Uncertain how she should respond, Emma raised a timid shoulder—a half-shrug that Merrick would recognize. She'd made the human gesture often over the years—each time he revealed embarrassing details of Mer living.

"Very well." He blinked, still clearly confused, and offered Emma his elbow. "I shall accompany you in the market, and perhaps assist your choices."

"Thank you." Though she'd vowed to avoid Merrick—forever, if possible—their recent experience left her traumatized, shaken. She may not want him for a husband, but she'd happily accept him as her shopping guardian for a day.

Merrick indicated the mermaids in the square, layered with long—multi-colored strands of pearls and coral—many of which appeared to be selling the adornments straight off their bodies. "Perhaps something here?"

"Jewels." Maia steered them down another row. "For her neck. Rare jewels."

Merrick's eyebrow twitched in amusement, though Emma didn't want to guess about what he found funny. "The Sea King has outlawed rare jewels, even in neckwear."

Maia froze, falling behind for the length of a breath, and then rushing to catch up. "Legal jewels. Something no other mermaid can replicate."

"But also, something popular," Emma added, disturbed by the ease with which Maia lied, a fact which overturned her earlier assessment that the Mer culture lacked guile. To solidify the fraud, she added a thread of truth. "I'm so different from the other mermaids. I would like to find something that will help me fit in—except for the joining ceremony. That's an occasion where I intend to be unique."

At the mention of a joining ceremony, Merrick's chest puffed with enthusiasm. "Unique indeed, as the Sea Princess of Atlantis shall always remain. You were not born to *fit in*, Emmalina. No royal ever is." He patted the hand holding tight to his arm. "Nothing would delight me more than to purchase your adornments this tide."

As much as she'd hated Merrick, she had to admit that when he wanted to be charming, he did a damn good job. It was too bad he acted this way so rarely.

# Chapter Nine

## James

**March 26**
*31 days gone*

JAMES HEFTED THE LEFTOVER BAG of grout into the bed of the truck, and swiped his wrist across his forehead, catching the sweat before it could drip into his eyes. Late afternoon sun burned bright and hot through the windshield as he climbed into the driver's seat. This degree of heat was unusual so early in the season, but the reminder left him grateful that he had another two months of school, which allowed him to only work half-days. Come graduation, that would change, and he'd likely find himself slaving away in this heat from sunup to sundown.

When he got back to the office, he entered the air-conditioned building, sighing as he hovered over a vent. "You're done early today," Ryan remarked. "Did you finish grouting both the kitchen and bathroom at that job?"

"Yup." The cool air seeped through James' sweat-soaked clothes as he filled out his timecard and put away his tool belt. "At a standstill until the grout dries, but tomorrow I'll caulk the fixtures and seal the stone. Turned out pretty. I liked their accent choices."

"Yeah, those clients have great taste." Ryan tapped a pencil on the papers he'd been leafing through, scrutinizing James as he moved about the shop. "I've been hoping to catch up with you all week. Started to wonder if you're avoiding me. You've been leaving the shop pretty fast."

"Sorry. I'm not avoiding you," he lied. "Just got to keep up with my classes. Finals are coming up. I'm juggling."

Ryan set his pencil down and leaned back in his chair. "Noticed you've been riding the bus. Something wrong with your motorcycle again? My friend who fixed it guarantees his work. I'm sure he'd look at it for you again, no charge."

Ache screamed through James' veins, but he kept his answer short. "No. Runs great."

His uncle folded his arms, his eyes never leaving James. "Wanna tell me what's going on?"

James dropped his timecard on the desk, leaning his hip against the sturdy oak. "Which part? I assumed my dad's kept you up-to-date." He'd suspected that Ryan and his father were communicating behind his back, and Ryan's deer-in-the-headlights expression confirmed those suspicions to be true.

Ryan blew out a long breath. "I'm worried about you. I don't want to see you unravel the way your mother did, or the way your father has been known to do. Your well-being matters to me."

James scrubbed his hands over his face and into his dusty hair. "I know."

Ryan stood from his chair and came around the desk, leaning on it next to James. "Your dad told me you're a suspect in that girl's disappearance. This is a big deal, James. You're going to need all the support you can get. I want to help. Do you need me to find you a lawyer?"

"I don't know." Since selling Lola, he'd resigned to being represented by a public defender—but when it came to sharing the decision with his father and uncle, his brain simply shut down.

"Do you need money?" When James shrugged in response, Ryan's tone turned to cajoling. "An escape plan? An alibi?"

That broke through James' stress enough for him to crack half a smile. "Yes, to all three. And probably the lawyer, too."

Ryan straightened, opening a notepad and retrieving his pencil. "Let's figure this out together. Tell me what you've done so far."

James glanced at his watch, always conscious of the time. "I sold my motorcycle and signed up for a scuba class."

Ryan's writing hand stilled. "You . . . what? What does scuba have to do with anything? Why would you sell your bike? We just barely got it running."

As much as Ryan had always remained a confidant and true friend, there were limits to what he would believe. Besides, he'd promised to keep Emma's secret from everyone, and that included Ryan. He couldn't, wouldn't betray that, even if he thought his uncle might believe him—which he didn't. Not now, anyway. "My dad offered to sell his car so I would have money to run. Figured I'd save him the trouble." James plucked a paperclip off the desk, fiddling with it while his mind scrambled for a believable explanation. "Cops know my bike already."

"And you're planning to . . . " Ryan paused, raising a brow. "Escape by way of the ocean? To swim your way to freedom? Do you even hear how absurd that sounds?"

Hearing the words from someone else's mouth made the *real* plan even sound ludicrous. "It gives me something to do when I've felt like there was nothing else. Swimming always cleared Emma's head, so I thought maybe it would help me too."

Ryan's large hand clasped James' shoulder. "You won't find her by diving." His expression softened into sympathy. "I know you don't want to hear this. I don't want to say it, but at this point I have a duty. If Emma truly left by swimming out to sea, as you claim, she's gone. Been dead for weeks. No one can survive in the ocean for that long without a boat or something."

The stark declaration gouged a hole in James' chest, even knowing Ryan didn't understand about the existence of Atlantis or the underwater world.

"Maybe it was sharks. The rocks. A rip current. Maybe she swam too far and got tired." Ryan squeezed both of James' shoulders as if to prevent him from melting into the floor—which James wished badly he could do. "You won't find her out there. Not even below. I know you're scared, and life feels completely out of control, but you need to let her go."

"I can't." Inside his head, the words roared, echoing back to him over and over, but from his mouth nor more than a fierce whisper. Fire burned in his chest, its flames rising to his throat, into his eyes until he couldn't see, couldn't breathe. "She's out there, Ryan. All alone. And she's alive. I know it. I *feel* it.

Meanwhile, I'm about to be charged for a crime that no one committed, a murder that never happened. My life has been turned upside-down. Even if I wanted to, I can't ignore what's happening. Something has to give, and I'd really prefer to solve everything by finding her and bringing her home."

Ryan clenched his jaw, breath heaving. "You need to see a therapist. This is not rational thinking, bud. I understand that denial is a stage of grief, a valid one, but this is the most dangerous variety. You've been through a lot of heartache this last few years. In your current mental state, you shouldn't be trying to learn scuba, or skydiving, cliff-jumping—or anything else that could result in death."

"I'm not crazy." James lurched away from his uncle, seizing his lunch pack and keys. "Believe me, my mental state has never been clearer. Learning to dive gives me hope. You can't keep me from it, so please don't try."

Ryan scrubbed his hands over his face, dropping onto the couch in the corner. "At least promise me you'll never dive alone. And that you're saving what's left of the money so I can help you buy your motorcycle back."

"Smart divers never scuba alone." James yanked the door open. "And there's approximately four grand stashed in a broken gas can in the carport storage closet. Emergency money."

"Okay." Ryan nodded, resigned. "Okay. Do your thing. Take your class. But James, if you love me, please trust me to help you. Don't run away until we consult with an attorney. I'll never forgive myself if you end up dead in a foreign country because you were afraid to face what's happening here."

James swallowed, numbness spreading to his ears. "Not planning to run. Yet."

"Good. Give me some time to track down a lawyer. Meanwhile, keep your head down and stay out of trouble. We'll get you through this."

James' feet weighed like bricks in his shoes as he lumbered to the bus stop. No matter how he tried to construct the scuba excuse so it made sense, no part of his life made sense at the moment. Ryan was right to believe that James wouldn't find Emma. That he might never see her again.

But James refused to give up and accept that.

He arrived at the beach earlier than usual, allowing time for a rare solid meal. He shouldered his backpack, scanning the length of coastal road, and letting his nose lead the way. Hand in his pocket and eyes on the ground, he inadvertently bumped into someone going the opposite direction.

"Sorry. I'm really sorry, I . . . " He squinted in the brilliant sun, and took a hasty step back when he encountered the deadly frost of Heather's glare.

"What are you doing here?" Hands on hips and shoulders squared, James could see how she held up the bottom of the cheerleader pyramids.

*Be nice! Head down and out of trouble, like Ryan said.* He took a calming breath and counted to five, before forcing the best smile he could muster. "Hey, Heather. It's nice to see you. I actually have a class nearby tonight." He hitched his dive bag higher for emphasis, proud of his self-restraint.

Her cobalt eyes shot shards at his face as she folded her arms like a gangster preparing for a fight. "I can't believe you're not in jail yet. You're a menace to society. I hope they throw away the key."

James' neck muscles tensed with anxiety that suddenly felt too familiar. *Be nice, be nice, be nice.* He kept his smile in place, though it took everything he had to leave it there. "I'm pretty sure they don't throw innocent people in jail. Especially when there's no evidence—like, I don't know, a body? Just a thought."

Her malicious grin grew. "Oh, they have evidence. I've seen it. They're just busy gathering their eggs— building a strong enough case to ensure that you never see daylight again."

"I love Emma. I'm as desperate to get her back as anyone." Unable to keep up the act any longer, James sidestepped Heather, anxious to escape before she produced a weapon and stabbed him.

"Then why haven't you been to her house to visit her parents? Or Keith?"

James froze, mid-stride. He'd asked himself the same question more often than he could count. "Last time I saw Keith, he threw a stapler at my head and told me to never come back. I don't want to further traumatize him. And I've never met Emma's parents. Haven't known how to approach them. Not sure how they'd react to a visit from the guy who's a *person of interest* in their daughter's disappearance. It's a respect thing."

Heather pivoted, somehow up in his face before he realized she'd moved. "Emma's parents are super chill. You want to find her? Go see them. Tell them the truth. The only reason I can think that you wouldn't visit them is guilt. And why would you have guilt, if you're innocent?"

Since Emma left, he'd avoided doing a lot of important things. Zero desire, zero motivation. Losing Emma had stolen both. But Heather hit on a point James could no longer ignore. The Harris' had been in Greece when Emma's change transpired, and Keith traumatized beyond repair, after being kidnapped and held captive in the underwater city.

But Keith, the only other witness that night, could be James' strongest ally if someone could get him talking. What if Emma's parents knew more than Emma thought? The grandmother couldn't be the only person who recognized what was happening. Realizing that it was way past time, he decided one visit couldn't hurt. Then at least he'd know where they stood.

Either way, Heather's wild accusations didn't help. "Not avoiding it. I've been working whenever I'm not at school."

"Whatever." Heather rolled her eyes in disgust and swiveled away. "Can't wait to see you rot in a cell for eternity."

Vicious as they were, Heather's words drove home a point James had neglected to make. Emma's parents should have more motivation than anyone to locate their daughter, to protect her—at any cost. Maybe it was time to call on Emma's grandmother so he could figure out who he should trust with his love's life-threatening secret, and who he could not.

# Chapter Ten

## Emma

Time was kept differently in Atlantis, but after what—Emma guessed—had been several weeks, she'd begun to sense the tidal shifts caused by the moon's gravitational pull, and an extra level of warmth each time the sun above hit its midday apex. The Mer kept no clocks, no visual time-gauges, but whenever the current shifted from one side to the next, market merchants pulled their partitions, packed up their goods, and headed home, and the royals in the palace prepared for sleep tide.

And while the palace occupants slept, Emma explored, roaming the empty halls alone.

One such night, she ventured out with two goals in mind. To find her necklace, and a map that would lead her to Oceania, where she would choose her own fate. Either option would work.

The empty, half-lit halls, vibrated with eeriness, an extra layer of cold in the water that left her shivering. She floated through a dining space, past the throne room, and down the servant's corridor. She'd never encountered a kitchen, where food was prepared, but knew one must exist. She couldn't think of a better place to make new friends who might unwittingly help orchestrate her escape. In this section of the palace, she found neither doors, nor privacy curtains. Each chamber gaped like the mouth of a tunnel, providing enough privacy that Emma couldn't see in—and only the tiniest speck of light crept along the floor of the ones that must be occupied.

Ahead, the water rippled with movement, followed by a clang that reminded her of a slamming door. Emma scooted along in the shadows, peering stealthily around the corner, and was surprised to discover a wide, open cavern. Rock and ice walls lined the room, stocked with shelves of mismatched storage vessels, and cages of wriggling sea life that would soon become the featured meal. A salvaged treasure chest, a metal container covered by a smooth, flat shell, baskets woven from sea grasses and live coral, rows and rows of seashell bowls covered in filmy netting and filled with various colorful fishes. Near the center, stood a tall, stone pedestal, stained with puddles of red, green, and yellow. And to one side stood a tall door made of thick, opaque ice. *This must be where the food's prepared.*

She pressed her face against the foggy wall, trying to determine if it was another passage, or a storage locker for more food. When she couldn't see well enough to tell, she slid the door aside, revealing half a sword fish carcass, a basket filled with happily swimming shrimp, and a tub of snapping crabs. She helped herself to a handful of wriggling shrimp, shoving one into her mouth the way Keith shoveled potato chips in his.

Seafood here was distinctive from the kind she'd loved on land. The little blue shrimp wriggled inside her mouth, but she'd become accustomed to the grainy, crunchy texture. She would never stop missing spices and condiments. Cocktail sauce and butter would fill a serious gap her taste buds had discovered.

The noise clamored again, followed up by a rhythmic, musical beat that increased in volume. The Mer had proven a comparable species to humans, not so different in nature, so she'd expected the kitchen to be a hive of activity—even during sleep tide. To find It empty left her confused, and hearing these new sounds only amplified her disorientation.

She took another handful of shrimp, debating whether or not she should continue to explore, or give up for the night and go to bed, but when a din of voices joined the musical noise, she couldn't ignore that something was happening. An assembly had gathered. She continued down the corridor, past multiple caverns before arriving at one that threw a swath of amethyst light across the passage, casting a ghost-like image on the opposite wall. Laughter rang from within, and more clanking, the swish of fins and clacking of neck adornments, all joined by a steady beating of drums.

Nerves tugged in Emma's stomach and knotted the muscles between her shoulders as she ventured around the passage and into the open. In the corner opposite her, a band of Mer, produced a haunting melody with strange-looking instruments. To one side, an entire wall had been lined with shelves of colorful containers of textured substances. A high, stone table, lined with a variety of foods popular among the Mer, had drawn a small crowd. Everywhere she looked, Mer of all sizes and varieties mingled, some as singles, others in social clusters, and others wheeling together in what appeared to be dancing.

No one seemed to notice her arrival, allowing Emma to watch from the shadows, and blend into the growing crowd. A thin-boned, mermaid carried a container of glowing red plankton to the top of the palace wall, where she scooped a portion into the already glowing light source. Before the mermaid had the container's lid replaced, the light that had slowly faded to blue altered back to purple. Waiters served the guests food on flat, coral platters, and drink in snail shells bigger than Emma's fist.

Most of the party-goers carried their platters with them, devouring the snacks, and then setting the trays aside to join the dancing. Another cluster hovered near the stone counter that stood directly in front of the shelves, flirting, and consuming a continual stream of the multi-colored substances. Feeling timid and out of her element, Emma approached the counter and leaned on the cool stone top. The mermaid returned to her post on the other side, beaming at Emma and indicating the array of substances. "What can I get you?"

Had she been ashore, Emma would have ordered ice water or a soda, but here, neither was an option. Lips pressed together, she contemplated the containers, wondering what they held. After far too long, the mermaid-bartender inched closer. "Shall I make a suggestion?"

Emma's gills inhaled salt water as she forced a timid smile. "What is it?"

The mermaid flashed a devious grin. "You are new to this. Do not be afraid. The effects of paihana usually wear off by the rising tide. Completing your palace duties should not be extra difficult."

Next to her, a wrinkled merman let out an effervescent snore, having fallen asleep, upright, a gel-filled vessel in his hand. "What effects, exactly?" Emma asked.

"Laine." The mermaid beckoned someone over, catching the shell as it slid from the sleeping merman's hand. Another merman, burly, dark-haired, and wearing the wrist-cuffs of a guard, scooped up the sleeping merman and hauled him out the door. The bartender returned her attention to Emma, eyes lit with merriment. "I am called Marietta."

"Emma." She offered a hand for shaking, but pulled it back quickly when Marietta stared at it, confused.

"You are new to Atlantis."

She fought the instinct to nod, because nodding was not a recognized response among the Mer. "I am called Emma." Marietta had laid her arm across her chest, which Emma took as a form of greeting, so she imitated the move. "And yes, I am new here."

Marietta chose a yellow container, and scooped a portion into an empty shell, which she offered to Emma. "Paihana. This is a delicacy, shared among royals—and occasionally the servants who live in the palace."

While Marietta curved away to serve someone at the other end of the bar, Emma sniffed at the gelatinous substance, finding its scent no different from the same water she breathed, day in and day out. When the paihana jiggled, she poked her finger in, pleased when the warm, thick jelly slurped around it.

Marietta returned, setting aside another empty shell, so Emma asked, "What does it do?"

"It gives you an extra portion of joy." Marietta tapped her long, pointed nail on the yellow container, eliciting a musical ping. "This one is created using hearts of yellow sea anemone, mixed with the underbelly of stonefish."

Emma raised her vessel to eye-level, peering more closely at the sticky substance. "Aren't both of those creatures poisonous?"

Marietta dipped her finger in Emma's shell and scooped some into her mouth. "Only if you touch their spines. Paihana is made from the milder, vulnerable insides of those creatures, where the poison is not so prevalent. It alters your mind and body for a time, but not in a way that will cause permanent harm."

Marietta sucked the goop off her finger and continued her work. From the amount of people drinking, Emma gathered that imbibing of paihana was a popular pastime for the Mer.

Intrigued by the fascinating substance, Emma licked the yellow goo off her finger. A tart, sweet flavor burst across her tongue, seducing her with promises of delight. Immediately wanting more, she raised the shell to her lips and gulped, appreciating how it slid down her throat as if it crawled down of its own volition, requiring no effort to swallow. She had once tried alcohol with Tom—it had been bitter, smelly, and seared her mouth, throat, and stomach after a single sip. But paihana zinged inside her mouth, sweet and tangy at once, appealing to the same under-used taste buds that still longed for condiments like butter and lemon.

By the time Marietta returned, Emma had emptied her vessel, and was already contemplating the next one she should try. "Did you like it?"

"It's delicious!" Emma spouted, hearing her voice as though amplified by a microphone, much louder than she'd intended to speak. With an embarrassed pat to her lips, she lowered the volume. "I loved it very much, and now I'd like to try another. What else is good?" Momentarily unconcerned about boundaries, Emma reeled across the counter and up the well-lit wall. She elected a speckled container filled with bright green gel, significantly thicker than the yellow. "This is a pretty color. What's it made of?"

Marietta snatched the container and replaced it on the shelf. "Oh, you do not want to try that one. Not this tide."

"Why not?" Emma persisted, poking her lips out to pout—again, like a human. "It's pretty, and I like the taste of most green things."

"This is not naturally green." Marietta steered Emma back around the counter. "It is made from the poisons that begin blue and yellow, which turn green when mixed together. This paihana is too strong for someone who does not regularly imbibe."

"Have you tried it?" Emma asked, leaning her elbows on the counter to keep herself from floating away.

Marietta ignored Emma's question, searching a lower shelf, until she landed on an ornate container stained bright pink. "Are you feeling joyous yet?"

Emma caught her legs floating level to the counter, where she'd rested her chin on her hands. "Happier than I've felt since I got here." However short-term the results, maybe if she drank enough of the flavor-packed concoctions she could somehow conjure a laugh. That was another thing she missed about home—laughing. She couldn't remember the last time she'd done it. Desperate for more paihana, she reached across the counter with molasses-slow arms, knocking Marietta's empty shells to the stony ground, where one split apart on impact. "Oops." She lurched back, and banged into a dancing couple, who shoved her away as she blinked to focus her eyes.

Disoriented by the way the world had blurred, and sensing that she was losing control of her body, she flexed her fingers, frantic to grab hold of any steady thing. A tremor of panic shuddered through her, and pressure burst in her head. With her last thread of logic, she realized that she'd put herself in a horribly dangerous situation from which it was imperative that she extract herself. "I need to go," she said to no one. "Back to my room."

Between her flailing movements, and with the help of the in-room current, she'd drifted away from the counter and into the crowd. No longer able to see Marietta, the bar, or the exit. She was surrounded by strangers, all equally disoriented by their own paihana choices. No one noticed the panic attack that threatened to explode in Emma's chest. "I need to go back." Her head spun, noise magnified, every motion and light turning in her stomach until it bubbled and squeezed with pain.

She propelled herself forward, first aiming for the ceiling, and when that only intensified her stress, shot lower, using the ground as her anchor. After several minutes of panicked confusion, a warm hand grasped her elbow. "This way, Princess." Laine, the merman who had carried out the sleeping patron, guided her to the exit.

"Thank you." Frightened, and torn about allowing a stranger to touch her, she submitted to Laine's lead.

A drunken merman, dark of hair and fin, crashed into her, but Laine shoved the merman aside with a muttered curse. "I'll be back for you."

Emma rolled her head around, hoping for a glimpse of the merman, and suddenly the cavern was populated with mermen who all had the same face as James. His voice echoed in the music, compelling her to swim into the arms of the nearest James, seeking comfort. Confusion clawed at her insides, upsetting her already churning gut. Her fingers tingled, her eyes refused to focus, and her skin had numbed in places she didn't realize existed.

Laine tugged at her elbow, indicating the exit. "Do you not wish to leave?"

"Yes." She closed her eyes against the onslaught. "Please."

He escorted her to her room, silent, but for the rhythm of breath bubbling from his gills. When they arrived at the curtained door, he released her elbow, dismissing her with a curt bow. "You would be wise to avoid paihana parties, Princess Emmalina. Such a gathering is not a safe, or proper place for the Sea King's granddaughter."

"There is no proper place for me." Emma parted the curtain. "Thank you for escorting me. I'll remember your kindness, Laine."

His face distorted in her already fraying vision as he nudged her into her room and tugged the curtain closed. "You should not wander the halls this tide. Sleep well."

Emma fell into her bed and let the swaying motion lull her racing pulse. Fragmented memories of James overtook her thoughts, so real that she could feel the weight of his arms around her, and the warmth. His lips pressed to her forehead, breath in her hair while their legs tangled together. When his heartbeat finally matched rhythm with hers, she slept in James' arms, as she had been on that last night in her true home.

And in her sleep, she smiled.

# Chapter Eleven

## James

**March 31**
*36 days gone*

ON THE DAY OF HIS first pool-dive, James decided that he would love diving, even if he'd never met Emma. While Tony worked with the claustrophobic class members, James sank to the bottom of the deep end, bobbing as he practiced breathing with a regulator.

He switched between the main REG, and the backup one, following the procedure he'd learned from the videos. When water leaked into his mask, he adjusted it, and even stayed calm when Tony encouraged him to force out the leaked water, without surfacing. He even inflated and deflated his buoyancy control device, experimenting with weights to learn how to achieve neutral buoyancy.

Tony caught up to him after class. "I'm impressed. You're a fast learner. From your build, I'm guessing you're an athlete."

The contentment of pleasure soaked in as James packed his mask and snorkel into his mesh equipment bag. "Basketball."

Tony squatted, holding the bag open while James crammed in his flippers. "All divers should be physically fit. Could save your life."

"I'm a strong swimmer." James pulled the drawstring and stood, rubbing his hair with a towel.

"I would guess that of you." Tony straightened too, one hand bracing his back. "Can I be nosey and ask why you're in such a hurry to certify?"

James slung the strap over his shoulder, unable to look Tony in the eyes. "My girlfriend loves to dive. She's gone for a while, but I hope to surprise her when she gets back."

"Oh yeah? Maybe I know her. What's her name? Where did she certify?" A young couple interrupted with a question, and James waited politely while Tony addressed them, fighting the urge to flee. When the couple had departed, Tony returned his attention to James. "You planning to take your girl on a fun trip? Somewhere romantic?"

*I wish. Too bad I'm not allowed to leave town.* "Maybe someday. Hopefully in the near future."

"You're young. Plenty of time." Tony waved goodbye to an older gentleman, and then began to rearrange a haphazard display. "Where did you say she certified?"

James swallowed, inching toward the door. The direction these questions were moving left him prickling with discomfort. "I'm not sure. She's been diving for years." Hearing the words, James could almost predict the next question word for word. "She's not from around here, though. I doubt you'd know her."

"You'd be surprised. It's a small world." Tony's grin flashed as he deployed to the register, where a customer waited. "Anyway, it's no big deal whether I know her or not. I just noticed that you've attacked this class with more dedication than anyone I've ever seen. Feels like you're pretty seriously about this girl."

*My life and future are dependent on her.* "I am."

Tony paused, informing the customer that he'd be right there. "If she loves diving the way you claim, you should hang on to her. Nothing on Earth shapes a person quite like becoming one with the sea."

A heavy ball of fear settled on James' chest. Tony had just hit on his biggest fear. Emma loved swimming. She loved the ocean and all its inhabitants. It was the one and only place that brought her peace when she was stressed. By now, she must have learned her purpose, met her family, and visited her home in Atlantis. What if she loved all of them too?

Unease crackled in his fatigued muscles. The more he learned about diving, the better he understood that with each day that Emma stayed gone, her chances of returning withered away.

Exhaustion weighed like boulders sitting on his neck, and a migraine throbbed behind his eyes, urging James to escape the dive shop, fast. Once again, Tony offered him a ride, but since the students had used their new equipment for the first time, a number of them lingered longer than usual, perusing accessories and additions. Knowing that Tony couldn't leave for a while, James slipped out the door.

Water dripped through the bag, down his leg and into his shoe, but James hardly noticed as he plopped onto the bus stop bench, breathing a sigh of relief just to be outside. He opened his transportation app, blinking to de-fog his eyes, which landed on a route that would bring him past Emma's family home.

Heather's reprimand echoed in his mind. She was right that he needed to go there. At some point, he would have to meet them. Better that it not be in a courtroom facing murder charges. Still, apprehension threatened to grind him into the bench. Every memory he and Emma had made in that house was imprinted on his brain, more vivid, more accurate than if he'd recorded them.

When a bus approached, James checked the schedule again, deciding to board either way. If this bus took him home, great. He'd give himself a breather for tonight. But if it took him to Emma's house—he'd consider it fate.

It wasn't long before James realized he was going for a visit. What would he say to them? Would they let him in or send him away? Or call the police to arrest him? Did they consider him guilty? The taste of blood filled his mouth from chewing the inside of his cheek—a recently developed habit.

Maybe Heather was right. Maybe it was his fault. Maybe if he'd stayed out of her life, resisted the attraction—maybe she'd have been allowed to finish high school. And who knew? Maybe Emma would've wanted the chance for a new life in Atlantis. And maybe James wouldn't feel so lost.

Did Emma feel a similar loss, or had she adjusted? Had she married that merman-dude? And if so, was it by force or choice? Maybe she'd made friends, met her long-lost family. Maybe. He wanted her to be happy, and at the same time, prayed she was still uncomfortable in Atlantis. He couldn't stand the idea that she'd spent the last several weeks in misery, but he needed her back, and terror continually besieged him—insisting that she would adapt and forget.

"And I'll be in prison," he mumbled, shaking his head at the pathetic turn his life had taken.

A woman sitting on the row opposite him looked up from her smartphone. "I'm sorry, did you say something?"

James shook his head. "Just thinking aloud."

With a suspicious hum, the woman scooted down the row and resumed scrolling her phone.

Minutes later, the bus pulled to a stop near the Harrisons' street, and the door opened. James rose, heart pounding in his temples as he compelled his trembling legs to move, forcefully placing one foot in front of the other until he stood on the sidewalk at the end of Emma's street.

A downpour of memories saturated him until one settled, gelled. Police cars parked in the road, lights flashing, and officers searching for the man who broke Emma's window. Valentine's Day seemed like years ago, rather than months.

Entering the neighborhood felt forbidden and wrong—like encroaching on territory that was no longer his. When he arrived at the familiar house, he stopped at the edge of the driveway, eyes drawn to the bedroom window. They'd watched a torrential storm through that window, while James held Emma together on the night her brother disappeared.

The light was off, of course, as were the rest. The home behind the glass lacked warmth, and the vivacious energy James knew had once existed inside. All over again, loss punched him in the gut, stealing his breath as if he'd found her cold and still, her eyes staring, with nothing behind them.

Emma's red convertible sat in the driveway, dusty and un-driven.

Across the street, a porch light flickered on, and the woman who cared for Keith stepped out, hands on hips, straining to see through the dark. Not in the mood to chat with a neighborhood gossip, James stole a last look at Emma's house, and continued down the street.

The next day, James worked with Matthew to finish up a tile job. The solid, back-breaking labor went a long way to soothing his frustration, even as his muscles protested. There was something immeasurably therapeutic about lifting and hauling heavy tiles, and then using them to create beautiful designs. Because of a tight deadline, Matthew started before dawn, and

James joined him just after two, immediately following his final class of the day.

By six, they'd laid all the stone, leaving only finish work to be completed after the tile had dried and set. James used the edge of his shirt to wipe a sweat river from his forehead. "That went fast. Hope we didn't mess anything up."

"Me too. I think that's a record for me. We work well together." Matthew guzzled from a jug he brought with him every day. "You finished the backsplash in the master bathroom, right?"

"Yep. And the decorative shower strip." They double-checked each other's work, finding only perfectly patterned segments. "Unless we missed an entire room, we're done until we can grout tomorrow."

Matthew pulled off his work gloves and checked his dusty, beat-up watch. "It's early. Do you want to grab some dinner?"

While Matthew had worked in the kitchen, and James handled the bathroom, he'd tuned out the world with earbuds and music. Somewhere between finishing the shower pan and the backsplash, he'd rekindled the dream of buying that boat from the dealership. Felt like ages since he'd been to the cove, and he itched to *do something*. Anything. "I'm driving Ryan's work truck, so I should probably get it back to him soon. Raincheck?"

Matthew shrugged, gulping more water. "Sure. Another time, then. Let's load up the equipment and cut out of here."

Half an hour later, James pulled into the parking lot of the dealership where he'd sold Lola. Tile-dust coated his hair, skin, and clothes—even his eyelashes, but now that he'd made up his mind, he hadn't dared take the time to go home and shower, lest the warm water bring him to his senses.

The boat he'd looked at was gone.

Lola too.

He couldn't afford to buy Lola back, so there was no use in waxing nostalgic. But the boat—there weren't a lot of boats available in his price range, nor did he have time to hunt one down. Nausea tumbled like rocks. Why had he waited? He should have bought it the minute he'd had that money in hand. *Maybe it wasn't meant to be.*

Still, he couldn't leave without making sure.

This time, a different salesman met him in the lot. Patchy facial hair announced his youth, eyes filled with a hunger that screamed *beginner*. He shoved his hands in the pockets of perfectly creased pants, rocking back on his heels. "Whatcha looking for today?"

James pursed his lips, fighting the urge to laugh. If only this kid could see how identically his actions mirrored the behavior of the other salesman. Either body language was part of their training, or vehicle sales required a specific personality type. "I was here a few days ago, and looked at a boat that was parked on the other side of the building. Has it been sold?"

The scrawny kid regarded the lot, evidently unaware that any such vehicle has been available. "Probably. We're competitively priced to keep our inventory moving. High turnover rates."

Feeling like tile mortar had spilled in his guts, already half solidified, James somehow avoided snapping. "Could you please find out if it's been moved?"

The salesman led him inside, where he scrolled a computer log, brow crumpled in concentration. After several tense minutes, he refocused on James. "Sorry. I can't see a boat listed. Someone must have sold it. I'm happy to show you a car, though. Or a camp trailer?"

"Unless you're selling a car that floats on water, I'm not interested." Outside, the sun's last rays lit the horizon pink and gold, but inside the run-down building, a black hole of darkness opened, threatening to swallow James.

"I might have a—"

He slammed the door, livid with himself for not buying the boat when he had the chance. His tires squealed as he tore out of the lot, setting his sights on the beach.

Though he wasn't born of the sea in the same way as Emma, its enduring rhythm sang to him, symphonies of peace and truth that provided clarity for a mind besieged with turmoil. He hadn't returned to the cove since Peters cautioned him away, the loss a lingering, unreachable itch. What if she came in search of a message, only to find the place swept clean? Would she imagine he'd given up on her?

Though cliffs concealed the inlet, obscuring the cove from view, a tall sandstone arch—which Emma claimed stood as a marker for the entrance to Atlantis—stood over a mile out, and would be visible from the boat harbor south of Tony's scuba shop. The harbor would not offer the same privacy that had allowed him to sit alone on the sand, talking to Emma as though she sat with him, but he could at least perch from the edge of the dock, feet dangling above the sapphire waves as they crashed against the pilings.

He parked in a lot and paid the fee, then strode onto the concrete pier, squinting against the glare in search of the formation. From this perspective, it appeared no more than a speck on the distant horizon, but if brought a pair of binoculars, next time he'd have a better view. Maybe it was more than a mile, as he'd first believed. "That's a long way out."

Rather than sit, he wore a line in the salty buildup at the end of the dock, rehashing the events of that night at least a hundred times. Given his new dive training, he finally understood that without a boat, any attempt to reach that arch would be nothing less than suicide. Maybe, possibly if he'd spent his life training as an Olympic swimmer, with a support team as backup—but he didn't have either of those things, and knew he never would. Even a BCD and dive tank be empty long before he got there—he doubted he'd even make it halfway. When he tired from pacing, he removed his shoes and stretched out on the dock, swinging his feet over the edge so that every time a wave splashed the wooden pillars, a fine mist sprayed up his ankles, and sometimes to his knees.

Overhead, a pelican circled, scoping the potential. James thought it might land nearby, but instead it dove like an arrow into the seawater, emerging with a mouthful of a nicely-sized fish. "What do I do?" he yelled. Again, doubting Emma could hear, but remembering how his one-sided conversations had always alleviated stress. "I'm trying really hard, but every day fate throws me a new curveball. It's like, no matter how I try, what I do, I'm doomed to fail." As always, the ocean responded with a steady rush of waves.

After a while, the sun made its nightly dip into the flat edge of the sea, hot enough to burn through his clothes so sweat to rolled down his back. The time had come to return his uncle's company truck. He retraced his original path, so lost in thought that he nearly missed the bright white boat being towed out of a storage bay at Steadman's Recreational. He hit the brakes, swerving into the parking lot, and narrowly avoiding a collision with a car in the next lane over. "Sorry," he yelled, but continued skidding into the lot, refusing to stop until he'd parked next to the boat. He waved down the towing driver while a seed of hope fought through his mortar.

"Do you work here? Do you own this boat?"

The man rolled down his window. "I work in the service bay. Tuned up the motor to help it sell. Great little machine, just needed a new battery."

*It's here. The sea gods have responded.* "Okay, well don't worry about parking it anywhere. I'm about to buy it." He turned off his engine and bolted inside to start the paperwork before the place closed. No way he would leave without that boat. He only hoped Ryan would let him keep the truck for a few more hours while James figured out where to store his new purchase.

# Chapter Twelve

## Emma

EMMA WOKE WITH A SOUR stomach and a massive migraine. Her insides growled with a mixture of hunger and opposition to food, and the temperature in her room had risen. She stirred to sit up, but her feet were tangled in the bed's seaweed webbing.

"There now, Princess. No need to move. I shall fetch you an anemone heart from the healer, and you will be well again."

"I'm not sick." But when she again tried to rise out of bed, the weight of her body held her in place, limbs heavier than ever before. "Okay, maybe I am."

Maia arranged Emma's breakfast on the coral table next to her bed, then swished through the privacy curtain. The galley Mer had sent more oysters, and a tiny blue crab. Eating required energy, but Emma reached for the crab, relieved that this morning—of all days—her provided meal included something that had always been a favorite.

But after wrestling with the outer shell for longer than should have been necessary, she decided the meaty, buttery crab would involve more effort than she could manage, and the thought of biting into the shell turned her stomach with even more enthusiasm. Setting aside her first choice, she selected an oyster and began the tedious process of prying open the sealed shell with a sharp, whale-bone tool. She used the same instrument to stab the meat, pleased when her hard work yielded her not one, but two beautiful, pink pearls, and a large, juicy slab of oyster meat.

"Congratulations, Mrs. Oyster," she joked. "You've given birth to twins." She closed the pearls into the pouch she wore around her wrist, then worked the meat free and slipped it into her mouth, trying not to shudder when it slithered all the way down.

"Oh, Princess. You should not eat until you are well." Maia appeared next to the bed, a helping of gelatinous brown anemone stuck to the end of another eating tool. "The effects of Paihana can sometimes leave a maid unable to eat for many tides."

As if Maia had called it forth, Emma's stomach revolted, expelling the slimy meat—which was now glazed with bright yellow goo—and coating her mouth with the vile taste of poison. The remains of her one-bite breakfast floated around her head, refusing to disperse until Maia scooped it away and rubbed the puke into the fine, silt ground. "How did you know that would happen? How did you know I drank paihana?"

"Laine reported to me last tide, informing me that he saw you safely here." She checked the temperature on Emma's forehead. "But don't worry. I'll not betray you to the Sea King. Confessing such a thing would mean punishment for me as well as you, and I do not wish to lose my assignment. I enjoy your company, as friends."

Did she consider Maia a friend? By default, Maia was the only Mer that Emma regularly interacted with, and because she'd been assigned as Emma's maid, it was hard not to doubt her loyalty on a friendship level. After all, this was her job, and she had a lot to gain by keeping Emma happy.

Maia hovered, again offering the anemone. Emma accepted the skewer, frowning at the blob of goo. "Why am I taking this? I thought anemone are poisonous."

Maia blinked, which Emma took as meaning that this was one more thing she was expected to already know. Like it was common knowledge to everyone except her. "Anemone carry poison in their tentacles, but healing enzymes in their organs. This is the heart of a brown. It's strong, but will numb your pain and settle your insides so you will be able to consume your meal." She indicated what was left of the oysters and the tiny blue crab that had originally excited Emma.

"This is supposed to make me feel better?" she clarified, attempting, once again, to sit up.

"Yes, Princess. The enzymes will eat away what is left of the Paihana and make you well again."

Emma considered her mermaid servant, reminding herself that sarcasm and lies were not the way of the Mer. She stacked up her courage. "Okay then." Eyes closed, she shoved the brown substance into her mouth. The anemone slid down her throat easily, and within minutes, the spinning in her head eased.

While Emma lay in bed, Maia scooped away pockets of slimy, dark-colored water that Emma hadn't noticed until now. Several such spots dotted the water in her room, and as Maia scooped each one and then buried them in the sand, Emma realized that at some point, all of the disgusting substance had come from her.

"Is it working?" Maia asked, continuing her task.

Emma sat up, finally able to concentrate on untangling her feet. "I think so. How long before I should try eating again?"

Maia glanced over her shoulder, examining Emma's face. "When your insides roll with emptiness."

She refused to cause more work for Maia by eating too soon and risking the embarrassment of another vomiting episode. "Do you think I could swim? Or will that make it worse?" She rocked in her hammock, gathering the courage to move. "I'm sorry to be so much work. I'm new to this."

The humble admission earned her a smile from Maia. "Yes, Princess. As you are new to everything in Atlantis. Do not worry. You will learn quickly." A wistful look of nostalgia flickered in Maia's expression as she turned to deal with another dark patch. "You must remain still for now."

Soon, Emma's stomach rumbled loudly, and together, the mermaids broke open the oysters, harvesting the colorful pearls and saving them in Emma's pouch before she speared the meat into her mouth. Even cracking the crab wasn't as difficult as she had expected, and for the first time since her arrival, Emma cleared her meal tray.

Maia beamed. "You see, Princess? With enough time, you will learn to like your home below."

"Thanks." Emma tried to force a smile, but overwhelming sadness threatened to consume her. "But I'm not sure that's possible."

Maia clasped Emma's hand and helped her rise from the hammock. "Do not worry, Princess. It is good to know where you come from, even if you intend to leave again."

Emma couldn't argue that point. Her sweet, innocent maid had proven wiser and more observant than Emma gave her credit for.

When Maia returned to the galley with the empty tray, Emma sneaked out to begin a new search. The goal: her missing necklace. Where to look? The private quarters of last person who'd had it in his possession. Merrick.

With the exception accompanying the mermaids in the market, Merrick had kept his distance, as she'd asked, though everywhere she went, he lurked nearby. Perhaps he didn't live in the palace, at least not full time, but he must at least have a room. As her grandfather's Duke, and her intended, it would make sense.

The palace flourished with activity and noise, which elevated the risk of wake-tide snooping. But a sense of urgency thrust her forward. She stayed low, favoring shadows cast far from the glowing walls, and held her breath when necessary to avoid air bubbles giving her away.

Once she'd circumvented the public areas, she peered into every darkened chamber, assessing the probability of each. Could this be the room in which

Merrick had hidden the necklace? Could this? After a while, she happened upon an unkempt storage chamber. Mounds of random things—stacked taller than Emma could stand—overtook the available space, so that even a mermaid of her size could scarcely squeeze through. Metal slabs from ship wreckage, empty treasure chests covered in barnacles and growths, smashed shards of china and glass, a tarnished silver spoon, and a green fork made of either brass or copper. A veritable treasure trove of salvage.

She pressed her palm on a stone slab to propel herself, headlong, into the mess, and left a handprint in the silt. A similar touch to metal left a mark as well. Rounding the other side, she dragged a finger over a fragment of pottery, leaving another line. It appeared that no one had visited the artifacts in ages. If her pendant was hidden here, she would see more evidence of disturbance, or at the very least proof of entry. Despite her curiosity, it was time to move on.

Shelves lined the next room she encountered, as well as natural ledges and tables, all buried under stone tablets and sharp instruments used for etching. In the center a long, stone surface had been erected, and was now skewed with heaps of tablets-all etched in the language of Mer.

While she snooped, her grandfather's aide, Glan, entered, stone quill in hand and brow furrowed as if his head hurt from retaining the court's information.

He veered to the stone surface and began etching feverishly on the nearest tablet. "Princess. You should not be in this chamber."

Emma let out the breath she'd been holding while she hoped he hadn't seen her. "I'm sorry. I was just . . . " What? Exploring? Sneaking around without my handmaid? Snooping. "Looking for something to read— something written in English."

Glan continued etching. "You will find no human language in Atlantis, and no reading that would be of interest to you."

"Oh. Okay, then." She gulped, fighting the urge to argue that anyone intended to rule a place should be able to read the documents kept in it. But Glan was just an aide, and this wasn't a battle worth fighting.

Once she'd left the recording chamber, Emma decided to change tactics and target her grandfather's corridor. She'd never ventured in that direction, assuming the tunnel was dedicated only to the Sea King's private cavern, but now she wondered if she'd find Merrick's room down that hall as well. She changed course, curving around—and collided with a bottle-nose dolphin.

"Oh! I'm so sorry." She petted its flank noting that the creature carried a woven bag in his mouth. His forlorn eyes silently begged for freedom. "I hope I didn't hurt you." Emma ran her hands along his smooth underbelly until her fingers encountered a tangle of tough, seaweed netting wrapped around the dolphin's flukes. It bound the animal tight enough to prevent his escape, but lose enough so he could move about the palace. This was not the result of an encounter with a fisherman's net, but a device purposefully placed by the Mer.

Heartsick to know that anyone, human or Mer, could enslave such a magnificent creature, Emma continued to stroke his velvety skin, humming to keep him calm while she inspected his cargo. At first glance, the bag appeared to be filled with kelp and seaweed, but when she pinched a portion between her fingers, she perceived a glimmer—something shiny. Still humming, she attempted to pry the bag from the dolphin's mouth, but he jerked away, his eyes begging her to let him continue his task.

"Busy, are you?" She patted the sides of his face, meeting his eyes to gain his trust. "All right. Go on your way, then."

The dolphin continued his journey, and Emma followed. Her new friend disappeared into a tunnel, which later opened into a wide grotto. They passed beneath a fissure in the ceiling, through which a ribbon of sunlight glistened, curling toward the ground like a stream of gold poured from the far, distant sky. Momentarily distracted, Emma paused, allowing the glow to bathe her skin with light.

The dolphin continued down another tunnel and out of view, so reluctantly, she followed, rewarded when the tunnel ended in a massive cave that appeared to have been covered in glitter. She swam to the nearest ledge, and dipped her hand into a bowl filled with gemstones, watching them sparkle between her fingers while her brain worked to process what she held.

Blood red rubies, emeralds green as blades of grass, sapphires so dark they were nearly black, and bright white diamonds so large, a single one could possibly feed a third world country. There were other gemstones, too, and other treasures. Plates and chains and housewares made of gold and silver. Piles of coins that must be hundreds of years old. Weapons encrusted with jewels, and armor that bore tarnish, but no rust. Green copper servers and goblets and tools and antique jewelry on and on.

The collection would put the Smithsonian gem museum to shame. Probably the history one, too.

She pulled water through her gills, heart racing as her new scales crackled and tightened. Someone had created this place, and gone to a lot of trouble to keep it hidden. These were not like the adornments popular to the Mer; they were human jewels, treasures made by human hands and worth millions of dollars on land.

The dolphin dropped his cargo on a tall stone dais, then brushed against Emma's side as if to urge her to leave. Ignoring the warning, she approached the dais and spread the contents of the bag across the stone surface, digging through the debris to unearth more jewelry. "Where did this come from?" Again, the creature bumped her, urgency mounting.

"Okay, I'm coming." She caressed his skin, stealing one last glance at the collection. Whoever built this place—she guessed her grandfather—was unlikely to have a full inventory of every single item. And if they did, the list would be longer than a thousand-page paper book, and way more using Mer tablets. On her way out, she pilfered a gold and diamond necklace, and a jeweled tiara, hiding them in her wild hair to conceal them from view.

Her grandfather had made known his vile hatred of all-things human, so while logically it made sense that the treasure must be his, Emma had her doubts. Lies and guile weren't part of the Mer culture. In fact, she believed most Mer incapable of voicing a single untruth.

But there was one who had experience with human trickery. One she knew well, and who had access to the surface, somewhere from which to steal even *more* valuable human treasures. Aside from Emma, there was only one Mer in Atlantis also gifted with feet, and the ability to walk on land.

*Merrick.*

# Chapter Thirteen

## James

**April 2**
*38 days gone*

"YOU DID WHAT?" RYAN PACED in his office, eyes firing daggers through the window at the boat hitched to his company truck.

"It's not as stupid as it sounds." James leaned on the door frame, unwilling to make it possible for Ryan to close them both inside. Why had he told his uncle about the boat? He should have just asked to keep the truck overnight and given Ryan a lame excuse about having a date—or something.

Ryan scrubbed a hand over his face. "See, this is where we disagree. I can't think of *any* reason why it makes an ounce of sense that you sold your bike and bought a boat that you can't even tow. What're you going to do with it? Can't boat to work. Can't boat to school. Can't use it to pay for a lawyer." Ryan slammed his hand on the desk, leaning on his knuckles as he stood, quivering with fury. "What has gotten into you, James? I don't even know who you are, anymore. Do you *want* to go to jail?"

"Of course not." The mortar in his gut had fully solidified, leaving James to function around a solid mass of anxiety. Even though buying a boat and learning scuba felt right, and made complete sense to *him*, James couldn't explain to anyone *why*. To protect Emma, to provide her a chance to live a normal life if—when—she came back, he had to keep her secret locked in a vault. But he also needed to give Ryan a plausible reason for what he'd done. One that made sense of all the madness. "Look, I know a lawyer's going to cost a lot of money. There's a strong market for inexpensive boats around here, so I thought I'd put in some work to fix it up, and then sell it—see if I can make enough profit to help offset my legal expenses."

Ryan blinked, his boiling rage calming to a simmer. "That still doesn't make sense to me, James. You outright owned a very nice motorcycle that got you to work, and school, and practice, partly because I called in some significant favors to help you keep it running." He jabbed his finger in the direction of the boat they could see from the window. "You don't even have a vehicle to tow that thing, let alone transport you to and from work. How do you expect to fix up a boat, if you can't drive yourself to wherever it's moored?"

"I'm doing fine with the bus."

"You shouldn't *have* to ride the bus." A vein throbbed in Ryan's neck as he planted himself in a chair. "That was the whole point of my helping you get your bike fixed in the first place."

"I couldn't keep my motorcycle." Giving in, James fully entered the office, taking the seat opposite his uncle. "The cops recognize it. They were following me everywhere, scrutinizing everything I did. At least when I ride the bus, I can pretend to get lost for a minute."

Ryan leaned on the arms of his chair, thumping one hand repeatedly as if *he* was the suspect in a murder investigation. "Why didn't you tell me? We could have traded it in and got you something else. Why a boat? It just doesn't make sense."

James leaned his chair back, staring at the ceiling, and wishing, that he could open up and tell his uncle everything. "No matter what we bought, the cops would get to know that vehicle. And they would continue to spy on everywhere I go and everything I do. At least a boat is still worth something. Cash has to be hidden or put in a bank for the authorities to scrutinize. I'm going to drop this boat into the water, and rent a temporary slip at the dock. That way, I won't need to tow it. And then, even if the cops follow me to the dock, at least they'll know I'm not doing anything illegal. No one in his right mind would try to escape the country in a thirty-year-old seventeen-foot speed boat."

"No one in his right mind." Ryan stopped beating the chair's arm and narrowed his eyes at James. "But you're not in your right mind, are you? Swear to me that you're not planning some elaborate escape by boat, because now that you've brought it up, there's one more thing to be concerned about."

"I swear." James laughed out loud, grateful that this was one thing he admit to his uncle in all honesty. "Don't worry. Running would make me look guilty."

"Okay." The anger lines on Ryan's face relaxed, but his brows remained furrowed. "I'm not going to lie and tell you that I'm not extremely worried about your state of mind. But in a convoluted, unrealistic way, I can kind of see where you're finding your logic. I *am* concerned about the fact that you know less than nothing about fixing up a speed boat. And not sure how you plan to pay for parts. There are so many factors you haven't considered."

"I'm going to teach myself." James squeezed the arms of his chair, preparing to bolt, while he waited for the ridiculous conversation to finally end. "I've been watching a lot of you-tube tutorials. And I've saved a good chunk of my paychecks so I can pay for parts gradually, the way I did for my motorcycle."

"You might not have much time to play mechanic," Ryan pointed out. "Without a phenomenal lawyer, you're looking at jail time, sooner than later."

"No one knows that better than I do." James burned his uncle with a gaze of steely determination. "Do you think it's easy to get up every morning and pretend that my girlfriend hasn't been missing for weeks? Knowing that I've probably blown my chance for a basketball scholarship, because losing her was crazy hard? Do you think I actually sleep at night, ever? Trust me, Ryan, I've thought this through on every level, and every aspect. There's nothing I can do about Emma being gone right now, and until I can get past these legal troubles, not a lot I can do to salvage my chance of going to college. I have to do something with my time, or risk going madder than I already am. I'm making a project out of fixing up this boat. I'm sorry that you think I'm wasting my time, and my money. Sorry if you resent that I need your help retaining a lawyer. You have my word, that whatever the cost, I'll pay it back. As soon as is physically possible. Right now, as long as I keep showing up for work, please let me cope however I can." James stood, bouncing the keys in his palm. "I'll bring the truck back tomorrow, as soon as I rent a slip."

Ryan stood, lips pressed together as if holding in the remainder of his thoughts. "Nah. Go ahead and keep it for a few days. Matthew has his own, and as long as you show up for work, I'm not out anything by letting you borrow it."

Relief bloomed in James' chest. He hated lying to Ryan worse than about anything in the world, but the more he thought about it, the more he realized that turning this lie into reality could be doubly beneficial for him. "Thank you. I owe you bigtime."

"Yes, you do." Ryan pulled him in for a manly hug. "How about next time you decide to spend large amounts of money while attempting to fill a hole in your life, you call me first. I can't help you with anything if you don't communicate."

James drew away, itching to escape and get to the marina before scuba class. "I promise, I won't let you down."

But as he climbed into the driver's seat of the beat up old Ford, his throat clogged with guilt. No matter how things went down, his most recent, important promise was one that was simply impossible to keep.

Though he'd flown as fast as he could, he missed the marina's office hours by fifteen ridiculous minutes.

Squeezing his eyes shut, he pressed his forehead against the glass door, wondering when—if ever—life would cut him a break. Worse, if rush hour traffic hadn't let up, he was about to be late to class, too. On top of all that, he hadn't eaten since the cheap-o, miniscule school lunch he'd forced down around eleven-thirty, and his mood was rapidly deteriorating into hangry mode.

But scuba class, being the top priority on his list, took precedence over everything else, so James hauled his new boat to the beach-front shop, and parked in the public lot across the street—paying for two parking stalls, just in case. Knowing Tony and the class would be waiting, he changed with record speed and met the group out back on the pool deck, apologizing the minute he stepped outside.

They worked on the same skills as last time, with the added pressure of having Tony turn off the oxygen tank so they would know what it feels like to run out of air. By the end of the session, James passed off the required skills, and gained the right to attend the first of his supervised open-water dives.

Even after he'd aced the required pool skills, his nerves frayed like a sweater unraveling. A single thread, caught on one small thing, unlooping the rest into a jumbled mess of yarn. In two days, he'd finally enter the ocean, below the surface, swimming in the same manner that Emma did—only wearing significantly more equipment. His chances of seeing her during the first dive were less than a billion to one, but in those moments of subaquatic freedom, he would be closer to her than he had in over a month. By the time he changed and turned in his tank, anticipation had him bouncing on the balls of his feet.

"What's got you so excited?" Tony asked, cataloguing the equipment and making notes on his ever-present dive log. "Your girlfriend coming home? Got a hot date?"

James leaned against the counter, fiddling with the pearl in his pocket and grinning wider than he had in a long time. "Looking forward to our open water dive. Can't wait to get out there."

Tony finished logging the tanks and set the log on top of a precarious stack of papers behind the register. "I'm glad to see you're still excited."

"I'll always be excited about diving." James turned his attention to the fish tank, dominating the wall opposite him. "I love to swim. Think diving's my new favorite sport."

Tony raised a brow, moving closer to the tank, as James did. "I thought you were a basketball star? Even saw your picture on the front page of the community paper at a gas station not long ago."

A tiny seahorse emerged from behind a waving plant, poking his nose into a fake rock tunnel. James looked forward to seeing such fish in the wild. "That was before. Lately . . . I don't know. I guess swimming has become more important."

"Don't get me wrong. It's always incredible to find a new passion. I'm just saying don't give up on the old ones. It's possible to do both, to love both. You'll be happier in the long run." Tony returned to the task of putting away the equipment, hauling tanks, BCDs, and tubes into the enormous closet where he kept them, and James stepped in to help. When they'd finished, Tony asked, "Do you need a ride home? I have the time."

James picked up his dripping mesh bag, this time wise enough to hold it at his side and avoid having it drip down his shorts. "Thanks, but I have wheels tonight."

Intrigued, Tony craned his neck trying to see out the window. "Oh yeah? You get a new car?"

"Not exactly." Face twisted in a pained grimace, James led Tony to the door and opened it, indicating the dim lot, and the dark outline of his new boat.

Tony whistled, impressed. "That's yours?"

"Not the truck, just the boat." In the few hours he'd owned the craft, it already felt like such a lifeline. "She's solid. Going to fix her up and turn her into a diving vessel."

Shaking his head, Tony returned to the cash wrap and began the closing procedure. "Most nineteen-year-olds obsess over having a car. What possessed you to buy a boat?"

James let the door swing closed, leaning on the wall near the mask display. "Just felt like something that might make me happy."

Tony scooped change from the drawer, preparing to count it. "Well, I admit, boating certainly makes me happy, so I don't blame you there. Where are you planning to keep her?"

"Not sure," James admitted, squirming with discomfort. "The salesman told me I could rent a slip at the marina. I hope it's affordable, because at some point, I have to return that truck."

Tony blew out a disapproving breath. "It's only affordable if you're loaded. Those slips come at a premium, and you, my friend, aren't rich."

"I'm not." The revelation hit James like a punch to the gut, and he straightened, knocking down a row of masks and then bending to pick them up again. "There has to be somewhere I can moor her. Somewhere affordable." He had nowhere to park a boat. It was hard enough figuring out where to park Ryan's truck when he had it.

Tony stroked his chin stubble, thinking. "Tell you what. I know someone who owns a private dock. Residential. It's not my house, but someone close to me, and I see him a lot. If you have time to hang out for a bit, I'll make a call and see if he has room, and if he'd maybe work you a short-term deal." He recounted a stack of ones, then dropped the set amount into the till and slid the rest into a bank envelope. "Hopefully long enough for you to make those repairs."

Gratitude jammed into James' throat. He couldn't remember the last time a veritable stranger went out on a limb for him, and Tony had already been more kind than most people. "Oh man, that would be awesome. I appreciate you so much, Tony. Please tell your friend that as well."

"Don't thank me yet. He might not have room." Tony scrolled through his phone contacts, and landed on a number. "If I'm going to cash in a favor, you're taking me for out diving once she's running."

"She runs now." He prayed the motor worked as well as it had when they'd started it in the lot. "Just needs some TLC. But *of course* I'll take you out. Always up for a dive buddy, once you set me free." He couldn't bring Tony on the search for Emma, but he wouldn't turn down a buddy—especially an instructor—for his first unsupervised dives.

"Perfect. It's a deal." Tony punched the dial command on his phone as he switched off the shop lights, leading James outside and locking the door behind them.

Some days James felt like the world was against him, but others—like today—he couldn't believe his luck.

James stood outside the nursing home where Emma's grandmother lived. Renewed hope had given him the courage to follow through with a promise he'd made when Emma left. Mona Harris was the only person besides James who knew what Emma truly was, and with his open-water dive approaching, optimism had temporarily replaced his depression to the degree that he simply *had* to talk about it, or risk blurting it out to a stranger. Or Tony. He'd been sorely tempted to tell Tony, and that wouldn't help either.

He made his way into the large, stone building, taken aback by the grandeur of the lobby and the quiet elegance that brought his eyes to the smallest details. Gold gilded accents added a touch of glamour, and the sleek, marble flooring was covered in thick, luxurious rugs that brought attention to the wood beams stretching across the ceiling. Even the check-in desk matched the same rich materials.

The woman behind the desk had gently-wrinkled skin and bright, kind eyes that helped in calming his nerves. "Can I help you?"

James dragged his fingers over the rough-hewn desk. "I'm looking for Mona Harris, but I don't remember her room number."

The woman tapped her computer keys. "Are you a relative?"

"Family friend." He coughed, tension itching his throat.

"Is she expecting you?"

"No." He shifted his weight from one foot to the other, realized what he was doing, and silently berated himself for fidgeting. "I'm surprising her."

"She'll love that, I'm sure. It's been weeks since her granddaughter visited—she used to come every few days." The woman regarded James, as if testing him for ill intent, then wrote the room number on a post-it and handed it to him. "Two-fifty-five. You should knock first, let her know you're out there. She has her good moments, but a lot of defensive paranoia."

Emma had said something similar. "I'll definitely knock. Thanks." He followed the posted signs, and soon stood outside Mona's room. He took a deep breath and bounced on his feet, shaking his tight muscles loose before rapping on the door.

A feeble voice called for him to come in, and he entered, scrunching his nose at the mixed fragrance of menthol and roses. The gray-haired woman rocked in a chair, a navy and white afghan covering her lap. Throughout the room, she'd carefully placed bits and pieces, reminders of the sea. Seashells on the window sill, on the wall above her bed, a framed blow-up of waves breaking against a cliff, on the nightstand, a glass bowl filled with multi-colored pearls.

The shape of her forehead, the placement of her cheekbones, the last remaining hints of red in her wavy hair were probably a trick of his mind, but James could swear that Mona and Emma looked crazy alike, which shouldn't be possible for an adopted family member. "Are you Emma Harris's grandmother?"

The rocking stilled, her eyes widening with alarm. "You're not a reporter? Investigator?"

He stepped closer, speculating how Emma and her Gran had such similar eyes. He saw Emma in everything these days, and now everyone. "No. Not either of those. I'm Emma's . . . she was my girlfriend. Is my girlfriend. I'm James."

"James." Mona pressed her lips together, setting the chair in motion again. "Yes. You're the boy she loved. I told her to break up with you, spare you the pain of her leaving."

James dragged a chair from the corner and situated it near the rocker, then took a seat. "She tried, but it didn't stick. She can't get rid of me that easily."

"And now you've come, wanting my help to bring her back." She reached beneath the blanket and retrieved string of beads, rubbing them between her fingers.

"Yes," he admitted. "That's the ultimate goal."

"She can't come back." Mona's grip on the beads tightened, her misshapen knuckles cracking from the effort. "None of them can. While her gills developed, her lungs shrank, eventually becoming useless. Emma now gets her oxygen from the water, instead of air. She would die here."

"That merman has lungs." James leaned his elbows on his knees, refusing to accept the finality of Mona's response. "The one who tricked her, who took Keith hostage. He came ashore for hours, maybe even days. I've saw him, talked to him. He's always breathed just fine."

"Merrick." The blanket slipped, catching beneath the rocker, so Mona stopped rocking and tugged it free. "He can survive for hours, at most. He, too, would die if he stayed long enough ashore."

James fisted his hands, wedging them between his knees to hold in the building frustration. "If Emma can visit the way he does, maybe she can reverse the use of her gills, re-inflate her lungs and adapt, the way she adjusted to breathing under water."

"My dear boy." Mona rested her wrinkled, weathered hand on his forearm, her weak grip shaky. "Emma is lost to you, as she is lost to us all. We can do nothing to bring her back, except savor her memory as a priceless treasure."

He covered Mona's hand with his own, refusing to accept this as a final answer. "I would love to savor her memory. Everything about every moment with her is more precious to me than those pearls in your hand. But if Emma doesn't come back, at least for a visit, I'll be savoring my memories from a jail cell."

"Oh dear." She removed her hand to cover her mouth. "Do the authorities believe you've hurt her? That you played a part in her leaving?"

James sat back in his chair, pinching the bridge of his nose. "Someone from school followed me to the cove, found Emma's things. I have no alibi for the night she disappeared, because I was with her—and both of our cell phones left a timestamp on the nearby cell tower. Even Keith believes I'm guilty, but all I did was help her rescue him, and then bring him home. The evidence against me is stacked against me, and I would be stupid to ignore it. If the situation were reversed, even *I* would believe I was guilty."

"But you're not. This is no one's fault." The rocker tracks squeaked against the floor tiles as if protesting.

He switched to rubbing his temples, reminding himself to be excessively patient with the woman. "The problem is that no one outside this room understands what Emma is, or where she was forced to go. They only know she's gone, and someone must be blamed. Sadly, that person's going to be me."

"I can't allow you to be imprisoned, simply for being part of her life." Mona tossed the afghan on the ground, pushing off the arms of the chair so she could stand.

James stood with her, placing a steadying hand on her elbow as she reached for her walker. "We can't tell people about Atlantis, either. I promised."

"No, we can't. But something must be done." She scooted across the room, opening a dresser drawer and removing a handbag. "Let's go for a ride. If you wouldn't mind driving, I'd like to visit my son."

Something in her eyes, the set of her lips, sent a tingle down James' spine. "I . . . um, I mean, sure, I'll drive you. It's just—I haven't met Emma's parents, yet. And I haven't seen Keith since Emma left. What if they believe I hurt her, too? Won't that be awkward?"

She set the purse in the walker's carriage and slung a cardigan over the top. "I intend to set them straight. But, my boy, you must give Emma's parents credit. They've raised that girl, and even though I never warned them—never even told them what was coming—my son is a highly intelligent man of compassion. Tell him your version—the real one. I suspect they'll believe you, with or without my testimony."

"I doubt that." James stayed close in case the frail woman needed a hand, and was surprised when she manipulated the walker one-handed and reached for his arm with the other.

"Anyway, it is not Russ we're going to see tonight." Her fingers tightened on his elbow. "We're going to a grave on the hill. I'd like to tell you a secret story of my own. One I've not shared with anyone before, ever. Not even Emma."

She opened her fist, and lowered the strand of pearls into his open palm. It wasn't until he looked closer that he recognized the pendant Emma had worn every day for as long as he'd known her—until that very last one. His eyes shot to Mona and she nodded.

He felt as though the air had been sucked from his lungs. "How do you have this?"

Mona pointed at the ceiling, where a dark bubble covered a security camera. "Not here. Let's go for a ride."

# Chapter Fourteen

## Emma

AFTER SHE'D LET MERRICK BUY her neck adornments from the market, Emma had asked Maia to find her a container in which to keep them. Maia had left for several hours, and returned with a large, empty clamshell that was roughly the size of one of Emma's mother's Tupperware bowls. At the time, she wasn't concerned about security, because nothing in Atlantis held specific sentimental value, aside from the pendant—and when she found that, there would be no further need for storage.

But as she lifted the heavy lid from the clamshell and buried her newest acquisitions beneath the rest, unease rippled along her scales. There was no telling what her grandfather would do to her if she got caught with the stolen, illegal treasures. Probably a lengthy trip to the dungeon, and that was not a place she intended to revisit. She added finding a secure hiding place to her priority list, but for now, piled on every random thing she could find.

When Maia returned, carrying yet *another* tray, Emma was back to lying in her hammock, watching her hair swirl and wondering how the Mer kept occupied. She wasn't relaxed, so much as bored to insanity. "Another meal, already? I just ate."

Maia set the tray on the taller of two brightly-colored, flat-topped corals near the door. "I am to prepare you for receiving suitors at a Guiding Tide celebration."

"Suitors?" Emma sat up, confused, but eager. "We're having a party? Will we be serving paihana?"

Maia urged Emma out of bed and directed her to perch on the coral stool in front of her dressing table. "I do not know what party means. Is it a human word?"

"Yes. Party means . . . it's another word for celebration."

"Ah. I see." Maia got to work weaving colored plants, shells, and lustrous pearls into Emma's hair, plaiting it in an intricate braid like nothing Emma had ever seen done before.

She asked again. "Is this the kind of celebration where Paihana will be served?"

"Perhaps, Princess. After the merman suiters have been presented." Emma gasped from a particularly strong tug to her hair. "I am sorry," Maia muttered. "Have I hurt you?"

"Please don't pull so hard." Emma chewed on her bottom lip, emotions whirling like a cyclone. The Sea King had planned a party to help her find another mate. She hadn't asked for his help, but she'd begged—multiple times—to be freed from her betrothal to Merrick. Since he'd granted her time to find another option, he must have known she would have no way of meeting eligible mermen. Had her grandfather strayed from societal custom in lieu of her happiness? Appearances insisted that he had, but doubt had her biting her lip until she tasted blood. Something about this situation felt wrong.

When Maia finished with the intricate creation of Emma's hair, she tugged at the threadbare straps on Emma's swimsuit top. Emma slapped the offending hand away, whirling to face the maid. "What are you doing?"

Maia floated backward, eyes widening. "I . . . I am removing your human covering, as the Sea King has commanded."

Emma crossed her arms over her chest, mortified that she was expected to parade around topless while trying to find a mate. Even though this behavior was customary in Atlantis—and covering up was more noticeable than baring it all—she couldn't bring herself to follow this particular tradition. Not yet. "I'm not comfortable with that."

Maia released a stream of bubbles from her gills. "Do not worry. Your adornments will be sufficient covering over your scales."

"It's not the scales I want covered," Emma muttered. The Mer hadn't been conditioned to be embarrassed by, or self-conscious about their nakedness, but Emma *had*. For nearly eighteen years she'd dressed with a certain degree of modesty in mind, and the *one time* she'd ventured out of that comfort zone and let Heather help pick her prom dress, things had gone terribly, horribly wrong. She could not fathom going completely topless to a party where she knew no one. Not even if everyone was doing it.

Once again, Maia tried to untie what was left of Emma's worn bikini, and again, Emma slapped her hand away—this time, more forcefully. "I said no. Keep your hands off me."

Those scaled hands squeezed into fists as another gust of bubbles whooshed from Maia's gills. "Princess, the Sea King has insisted. He does not wish to display reminders of your human side. Doing so could turn away eligible suitors."

Mortified, Emma floated off the stool and spun away from her maid, arms tightened against her breasts. If she were home with James, alone, would she have the courage to parade topless then? Would she have reclaimed enough freedom of her body that she would feel confident in letting him see it? And if that precious, intimate event happened between them, could she overcome the anxious remnants of her scarred past?

In the days before she'd left home, she'd planned to fully give herself to James. They'd even had a brief conversation about it. But until it happened, she couldn't know if she was brave enough to see it through. She *did* know that she wasn't ready to show herself to strangers.

"Maia, I can't. Please understand. If the Sea King insists on removing my top, I won't attend the party."

"Princess Emmalina." Maia approached, halting feet away, as if torn. "Such an infraction could cost me this position as your maid."

That would be bad. They'd established a sort-of friendship, developed a routine, a couple of understandings. If Maia was reassigned, there was no predicting what her next maid would be like, and Emma couldn't afford to take such a risk. She fiddled with a thread that had unraveled, and the straps came loose, hanging by thin fabric that she knew wouldn't last much longer.

She was in no way ready for this party.

The last time she danced was at prom. Because it felt like another lifetime, she managed to think back on her dress and remember how elegant she'd felt wearing it. How regal—and ironically, royal. Being the Royal Princess of Atlantis, and an intriguing new member of the society, perhaps she could start a trend. "Maia, I have an idea."

Emma described the seashell bras seen in animated movies she'd loved as a child, adding thoughts as she went, and soon, Maia incorporated some ideas of her own, until they'd reached a suitable compromise that excited them both.

Maia gauged the time according to the shifting current. "You are required, post-haste. How will we create such an article in time?"

"We must be quick." Emma directed her to the privacy curtain. "I'll need shells. Clams, sand dollars, mother of pearl, starfish. Even crab shells might work, if they're whole." She measured the cups on her current top, then snapped a similar-sized length of kelp from her privacy curtain and pressed it into Maia's hand. "This size. Find as many options as you can, and bring them to me. Be quick."

The look on Maia's face could only be described as sheer panic. "Princess, you are expected in moments."

"I know. You should hurry." Wishing she'd thought of this days ago, Emma sifted through the contents of her clam, and came up with long strands of pearls, thick coils of seaweed, pliable coral tubes, and banana leaves that had acted as serving plates. "I can work with this."

She cleared the dressing table to use as a work surface, and caught a glimpse of her reflection in the iridescent sea-glass mirror. Maia had woven her hair into a wild, Atlantian style, interlaced with expensive strands of rare corals, colorful sea grass, and underwater blooms. It was, Emma decided, inherently striking in the way of the Mer. "Impressive."

She braided strands of seagrass and experimented with her other materials, determining the strongest, most pliable options, and when Maia returned, wasted no time digging through the basket of options. She used her clam-shucking tool, along with a heavy stone, to drill holes into the top half of an empty turtle shell.

Thanks to the soft inner layer, and Emma's cheerleading muscle, she drilled a hole, through which she threaded her thickest seagrass braid. Maia drilled the hole in a second shell, while Emma added strung pearls to reinforce the braids.

When the piece was finished, Emma tried it on, impressed with their combined creativity. "We make a good team."

In lieu of a response, Maia tilted her head, frowning.

Emma peered closer at the sea-glass mirror. "What? Is something wrong with it?"

"Something is not right. One moment." Maia seized a leftover bloom from the dressing table and twisted it into the braided strand between the two shells. "Much better. Now your covering and your hair appear to have been a planned combination."

"It's perfect." The piece had turned out even prettier than Emma expected.

Maia arced around Emma, checking their creation from every angle. "Emmalina, I do not understand why you must cover yourself, but I like this adornment very much. It is different from typical Atlantian neck adornments. A stimulating change."

"Agreed." Emma chose two colorful strands—one of pearls, and one of tiny corals—to accessorize her new top, while allowing the unique turtle shells to shine through as a creative new fashion statement. Finally prepared to be seen, she followed Maia into the crowded ballroom, where hundreds had already gathered.

Maia positioned herself in the shadows of an unlit wall, where she would wait with the other servants, and beckoned for Emma to join her grandfather at the far end of the room, where two tall, coral thrones had been erected on a platform. The mer-band played a complex, but enchanting melody, and couples danced—much more formal than the attendees of the underground paihana party. Servants interlaced between the guests, transporting platters crowded with goblets—which were carved from whalebone—and delicate snacks that Emma didn't recognize in the least. And there were mermen. Lots and lots of them, milling around the edges of the dancing space—not dancing— apparently scared to interact with females. These mermen, Emma decided, were here for her.

She sighed, sending tiny bubbles toward the ceiling. This was going to be an interesting party.

As she crossed the room and approached her grandfather's throne, the music stopped, dancing came to a halt, and the servants bowed, as all eyes fixed on her. The Sea King waved her closer, eyes narrowing as Emma alighted on the smaller throne—assuming her intended position, without invitation.

"Hello, Grandfather." Keeping her voice bright required great skill, as whatever heat that remained in her body had disintegrated on her journey across the room. He continued to stare, but didn't voice disapproval, so Emma, now shivering from the chill, addressed the subject of her fashion choice herself. "Do you like my creation? I enjoyed the process so much that I've considered making more to sell in the market."

Tangaroa's confusion melted into a nod of satisfied approval. "Your creation is lovely, Emmalina. Much improved from your human covering. I should like to see other mermaids wearing such designs."

A twinge of pain jabbed Emma's chest. She knew what he was doing. He was convincing himself, his staff, and his guests that tonight's fashion choice was not an imitation of her life on land, but a fresh, new fashion statement from the Sea Princess of Atlantis. In the coming days, her grandfather might not be happy with her for introducing human modesty to the unchanged culture of Mer, but this attempt to shield herself had just provided far more than fashion choices or body coverings.

Her mention of selling the creations provided a built-in excuse for leaving the palace to wander in the market. Someday it could open an opportunity to leave the city boundaries *in search of materials*. Of course, *someday* would be unlikely to arrive before her forced joining, and she intended to be long gone by then.

"I enjoy creating, Grandfather," she said, continuing to play her part. "It gives purpose to my waking tides."

"A mate will also do that." He signaled the band to play, and the guests to return to their revelries. "When you are joined, there will be much to do as you establish your dwelling. More still, once you produce younglings."

Emma coughed, a strange, effervescent sensation bubbling in her gills. The joining with a mate thing, she understood. She even kind of figured she'd be expected to reproduce. At some point, but not *immediately*. "Younglings?"

"Atlantis needs an heir, and as soon as possible." As the merriment continued, unfolding before them like an endless parade of jesters, the Sea King signaled for a servant to bring him a drink. "I cannot live forever, nor would I wish to, and neither will you. Our ancestral line must continue."

It sounded like something Gran would say, only a lot more intimidating coming from Emma's Sea King grandfather. He'd made it abundantly clear that he expected her to be rapidly . . . abundant. And the thought of bearing younglings at the crazy young age of eighteen petrified her. Added to that was the reminder that she was the Sea King's one, and only, heir. If she left Atlantis forever, who would rule the city when her grandfather became too old? Who would keep the Mer protected, and demand peace in the realm of the sea?

After years of arguing with Merrick, Emma finally understood why he'd been so insistent that her choices affected more lives than just her own. Maybe disastrous emotional choices—such as the one her father had made—were the reason that the Mer joined for procreation, rather than love.

Her view across the immense ballroom offered a unique perspective, as mermaids and mermen packed in, and still more continued to arrive. They laughed together, drinking paihana and dancing, eating and gossiping, and casting furtive glances at the peculiar Sea Princess and her odd fashion choices. This peaceful, loving community had thrived, thanks to her grandfather's leadership, and when he died, the Mer deserved another noble and proper leader—not a phony who might never let go of her human roots.

The summoned waiter arrived, baring a tray of the lovely whalebone goblets Emma had noticed earlier. He presented his offering to the Sea King, who flapped his hand in Emma's direction. "The Sea Princess will henceforth be the *first* attended, on every matter, as she is the key to our future and the link to our past."

The waiter adjusted his position, offering a goblet to Emma, as instructed. "Paihana, Princess?"

"Thank you." She selected a goblet of syrupy pink paihana and brought it to her nose out of habit, intending to sniff the bright liquid before drinking, as her parents did with wine. This time, she perceived a hint of earthy tang, unexpectedly pleased to discover that the last of her senses had progressed in the evolution for maximum pleasure.

As when she'd first arrived, their guests stilled, creating an invisible spotlight that centered on Emma. Out of courtesy, she waited for her grandfather's consent, only pressing the vessel to her lips after his nod of approval.

The slimy liquid had a texture like oil, and gushed down her throat and into her belly with the torrid heat of fire, much stronger than the Paihana she'd originally tried. Remembering her experience from last time, she set her goblet aside, still half full, and when the waiter attempted to top it off, refused with a hand over her cup and a shake of her head. "Grandfather, I was told I'm to meet suitors this tide. Might we begin, soon?" *Before they all end up drunk and obnoxious.*

Tangaroa drained the contents of his goblet, signaling for the waiter to remove both empty vessels, and then he beckoned his assistant to his side. "Glan, line up the suitors, and prepare them to be received by the Sea Princess."

"Yes, Sir." Glan started for the dancing space to round them all up.

Emma noticed that aside from the already joined couples, few mermaids dared venture to dance. "Actually, I think I'll be more comfortable greeting them out there. Can I do that?"

Glan returned to the dais, awaiting further instruction. "Improper behavior that undermines Mer tradition."

The Sea King tapped his fingers on the coral arm of his throne. "Remember, the merman you choose, will be expected to assist you in ruling Atlantis when I am no longer able. He must be strong, wise, and fair, with an abundance of knowledge of how to maintain peace within our society. I understand that you have no affection for Merrick, but he has served me since the death of Caspian, sacrificing much in doing so. He is not as bad a merman as you believe."

Anger tightened her jaw. She would not be manipulated. "He's not for me, Grandfather. Merrick will never make me happy the way . . . " she stopped herself just in time. It wouldn't help to remind him of the human man she'd claimed to have already joined with. "I will consider your wishes. But this tide, I shall meet my suitors among the rest of the Mer." She rose, gliding onto the dancing space, where multiple hands shot out, each one an invitation to dance. She accepted the first hand she reached, determined to meet as many as possible tonight, and prayed to find at least one eligible merman that she didn't hate.

By the end of the night, she'd made some acquaintances, besotted two mermen who were younger than Merrick, and ignited a new fashion trend among the mermaids. She danced with each merman brave enough to ask, which took much longer than expected. At a point when thirst parched her throat, she gave in and accepted more paihana, and from that point on, her goblet remained filled.

The most interesting dance partners asked about land, seeming genuinely interested in her responses.

Others yakked about themselves, concerned only with impressing her. Regardless of the company, Emma experienced a careless joviality she hadn't felt in longer than she remembered. It could be a side-effect of paihana, but she suspected that—as much as she wished otherwise—this new carefree feeling was more about the safety, the security she'd found within the palace walls. Plus, she fit with the Mer, in ways she never could with humans.

As the music wound down and the band declared that only two songs remained before the arrival of sleep tide, Emma returned to her throne, gulping the last of her paihana while her grandfather yawned. "Have you enjoyed the celebration, Emmalina?"

She relaxed against the coral seat, surprised at how much fun she'd had. "It's been a long time since I danced. And never with mermen, until now. Only humans."

"And have you chosen a potential mate to court?" The Sea King again signaled for a refill. "You are running out of tides."

"Why the rush?" Her hand fluttered onto his forearm—their first, ever, physical contact. "I'm still new here, and so young. Why can't I have more time?"

His chest rose and fell, as if breathing had become a struggle. "I am not new, nor am I young. Atlantis is now a peaceful colony, but has not always been. I do not wish for my people to fall into the strife of battle or dissension. There must always be a ruler in the palace, to maintain peace within our borders."

"Excuse me, Sea Princess. Might I have the pleasure of one final dance?"

Laine, who'd been the bouncer at her first paihana party, was draped in an impressive array of adornments, winding around his muscular frame from neck to shoulder. Emma set aside her empty goblet and accepted his hand. "Absolutely."

He led her to the dance space, pausing for a formal bow, and then rising with a mischievous grin. "You seem to have gained a tolerance for Paihana."

The drink fizzed in her stomach, forcing her to swallow a burp. "I'm sure I'll be sick later. Horribly sick."

Laine swung her into the graceful movement of Mer dance. "Did Maia administer the anemone heart, as I instructed? Paihana should not leave you so ill, if imbibed with caution."

"She did. Just not quick enough." They twirled in grand circles, cutting a path through the mingling Mer. "I fell asleep right after you left, and woke up feeling terrible."

"My first experience with paihana ended similarly." They dominated the dancing space, as he looped her into his arms, then rolled her out again. "It is not intended for the weak."

"Definitely not," she agreed, slightly out of breath. "But I like it."

Laine's muscles bunched as he pressed closer, wrapping his fin around Emma's legs in a move far more intimate than the others had dared to try. She had to give him credit for boldness. "So, Laine. When you're not playing bouncer at the servants' underground nightclub, what do you do?"

"I am battle advisor to the Sea King. Tangaroa is wise, and Atlantis has not known battle for the span of my life, or my father's. If ever we encounter a time when combat is the only solution, the Sea King will deploy me, along with my soldiers."

This piqued her interest. Commanding soldiers and advising the Sea King required strong leadership skills. Invaluable experience that not many could claim. Plus, her grandfather and Laine had an established relationship. "Do you live here in the palace?" she asked.

He dipped her back, following through with the motion, and sending them looping in a vertical circle. "I am assigned a living cavern, but spend most tides in a dwelling near the gates. I enjoy quiet, and living away from the city leaves me available if ever a predator threatens to breach our borders."

Dizzy, Emma stuck her toe in the sand, discontinuing the circular motion before her stomach could revolt. "Do predators get in often?"

"We are well experienced at driving away danger." A tiny silver angelfish scrambled by. Laine caught it in his palm, and zapped it dead before she could blink.

When the music ended, and Laine released his hold, Emma realized that the warmth she'd lost at the beginning of the night had been amply replaced, and then some. "May I visit your dwelling sometime? I'd like to learn about your duty guarding the city gate. And perhaps ask you to teach me how to zap things, the way you did that fish."

"I would love a visit, and will happily teach you, Princess Emmalina." He took her hand and escorted her back to her grandfather. "Might I call on you next tide?"

She nodded, disregarding that her nerves fluttered like stingrays, as a link in her broken chain of emotions welded back together. "I'd like that."

# Chapter Fifteen

## James

JAMES' EYE TWITCHED, HEAD SPIRALING with perplexity. In the last six months, he'd taken in more unreal information than his brain could hold. Receiving another large dose might send him into a level of overwhelm from which he might never recover.

Mona jostled her walker down the hall, across the rug in the foyer, and then outside while James held the door. He slowed to match her pace, wondering how to help her into the elevated cab of the dirty, old truck. "Which cemetery were you wanting to visit?"

"Not a cemetery." Mona huffed with the exertion of walking. "A private lot."

James opened the door of his truck and boosted Emma's Gran inside, surprised at how light she was. "Isn't it illegal to bury people on private property?"

Mona didn't even crack a smile as she buckled her seatbelt. "Only if the authorities know."

*Great. Because I need one more reason to be in trouble with the police.* He lifted her walker into the back, and climbed in the cab. "All right. Illegal graves on private property. I'm going to need an address."

When they arrived at the empty lot, Mona directed him to bump over the curb, drive across the thick grass, and park next to an enormous maple tree. The lone tree towered over the sloped lot, rising at a vantage point that overlooked both city and ocean, while shading the grassy yard over which it presided. The canopy of harvest leaves appeared to melt, starting with lush, dark green bursting from the top-most branches, and ending on the lowest ones in a shade of pale lemon chiffon, with an interesting hint of silver.

James brought the walker to the passenger side and helped Mona out, setting her on her feet. She clung tight to the handles, regarding the span of serene landscape as she compelled herself closer to the tree's trunk. When the wheels caught, and she could no longer traverse over the thick roots snaking through the grass, she let go and hobbled the last two steps. She pressed trembling hands against the bark, eyes glittering with tears. "Oh, Caspian, how I've missed you."

*Caspian? Emma's biological merman father Caspian?*

A tear dripped onto Mona's papery cheek as James eased her onto the ground, where she settled against the silver tree.

James settled on the grass as well, still clutching Emma's necklace, caressing each individual pearl as if through them, he could somehow find a spark of her essence. She'd spent her life believing she was abandoned as an infant on Mona's doorstep, and that she had no biological connection to her human family. Discovering that her Gran had lied, keeping the truth to herself for nearly eighteen years would be devastating to Emma.

Mona's deep green eyes revisited the horizon, and the expanse of wild, sapphire sea. "I was very young when Caspian was born. Too young. Hadn't even graduated high school yet. I'd become trapped within a cliché, wooed by the romance of young love. At that age, I had no fear. Just wide-eyed naivety and a streak of rebellion that led me to sneak out my window each night for a lone visit the beach.

"The beach had called to me, you see. Since before my earliest childhood memory. I belonged to it, and it to me, as if my very heart and soul had been formed in the same way as a pearl, from a single grain of sand."

*Just as Emma was called to the sea.* His attention was drawn to Mona's hands. Soft skin, delicate fingers, long, narrow nails that ended just past her fingertips. They were Emma's hands, only slightly older, misshapen by arthritis, and covered in a layer of wrinkled, spotted skin.

"One night as I stood knee-deep in the surf, dressed only in a nightgown, I encountered a young man. The waves reflected a starless sky, that night, coloring the world in a curtain of black, broken only by the occasional shimmer of sand. Even once my eyes adjusted, I couldn't see him well, but I noticed that he wore no shirt or shoes, and his shorts looked much too small. I assumed he'd experienced a growth spurt, typical of my friends at that time, and kept my giggles inside.

"He said very little, so I introduced myself, told him I'd come to say goodnight to the sea, and asked if he'd like to join me. He refused, so I waded in further, determined to change his mind." She folded her hands in her lap, repentant. "Clearly, this was during a time when the dangers of walking alone at night had not yet occurred to me.

"I asked his name, where he was from, why he was out so late. With each question, his eyes grew wider, as if my questions frightened him. And still, no response.

Eventually, I asked if he spoke English, to which he finally replied that, yes, he did.

"Oh, it took some persuading to get him talking, but after considerable prodding, I learned that his name was Tang—like the popular drink mix from my generation—and that he'd come visiting from far away. Sometime during those short moments of interaction, the handsome, mysterious stranger crept to the very top of my list of desires. Our conversation that night was short, and mostly one-sided, but I invited him to meet me in the same place and time the following evening."

Mona flicked an ant off her knee, clearing the mix of dirt and grass to rid her spot of others.

"After several more meetings, all of which took place in the same manner as the first, he relaxed enough to participate in entire conversations. We discussed every subject under the sky, except his family. I supposed that he'd experienced a tragedy, and would share it with me when he was ready. I knew little of his upbringing, and no matter where I looked, he couldn't be found during the day. This was before the time of cell phones, and when I asked for his home number, he changed the subject. After that, I didn't bother asking where he lived. If I had been wiser, his reluctance to share contact information would have been one of many red flags. But I was too young to be wise, and when we were together—well. I left all my smarts behind each time I climbed out the window."

A bird sang from high in the tree, a single, lonely trill that was left unanswered. James swallowed, thinking of all the times he'd behaved the way Mona had with Tang, how he'd left all caution behind, starting with the moment he'd met Emma.

Mona continued. "We continued our clandestine meetings throughout the summer, and naturally, our relationship progressed. Together, we lived a secret life of exhilaration and adventure, we discovered passions that left me hungry to take his hand and step out of the darkness and into bright sunlight. I loved him, you see. In the biggest way I knew of love, and I believed his affection was equal to mine." She sighed heavily, eyes glazed over as if her soul had traveled back in time to that beach. "And then, one night he didn't show up. I waited until sunrise, but he never came. I returned to our spot every night for weeks, but he never came back."

"Like Emma," James murmured, wondering how he would have felt if she'd never told him about that part of herself. If he hadn't been with her in the cove the night she left.

Mona reached out and took James' hand between both of hers, patting it lightly and then resting the bundle on her knee. "Long, dark hours of waiting released a hurricane inside me, endlessly screaming winds of anguish. Maybe he'd drowned, or died in an accident. Maybe his family was forced to flee the country. I convinced myself that *my* Tang would never choose leave without at least saying goodbye—not by choice." She freed his hand and framed her cheeks with both of hers, shaking her head in disbelief.

James positioned his palms on the grass and leaned back, angling his face to better see the treetop, eyes searching the lonely bird. "Did you ever see Tang again?"

"Not for a very long time. And yet, daily in my memories." Her gaze lingered on the horizon, in the place between where the sky gives way to the sea. "About a month into the next school year, I discovered I was pregnant."

James' chest tightened with sorrow, knowing how the consequences from one bad relationship had shaped her entire life. "How old were you?"

"Fifteen." Her eyes flicked toward him, then returned to the sea, cheeks stained blotchy rose. "There had been no other young men in my life, and my parents remained oblivious to my nightly escapades of the past summer. The idea of telling them I was expecting left me terrified." Her attention fell to the grass beneath her hands. She pulled up several blades, and then let them slip between her fingers. "In those days, an unwed teenage mother would inevitably become a source of family scandal, especially for my ultra-conservative parents. And so, desperate to spare my mother the grief of embarrassment, I ran away.

"My son was born in an apartment bathroom, one sunny afternoon the following spring. I named him Caspian, because for some reason, the name reminded me of Tang. And though I'd planned to never return to Oceanside, a few years later, my father fell ill, and I couldn't let him pass without ever having said my goodbyes. I'll never know what would have happened if I'd been smart enough to stay away.

"The day Caspian turned six, we shared a lovely picnic on the beach where I'd met his father. While Caspian played in the surf, I noticed a figure—far in the distance—walking on the beach toward us. It might have been his walk, or the unmistakable posture, or his long, wild hair—but I knew. From the very moment I saw him, I knew my Tang had returned. I leapt up and ran to greet him, both nervous and excited for the opportunity to introduce father and son, but Tang never said a word to me. He strode right past, took my baby in his arms, and dove into the sea."

James couldn't even imagine the panic, the heartache. "Did you have any idea, any warning, that your son was half merman? That you might lose him in that way?"

It took her a moment, but Mona nodded slowly, as if only now seeing what she should have known long ago. "I think I must have. Tang wasn't like other young men, that was apparent from the onset. And Caspian had so many of the legendary signs, from scars on his neck from the moment of birth, to an uncanny ability to swim without ever being taught. But whether or not I *knew*, I didn't consciously realize. I wasn't prepared to lose him.

"I became a woman possessed, both desperate and determined to recover my baby. The police got involved, and the coast guard, and the community rallied until boats covered the water like a shield, but eventually the search died. The authorities contended that my son had drowned, and that his body could not be recovered, but I knew—as I lived and breathed, so did Caspian. And someday, when he was old enough, he would return to me."

James opened Mona's hand and slid the necklace into it. "You were right, weren't you? Caspian came home."

"He did." She closed her fingers around the smooth, shiny beads, eyes lit with satisfaction. "Years later. Many, many years. By then I'd married, and raised another son. Emma's father, Russell, was away at college when I found Caspian wandering the beach."

"You recognized him? After all those years?"

She fiddled with the pendant, stroking the luminous beads in the same way James had. "Of course, I did. A mother always knows her son. Not to mention that he'd grown to look very much like his father."

"Did he recognize you?"

"I hadn't changed much. A bit of gray, a few more pounds and some new wrinkles—but the same me I had always been. I brought him home, dressed him in Russell's clothes, and stayed up until dawn listening to his stories, learning everything I could about his life in Atlantis. He expressed that on the day Tang abducted him, he vowed to return to me. And how, after all those lost years, he'd finally made it home."

She wiped a tear from the corner of her eye, but another fell in its place. She embraced the pearls against her chest. "Having him home felt like a miracle; too good to be true. With Russ away at college, and having lost my husband only months previous, the timing of Caspian's return felt like divine intervention. For the second time in my life, he brought me purpose—something I thought I'd lost. I taught him to read, to dress, to care for his skin and hair and teeth. All things he'd known before, but after twenty-odd years, he needed reminding."

"I can imagine," James murmured, though he wasn't sure if that was true. How would he feel if Emma came back to him years from now, only to find that he'd moved on with his life? "What took him so long?"

Mona shifted, bracing her hands against the tree while she endeavored to stand. "He was the Prince of Atlantis. Turned out that his father—whose full name was Tangaroa—had needed an heir. A mate, too, but apparently he wasn't happy with the one his parents chose—which explained his rebellion, and subsequent relationship with me. When he met Caspian and me on the beach that day, he understood that he already had an heir—problem solved. My poor Caspian lost his childhood, his teen years—all of his youth—learning the ways of the Mer. Tangaroa held him hostage in that city beneath the sea, until Tang's nephew, Maui, paid them a visit."

Assuming that Mona's walker would be useless on the uneven terrain, James stood and offered Mona his arm, escorting her to the top of the knoll, where the panoramic view spread farther than any eye could see. "Maui? Like the Hawaiian island?"

"Yes." Mona's wrinkled fingers tightened on his arm, her frail body trembling with strain. "According to Caspian, Maui was a progressive thinker who believed in choices. The two spent a lot of time together, Maui teaching Caspian the ways of Oceania, which is apparently another Mer colony. When Tang banished Maui from Atlantis, he left Caspian a gift."

She held up the necklace. "This bauble was the source of Caspian's breath when he came ashore. It allowed him to stay with me." The breeze ruffled her feathery, white hair, and she closed her eyes, breathing in the earthy brine.

James braced an arm behind her back to keep her steady. "How did he die?"

"He stopped breathing. But first, he fell in love. Married. *Truly living*, in ways he never could in Atlantis. My son was the very definition of happy. And then Emma was born." The bird from before sang again, and Mona opened her eyes in time to witness the glory as it broke through the topmost layer of leaves and took flight, casting a shadow five-times its size on the grass at their feet.

"Caspian loved Emma's mother with an intensity I hadn't seen since I was fifteen and in love with Tang. The way he focused, pinning his existence on one single person, frightened me, because I knew so well the devastation, the aftermath of that kind of love. And then Elise died in childbirth. On the day we buried her, the life drained from Caspian. Not his *actual life*, but the will to go on. It was a sudden freeze, the kind that causes a tree's leaves to drop while they're still green and bright—encased in ice, and trapped within the jaws of endless winter, never to age another day.

"That night while I slept, Caspian left Emma in my living room. He'd bundled her in her car seat, and tucked this inside with her." She presented the necklace to James so he could trace the lustrous pearls again. "She was so sweet, more perfect than a porcelain doll, and too stunning to be a real, human baby, with skin just a shade above blue. She never cried. Not once that day, though she was awake, and alert as the morning sun when I found her hours later, sucking on her fingers.”

So her parents *had* abandoned her. Suddenly, everything he knew about Emma made so much more sense.

“We located him later that evening,” Mona croaked. “Curled up on Elise’s grave—skin shriveled like a piece of fruit that had withered in the sun. When grief overwhelmed him, he’d simply stopped breathing.”

The sun dipped lower, unfolding the first rays of sunset, and scattering tiny prisms of gold across the rippling water. Mona teetered, wilting with exhaustion as James guided her down the knoll. “You brought him here?”

“I wanted to bury him next to Elise, but I worried. If I took him to the mortuary, a medical examiner would have to perform an autopsy to determine his cause of death, and if that person looked closely enough—and they always do—they might discover that Caspian was only *half* human. Down the line, that could potentially endanger Emma, and I couldn’t bear the thought of losing her, too.”

Mona reached for her walker, her wrinkled hands clutching the handles with uncharacteristic strength.

“But my son deserved the dignity of a burial. This lot had been in my husband’s family for decades, and when he died, he left it to me. What was I going to do with it? Build a house? No. So, I bought a shovel and dug a really big hole. And since I couldn't provide a headstone, I planted this tree as a reminder of his life."

James picked a silvery leaf from a low-hanging branch and slid it into his wallet, anger building in his chest. "Why didn't you tell Emma about her parents? She has a right to know."

"I've never told anyone," Mona admitted. "Russ never met his brother. I planned to introduce them, but felt the need to explain to Russell in person. Caspian's story was—hard to believe, even for me. Then Russell canceled coming home, and Caspian got married so suddenly, and before I knew it—Elise was gone, and then Caspian. Those months passed in a single blink. How could I explain my angelic little Emma to someone—stranger or son—who had never seen the truth of the Mer? I chose to spare Russ the pain of losing the brother he'd wished for as a child, but never met, and provided him and his new wife with a daughter. He's never known that Emma shares his DNA."

James' budding anger faded as they reached the truck. Whether he agreed with her or not, Mona had done the best she could in an impossible situation— one he hoped to never experience himself. "I still don't understand why you didn't tell Emma. She's known about the Mer for years, known she was becoming one of them, and neither of her parents ever suspected."

Mona bowed her head, heavy with regret. "I wanted to protect them—Emma, her parents, and Keith—from believing that she could ever come home, because I refuse to see her life end the way Caspian's did. Emma's home, the safest place for her, is in Atlantis with Tangaroa. He'll protect her in ways I can't. She's his only living heir, and with Caspian gone, he'll never let her go."

"He's not protecting her, he's imprisoned her." Though he'd suspected as much, the reminder charred like bitters in his mouth. How could he save her if no human could reach her?

"She's a Princess. And she'll live a good life below, with a safe home, healthy food, even servants to wait on her—more than everything she needs. Tangaroa will choose her a good husband, and eventually she'll be happy there." Mona reached for the handle and swung the door open, which James accepted as the signal that she was ready to leave.

He raised her into the cab, seething. "That *good husband* has a tendency toward violence. Did she tell you that? He burned her once, badly enough to scar. Then he kidnapped her brother—your *only* grandson—and forced Emma into Atlantis while her parents were still in Greece. She didn't even get to tell them goodbye. Those are not qualities of a good and loving spouse. I've met Merrick, and trust me, he won't take care of her *or* make her happy."

As Mona reached for her seatbelt, the confidence in her eyes drained, replaced by apprehension. "I . . . I trust Tangaroa to find her someone who will make her happy. I can't believe he will force her to marry an abuser."

"Are you serious right now?" Rage boiling over, James slammed Mona's door and pitched her walker in the back, then stomped around, yanked open the driver's side door and threw himself onto the seat. "How can you trust the man who lied to you? Who got you pregnant while you were *still a child* and then deserted you? The man who showed up out of the blue and kidnapped that child right in front of you, without a damn word? You haven't had a conversation with him since you were fifteen."

Mona pressed a calming hand on James' burning arm. "I *have* talked to Tangaroa. He visited me the day Caspian died, and knowing I couldn't ask anyone else, he helped me dig the grave where we buried our son. When everything was done, we talked about important things. Caspian came home in search of happiness, and that's how we both lost him. Neither of us will allow that to happen to Emma."

Emma's necklace dangled from the pocket of Mona's housedress, dredging up another question. "Emma wore that every day, until Merrick and I got in a fight. She was so angry, she tossed it into the ocean.

Now she's in Atlantis trying to find it. How did it get from the bottom of the ocean, and into your hands?"

Mona tilted her head as if the answer was obvious. "I may be old, but I haven't completely lost my mind. And I have a lot of experience in sneaking out windows, borrowing cars."

He pinched the bridge of his nose to fight off a headache. "Um, what? What are you saying?"

She took the keys from his hand and slid the right one into the ignition. "I'm saying I've seen the Sea King. Recently."

James left the keys dangling, motionless in the eye of a building hurricane.

"Seems our headstrong girl has him worried. So, he returned Caspian's pendant. Just in case."

# Chapter Sixteen

## Emma

THOUGH THE MER DIDN'T ACKNOWLEDGE the sun's movement, the moon controlled every push and pull of the tide, every rip and lag of current, every swirling mix of deep, brash heat and icy, deadly cold, creating a separation of days, even for the unenlightened Mer. Be they moon cycles or sun, Emma had discovered that they broke down the same, whether beneath sea or sky.

When blazing azure light faded into the soft, pale orange of sleep tide, Emma sneaked out of her room again. Given the excitement of the party, she should have been tired, but thoughts churned with confusion, and her heart tick-tocked like an internal timepiece that insisted it was not yet time for sleep. Hoping for an opportunity to socialize on a more casual level, she navigated to the servants' corridor. But on this night, no thriving beat or flashing lights drew her attention, and no other rebellious Mer mingled in the halls.

*Guess they've had enough partying for one night.* She swerved to the kitchen for a snack, but paused outside the entry when she overheard voices beyond the wall.

"I cannot do such things. The Sea King would not be happy to know I put the Princess in danger." The familiar female voice required that Emma peek inside. She needed no more than a back-side glimpse of the frail, blue-skinned maid to confirm that the speaker was, in fact, Maia.

Betrayal burned in Emma's stomach as she crouched lower to stay out of sight.

"The only danger to her would be from sharks, whales, and octopus during the journey. Emma knows the surface, understands it. As long as she returns to the sea before her gills contract, she will be healthier for it." Emma recognized this voice as well, and the burn scalded to a blistering mass as the conversation continued.

"She is healthy enough here. Has even begun to eat."

Merrick bubbled a sigh, and kitchen tools clanked together. "Maia, she is unhappy. Emmalina must adjust to her new life. She must cut her ties to the humans."

The water shifted, and the tools clanked again. Wondering what they were eating, Emma spied again, astonished at how intimately Maia had positioned herself against Merrick. She even toyed with his neck adornment, dragging his face near to hers. "She does not wish to adjust. She wishes to go back and stay."

"She cannot go back; she cannot stay. She must be joined with me, as the Sea King has declared." When Merrick didn't attempt to extricate himself, the wound spread into Emma's throat.

"Caspian stayed ashore," Maia argued. "And the Princess has requested a new match. She has refused you. I do not understand why you continue to pursue her."

"We are betrothed," Merrick breathed, his lips inches from Maia's. "I am to rule Atlantis, with Emmalina as the Sea Queen."

Maia was right. Emma did want to go home, and she'd never intended to join with Merrick. But she'd considered Maia her friend, someone she could trust with certain things. And Merrick claimed to have loved her since she was born. But the Mer couldn't possibly understand love, or friendship, in the same way as humans. Clandestine night tide meetings weren't typical symptoms of either type of love. The feelings of duty she'd begun to develop for Atlantis and the Mer disintegrated. *I can't stay here.*

Maia pressed closer to Merrick. "*You* often go ashore. Why do *you* not die?" Her lips pressed to his, and Merrick tangled his hands in her hair, deepening their shared connection.

Emma gulped, holding her breath to avoid releasing a torrent of bubbles, and pressed herself against the stone wall, tears stinging her eyes. *I have no friends, here.*

Merrick tore his lips from Maia's. "I can no longer go ashore. The creature is deceased, and with it, our source of venom. The hunters have not yet found a replacement for Maui's gift, and without it, I cannot breathe air."

Maia curled away from Merrick, wounded. "Emmalina is half human, and humans live ashore. There must be a way for her to return." Emma would have thought Maia was trying to help her get home, had she not just witnessed Maia's true nature. Now, all she could think was how badly Maia must want to send her away.

"Emmalina is also half Mer," Merrick reminded Maia. "Her gills have developed, and her human lungs shriveled. She must say goodbye to the land, if she does not wish to die as Caspian did."

"If we were to locate another creature . . ."

Maia's voice trailed off as Merrick approached her from behind, his hands spanning her narrow waist and drawing her into his chest. "The beasts are elusive, rare. And the Sea King does not wish to lose his granddaughter, the way he lost his son. Someone must inherit the kingdom, and by birthright, it shall be Emmalina."

"But you—"

"I am *Maui's* son, not Tangaroa's *true* heir. It is not for me to inherit Atlantis without the Princess."

Maia retreated from Merrick's embrace, defeated. "I do not understand why you reject the teachings of your father, of Oceania. Such thinking could set you free from the bonds your uncle has created—the ones that trap you here."

Merrick turned his back on Maia. "If I desired to depart, I would have returned to my father's kingdom long ago. I intend to remain in Atlantis and join with Emmalina. Together, we shall protect the remaining Mer. Oceania is left with no guards, a crumbling market, and a disassembled palace. The Mer in Maui's city disappear faster than they reproduce. Soon, his people will end. If our species are to survive, we must preserve Atlantis and cause the population to swell."

"Merrick." Agony wrung from every syllable of Maia's voice. "The Princess might not bear eggs. If she is more human than Mer, there will be no swelling of population from your joining. We cannot know the consequence of this until the joining has occurred, and then it will be too late. If you intend to save Atlantis through reproduction, the Princess becomes a risk."

Merrick kept his distance, face hardening. "You think I do not understand this? If the Princess cannot produce, I shall visit the preservation nest and select an unfertilized egg. With a youngling to care for, Emmalina will accept her duty to remain in Atlantis and raise it."

"You have made your choice, then." Maia clenched her fists against her hips. "I will not encounter you in secret again. I can help you no longer."

Since she'd arrived, Emma had believed the culture of Mer—all except Merrick—incapable of guile, more innocent than humans, but after witnessing the scene in the galley, she realized that she'd been wrong in supposing them naïve.

Tears of grief blurred her eyes as she sneaked into a nearby storage grotto to hide, awaiting the secret lovers' departure. She'd cried herself dry by the time she returned to her hammock, drowning in loneliness on an ocean occupied by one.

For the first time since she'd arrived, Emma slept deeply enough to dream. Clips involving underwater weddings, pregnant mermaids, and Paihana-fueled dance parties that ended with Emma swimming for her life as she was chased out of Atlantis by sharks. She saw her human mother, sobbing by the shore as Keith swam alone for the arch, yelling for Emma to come home. And then she saw James at the top of the hill near the cove. He stood hip deep inside a half-dug grave, sinking deeper and deeper in the shade of a giant silver maple.

She jolted awake, surprised and disoriented as homesickness slammed into her again. Blinking grit out of her swollen eyes, she tried to remember her mother's face, and then her father's, panic building in her chest when both appeared distant and unclear. She'd already begun to forget, as Merrick once promised. How much time would she have before the rest slipped away?

Unease propelled her out of her bed, where she nearly crashed into Maia, breakfast tray balanced between her hands. "Here, now, Princess. It is good to see you truly rest for a change."

Emma blinked, confused and miserable all over again as more recent memories fell around her like rain. Unable to meet Maia's eyes, she faced her dressing table. "I must have been exhausted."

"You are becoming comfortable here," Maia told her. "Perhaps the Sea King is right. With time, you will learn to be happy in your new home."

The wooden tenor of Maia's voice jolted Emma with awareness. If Merrick was Maui's son, that made him her cousin, and her grandfather's nephew. If she stayed and joined with him, he would become the new Sea King. If she ran away to live ashore, Merrick would still be the next heir to the throne of Atlantis. The only way he would *not* rule, was if Emma stayed, and found another suitable mate—one that her grandfather approved of—and by now, she was certain that Tangaroa would never allow that to happen. His successor was already chosen. Even if Emma was to disappear, that successor could then choose his own mate. *Maia hopes he'll choose her.*

"Princess?" Maia set the tray on the dressing table. "Your breakfast."

"Thank you." She turned away from the wriggling octopus tentacles and portion of bony pink fish, unable to consider eating.

Though Emma refused to do more than acknowledge Maia, the timid maid hovered, straightening the tools she'd used for styling Emma's hair the night before. "Is something wrong, Emmalina?"

Maia's use of her given name snapped Emma's attention. To reply might unleash a shriek of anger, an admittance of what she'd seen, heard, and how she wanted to punish them both for their betrayal, for the hurt she hadn't known either could cause. But when her eyes landed on Maia's face, cold misery—written in the set of her jaw, the droop of her eyes, her thin lips pressed together to keep them from quivering—served a sharp reminder that Emma should forget those who had betrayed her, and refocus on her initial goal.

Calling on the gods of cunning, she inhaled a calming breath. "I want to go back to the chamber of palace history. My tides pass slowly, and I would like to know about Atlantis. I'm interested in learning how paihana is made, and how venoms can be used for healing, as you did for me that time."

Maia's face brightened, her backbone straightening with pleasure. "The Sea King will be pleased with your reasoning. I shall ask permission for study, so that we may visit the great hall after you return from your visit with Laine. We will not have to hide this time, as it is permitted that Mer with an interest in healing should be allowed to study."

"Great. Thanks." Knowing she needed to eat, Emma picked at the slices of pink meat, poked at the slimy, still-moving tentacles. She caught sight of herself in the reflecting glass, and frowned, latching onto the other subject Maia brought up. On top of everything else, she had a date to see Laine's dwelling, and she looked atrocious.

In this strange culture of little body covering and many hair and neck adornments, how did one prepare for a casual date? "Speaking of Laine, what do I . . . um, I mean, how should I prepare for my visit?" She indicated her appearance.

Maia, already holding one of the hair tools, urged Emma to sit and got to work on her tangled locks. "Do not worry, Princess. I shall make you presentable."

This was why she needed to keep Maia around—for now.

**April 3**
*39 days gone*

JAMES PARKED IN FRONT OF the Harris's house and helped Mona out of the truck, attempting to hide his unsteady hands. "They think I did something horrible to their daughter. Are you sure they won't call the police?"

"I won't let them. Not without hearing me out." Mona stared up at Emma's empty bedroom window. "It's time I told my son the truth—all of it."

The door swung open, and Keith stepped onto the porch, glaring at James with pure hatred, as if they had never shared an ounce of friendship. James stopped, unwilling to cause the boy any more grief, but Mona continued up the walk, shaking her head at her grandson.

"Go away!" Keith shouted. "I won't let you take me back there."

"Keith." Mona huffed, completing her last few steps before stopping at the bottom of the concrete stairs. "That's no way to talk to your friends."

"He's not my friend," the boy shouted, pointing an accusing finger at James. "He left my sister in the ocean, and she'll never come home again."

In that one sentence, James realized that Keith hadn't lied to the police—he'd told the absolute truth, and *that* was the problem. When Mona struggled with her walker and the porch stairs, James stepped forward to help her. "Buddy, I didn't want to leave your sister. I wanted her to come with us, but she couldn't. Not then."

"It's all your fault." Keith rocked from foot to foot, half-stomping, half-dancing. "I'm not your buddy. My sister is gone and it's all your fault."

It had been weeks since James helped to calm his special needs friend, but he hadn't forgotten how easily a conversation with Keith could go off the rails. "I know. I'm sure you're right that it's my fault, somehow. But I want to fix it. I'm trying to find her and bring her home, but I need your help. And your parents' help. Will you let us in?"

When they reached the top of the stairs, a sullen-faced, dark-haired woman emerged from behind the door. Mona stretched a hand toward her daughter-in-law. "Cindy. How are you holding up?"

Cindy shook her head and walked away with a faint, "Let them in, Keith."

Keith's face twisted into the saddest mask of angry hurt James had ever seen, but did as he was told and led the visitors to his father's den.

The entire room was buried beneath a mountain of clutter, the lone desk spread with antique books, crumpled papers, and rolled up ancient texts. Russell wore two pairs of glasses—one balanced on the bridge of his nose, the other stuck in the nest of gray-brown hair on top of his head—scribbling furiously in a notebook, with one finger holding his place in a musty, old book. He didn't look up when they entered and sat. Mona waited until he'd finished his current, and then said, "We need to talk."

Russ looked up, blinking in surprise, like he hadn't heard them come in. "Mother. Hello. Yes, you're right. We do need to talk."

The elderly woman brushed dust off the arm of her chair, moving the walker with her foot to give her a clear view. "I've been hoping you'd come for a visit. You've been back in the country for some time, now."

Russ snapped his pen closed and set it in the book, then folded his hands together over the top. "My daughter's missing. I've been pre-occupied."

Mona pressed on. "Son, there are some things you should know. Things that might help you understand what's happened to Emma."

Sighing heavily, Russ removed the first pair of glasses, allowing the second to fall into place, and then, as if surprised by the presence of a second pair, he removed those too. "Does this mean you've finally decided to tell me about my brother?"

The blood drained from Mona's face, and she teetered in her seat. "You know about Caspian?"

Russ pinched the bridge of his nose and leaned back in his chair. "I've known for years, Mother. Since he first came to stay with you, and took over my room. I came home to surprise you one weekend, and found him in my bed, wearing *my* clothes, eating food out of *our* fridge, insisting that *his mother* would soon wake up—though it was the middle of the night."

Mona stared at her son with wide eyes, lips pressed into a thin line.

"I almost had him arrested, Mother. I had the phone in my hand, ready to dial the police, until he explained who he was. He had a picture in the nightstand. You, and a little boy who wasn't me—a boy who looked like him. We compared our faces in the mirror, finding multiple features that were nearly identical. I wanted to hate him, tried refusing to believe him, but I couldn't. It's like my soul recognized him as blood. As the brother I'd always wished I had. After that, Caspian told me everything. And though our communication was mostly long distance, we were friends—as brothers should be."

"Why didn't you tell me?" Mona pulled a throw pillow into her chest, clutching tight as if holding onto her long-lost baby.

Russ glared at his mother. "I've been wondering that exact thing for nineteen years. *I had a brother* who I never would have known existed, if I hadn't come home that weekend. *My own mother* took him—a grown man—into her home, her life, our family, and never told me one word about him. Like, in your mind, one of us couldn't exist when the other was around. We shared no holidays. No birthdays. No Sunday afternoon barbeques. I have so few memories of him. And then, when my brother died, you brought me and my brand-new wife his newborn daughter to raise. So Cindy and I did that. Emma's *our* daughter, through and through, and we love her. I love her. I've spent the last eighteen years pretending I didn't know exactly who and what she was. Knowing that, at any time, some Sea King could show up and steal her away.

"I've dedicated my life, my career, to searching for the source of the poison that brought Caspian home. I intended to safeguard Emma from ever experiencing what Caspian went through—the agony of being ripped away from her family. After all this time, and everything I've done to preserve his legacy, I'm still wondering why *our mother* has continued to keep him a secret."

Stunned, James shifted in his chair, unable to find words, because despite Russ's anger, and Mona's devastation, no one bothered to tell Emma, either. They all lied to each other. *And I thought* my *family was messed up.*

After an epic stare-down, Mona broke the silence. "I needed to protect you. Every day after Caspian returned, I lived in fear that he'd leave, go home to Atlantis. I wanted to spare you the pain of knowing that you had an older brother whose life we missed out on. And I was embarrassed telling you about my shadowed past, even though it happened long before I met your father. You were so protective, and I worried you'd think Caspian was a con artist who somehow fooled me. Then he got married so fast, and you and Cindy eloped, and Elise was on bedrest and—the timing was horrible. Then suddenly, Elise and Caspian were both gone, and it was too late to untie all my secrets."

Russ laughed out loud. "Did Caspian ever tell you how he met Elise?"

Mona straightened in her chair, indignant. "Of course. Caspian told me everything. He met her at the beach."

Russ leaned his elbows on the desk, the hint of a smile playing around his mouth. "Where at the beach?"

"I . . . I don't recall." Her voice faded, wrinkles deepening in her forehead.

"He met her that same weekend when I found him in my room. He knew literally nothing about women, so I took him to that outdoor bar with the live band to give him some pointers, help him learn to talk without being so awkward." Russ pined his horrified mother with a smirk of satisfaction. "He met her at a bar, Mom. I told him what to say. How to act. Helped him dress. I shared everything I know about human socializing. And it worked. And when he fell hard for Elise—we talked about sex, and marriage customs, and expectations. We had a relationship, and I didn't know about his funeral. Hell, I don't even know where he's buried, or *if* he's buried."

Mona waved an ambiguous hand at the window. "Your father's property on the bluff, beneath the maple tree. I wanted him to have a view of the ocean. Why didn't either of you confront me?"

Russ scrubbed a hand over his neck, eyes shining with hurt and betrayal. "We planned to, just never got the chance. When I realized he was gone, I was angry, so angry with you. It took everything in me to even speak to you about Emma, so how could I add in Caspian? At some point, I stopped hoping you would tell me the truth. And I was determined to save my daughter's life, so I switched majors, and took the job at the college because it allowed me to study every detail, every legend, every lead possible to protect my girl. Our girl."

Mona propped her arms on the chair's arm and dropped her head into her hands, muffling an anguished sob. "Oh, the tangled web."

For the first time since they'd arrived, Russ shifted his focus to James. "Son, I'm so sorry you've been caught in the middle of this. I want you to know that we don't blame you. Cindy and I are aware of what's happened. Or, at least where Emma's gone."

A wave of liberation crested over James. "Thank you. I can't tell you how relieved I am to hear that." Emotions rose into his throat, but he managed to croak, "Might still go to prison, but at least Emma will be protected."

Russ stood and rounded the desk, folding his arms across his chest as he leaned against the cluttered surface. "I don't want to believe it will come to that, but I'm prepared to do whatever I can to help, as long as it doesn't endanger Emma."

"Thank you." James didn't want to be endangered either, but decided this wasn't the ideal time to argue fairness and freedom for the innocent. "What do we do now?"

"First, we communicate with each other. No more secrets." Russ sent a sharp, pointed look to his mother. "None. Understand?"

Mona nodded, sniffling when her son supplied a handkerchief.

James stared at the bright green carpet, thinking of his boat, his nearly completed class. "I think we should look for Emma. I'm taking an accelerated scuba course, should be certified for open water by the next week. I'm supposed to always dive with a buddy, but I've given it a lot of thought, and I'm willing to risk diving alone." Emma's family responded with open-mouthed stares, so he continued, "I know finding her is like a billion to one chance, but I don't know what else to do. I'm no good with research, don't have access to information you haven't already seen, and I'm new to this *Mer* thing. Plus, the cops have me in their sights. Diving might be the only way I can help. I'm a strong swimmer, and I've been practicing my slow breathing every night, to maximize my air usage."

Russ responded by presenting his hand to shake. "We haven't been introduced. I'm sorry about that. Clearly, you care a great deal about my daughter."

"I love her." James stood, accepting the gesture. "I'm willing to do whatever it takes to bring her home.

Might sound silly, but I even bought a boat to get me out to the arch."

"Impressive." Russ took a business card from a holder on the desk, offering it to James. "Once you're fully certified, I want you to call me. There's no need to risk your life—I'll dive with you. Does this boat of yours need repairs?"

James' cheeks warmed with embarrassment. "Probably quite a few. But the engine runs so far, and she floats. Most important parts."

Russ tapped the card in James' hand. "I'll help with repairs, too, if you need them. Let's start as soon as possible."

Mona stuffed the handkerchief into her pocket and withdrew the pendant, presenting it to her son. "Finding her is one thing, but keeping her here, and breathing, is another problem entirely."

After several minutes of examination, Russ shook his head. "This isn't enough. Caspian claimed that the pendant only kept him breathing after being soaked in poison, or venom—he used both in our discussions. I've come to believe he was talking about venom from a rare, poisonous sea creature. He'd been led to believe that the venom would eventually lose potency, and obviously it has, since it stopped working for Emma."

"I don't know that it stopped working entirely." James grazed his fingers over the pearls that had kept his love breathing. "She gave it to that guy, Merrick, and a day later, went downhill, fast."

"Even so, it's wearing low." Mona scooted her walker over the rug to stand next to her son. "The need to swim had become necessary for Emma's survival. Several hours every day toward the end, even with the pendant. She missed a lot of school this last year."

"I suspected as much." Russ covered his mother's hand with his, the beginning of a healing bridge between their differences of opinion. "My studies have taken me across the globe, and I've analyzed every sea creature known to man. I've been diving in virtually every major body of water where diving is possible, but nothing I've found has matched what Caspian described."

"Maybe you should look again," Mona suggested. "Perhaps you missed one somewhere."

Russ seized the notebook off his desk, flipping back several pages. "The problem is that we know so little about the biology of the Mer. According to science, humans have no solid facts that the Mer even exist, let alone lessons about how their bodies work. This creature could be something as simple as a clownfish, or something with no name that's still undiscovered by humans. I have some personal theories, but nothing strong enough that I'd be willing to bank Emma's life on it."

Mona picked up a dusty book and turned it over in her hands. "I suppose that while you boys are out looking for our girl, Cindy, Keith, and I will go over your notes, see if a new set of eyes can find something."

The book wobbled in Mona's hand, so Russ took it from his mother and set it aside. "We have to be so thorough. The wrong venom could kill her. The main reason I've never tested any of my theories is because Emma only gets one shot. One. Getting it wrong will cost us her life."

Mona chose another book, shoving it in the handbag she'd hooked to her walker. "Then I think we cannot fail." Turning her back on her son, she skimmed into the hall. "Cindy! Keith! Come here. We have work to do."

It was nearly eleven when James arrived home. He turned the knob slowly to minimize the loud creek, every move intended to avoid waking his father. But as he entered the living room, Richard Phelps' deep baritone rumbled. "You're out late tonight. Not getting into more trouble, are you?"

"No. No trouble." Life would be so much easier if he could tell his father the truth. "Been working on a new hobby. Scuba lessons."

Richard adjusted, his well-worn recliner protesting with every movement. "What happened to basketball? Thought that was your ticket to college."

James folded his arms and leaned against the door frame. "I thought it was, but I've lost interest." He hadn't touched a ball since Emma left. Simply couldn't focus, and he hadn't wanted to let his team down during playoffs. Basketball just seemed such a minor need after losing Emma.

Richard switched on the side table lamp, a soft glow illuminating the distended body that was practically molded into the chair. "That recruiter keeps calling. Needs an answer, soon."

"What recruiter?"

"One that's been calling every day for the last six weeks. Think he's fed up, but must want you pretty bad, because he's persistent as hell."

James retrieved a bright orange post-it from the coffee table, intrigued. "This guy is from Orange Coast College."

"I know." His dad shifted again, huffing from the effort as he attempted to stand. "Could be something good, Son. Please don't blow it."

Understanding that Richard's inability to stand was the most likely reason he hadn't gone to bed yet, James pulled the man to his feet. "Pop, if you'd lost interest in a sport and then got an offer to play for a college, would you take it? Play anyway?"

Richard tapped James' shoulder, as close as he could get to a pat on the back. "In your position? I'd take whatever help I could get. Even if it meant scrubbing the locker room floor every night. You don't want to end up like me—single and alone, too overweight to move, and hardly able to get myself to work. I'm not that old, but my lifespan will undoubtedly be short. Learn from your father, boy, and take the offer if they make one. If you hope to have any kind of real future, you need to do this."

Touched by his father's rare show of concern, James tucked Richard in bed. All the things he'd learned today, the information he'd taken in melded together into a hot, tight ball of pain between his shoulder blades. Grownup life decisions were pretty damn tough. He wasn't sure he still wanted to be an adult. Until, of course, he remembered Emma.

# Chapter Eighteen

## Emma

LAINE MET HER IN THE gathering room, otherwise known as the ballroom, minus the decorations, the crowd, and the endless supply of paihana. Shimmering gold cuffs banded his wrists, and he'd tied his red-gold hair back with cords of seagrass. Unconcealed by fancy party adornments, his wide shoulders and sculpted physique couldn't be overlooked, each tight muscle straining against his skin.

A tingle rippled Emma's scales. She'd always considered Merrick well-built, even after observing a wide variety of Mer. But when she compared Merrick to Laine, the latter became the Mer equivalent of a body-builder. It didn't hurt that Laine was closer to

Emma's age. Early twenties, if she were to guess in human years.

If things were different, Emma might have asked Laine to court her. If she'd come to Atlantis willingly, intending to stay—if her heart weren't already committed through and through—she could imagine seeing him romantically, maybe joining down the road.

His lips blossomed into a bright smile, and he greeted her with a bow. "Atlantis suits you, Cynarina. This is no longer the tide of celebration, yet I am stunned by your allure."

"Thank you." She clamped down on her jittering nerves, twisting her pouch around her wrist. "What's a Cynarina?"

He brought her hand to his lips, kissing to the tips of her fingers in a Mer gesture of greeting. "Cynarina is a beautiful and rare form of coral. Bright enough to stand out as different, yet always part of the sea from which it came."

"Thank you. I've never been compared to coral before." Although, as Maia had wound decorative strands of pearls and seashells into her hair, she'd noticed in the looking glass that the blue hue of her skin had deepened, brightened, and the ends of her hair now streaked with purple.

Laine led her through the palace, past the air-pocket chambers she'd never dared visit, and the holding cavern where she'd been made to wait during her first moments inside the city borders. Here, the blue lights shone brighter than in the rest of the city, the rioting exhibition of colorful plants lush and thick—undeniably beautiful in a way she hadn't remembered.

They exited through the heavy pearl-encrusted doors, passing throngs of Mer. Most spun out of their path with haste, and all stopped to observe the Sea Princess as she paraded through the grand square and into the market. Laine stayed close, shooing away any who attempted to touch her, which made this market visit exceptionally less frightening than the last. They passed the populated section of city and crossed a wide field, dotted with gentle swells of rocky terrain, covered in of colorful anemone, whips, and kelp. Schools of guppies, clownfish, and shrimp darted here and there, in and out of the many-shaped plants. Before they reached the city gate, Laine swerved right, leading Emma to skirt the city barriers.

Laine's modest dwelling turned out to be little more than a hut. Made of the same clay bricks and stones as other city structures, minus additionally embedded decorations. Vines climbed the walls and covered the roof, twisting around corals and mingling with sea grasses in diverse assortment, creating a reef that rose high above the ocean floor.

The dwelling was secured by a lovely driftwood door, which Laine swung open, signaling for her to enter ahead of him. "It is not as attractive as the palace, but I find the outskirts quiet, and I am happier in quiet places."

"Me too." Despite the lack of any real décor, Emma found the cottage-like space pleasantly warm—a comfortable hideaway. In one corner hung Laine's hammock bed, swinging above the silt floor, and strategically placed shelves had been carved into the walls. One of those shelves held a treasure chest of wood and metal, others were stacked with seashells, spears, knives, and other tools. Some had been stacked with containers, or tablets like the ones in the hall of records.

Emma perched on one of two stone stools. "It's a lovely dwelling."

"Thank you, Princess. Not much of it to see. It is only where I sleep. Would you like to view the city barrier next? Or begin learning to channel your current?"

The tide had already passed by half, leaving Emma torn. Learning to defend herself was at the top of her to do list, but she ached for home with an intensity that implored her to ditch Laine and escape to the surface, even if only for a moment.

"The barrier."

Laine responded with a curt nod. "As you wish, Princess. But be aware, the barrier is not much. Simply a canopy through which predators will not swim, and a protection against human study."

The way he'd raised his eyebrows in challenge sent a vein of discomfort pumping into her. She schooled her voice to keep emotions from leaking into it. "Still important for me to learn. Especially if I'm to rule the city."

Laine plucked a round, heavy stone from a shelf, bouncing it in his hand. "If you are to rule the city, perhaps you should not depart from your escort to visit the surface."

Caught, Emma pulsed with embarrassment. "That wasn't . . . I'm not . . . How did you know?"

Laine tossed the stone from one strong hand to the other, a perceptive smile twisting his lips. "I am a city guardian. It is my job to know who passes through the barrier, and when."

She scrambled for an explanation, an excuse, but settled on the truth. "I just wanted to visit for a moment. I know I can't stay."

"You have a mate on the land."

Emma nodded, unable to speak around the misery growing in her throat.

"I cannot allow the Sea Princess to swim into dangerous waters unaccompanied and unprotected." He opened her hand and set the heavy stone in it. "Perhaps we might form an arrangement."

Emma bounced the stone as Laine had, testing the weight in her hand. "What kind of arrangement?"

"Meet me here each wake tide and learn to use your current for protection. Once I am assured of your proficiency, and during a time while I guard the gate, I will look away and allow you to pass through."

A fusion of hope and despair tugged on the misery still lodged in her throat. "How long will that take?"

He prodded her free hand until it covered the stone, adjusting her grip until it balanced equally between both. "Shock this."

Emma rose from the stool, focusing on the rock with all her might, but nothing happened. "I don't know how."

Laine acquired the stone, demonstrating with a jolt that flashed bright white and left a thin crack running down the side. "Like so." He replaced the object in her hands, directing her to tilt her chin and focus on his face. "In the heart of every Mer lies a current strong enough to shake the complete sea floor. We must dig deep within to uncover this power at times when it is most needed."

With her eyes locked on Laine's, and his hands covering hers, Emma tried again, reaching for the strength she knew lie buried—somewhere. Moments later, a trickle of power shivered over her scales, though it never reached the rock. Her enthusiasm grew. "What was that?"

"Princess Emmalina, you will learn quickly to channel your current. Perhaps ten to fourteen tides?"

As quickly as it had risen, her excitement splattered. "That's too long. I can't . . . I can't wait that long to visit the shore."

Laine replaced the stone on the shelf, positioning his body between Emma and the door. "I cannot allow a visit without protection from predators."

"Oh, I'll be fine. I've been swimming in the waters between Atlantis and the shore my whole life. Haven't died yet." She peered around him, knowing she wouldn't get past until he let her. "If I agree to this . . . arrangement, what do you get from it? What will it cost to me?"

"I owe a debt." His pleasure wilted, eyes cloudy as the storms Emma loved to watch rolling over the ocean. "When I was young, I joined a hunting party, believing that position could be my calling. But I am no hunter. Instead, sharks pursued me. This dolphin protected me by acting as a barrier, never allowing them access to me—escorting me into the city. But after seeing me safely home, this dolphin was taken captive and indentured to the Sea King, for the span of forever. I wish my protector to be freed."

She knew that dolphin. Had met him roaming the halls at night. "I don't know if I have enough influence to free a servant of the Sea King."

"No influence is necessary." He chose a knife from his assortment, slicing the water as if chopping through chains. "Only a tool sharp enough to break his bonds, and a path through which to escape."

In a convoluted way, Laine's strategy for the dolphin and his plot to help Emma seemed eerily similar. "And then?"

Laine pressed his fingertips to hers, a binding agreement between Mer. "In return, I will teach you currents, and afterward, look away as you depart the city barrier."

"Today." Emma swallowed, refusing to remove her fingers from his until she named a term of her own. "I want to visit shore today. Just once. I'll be fast, and promise to return before the tide change. I've seen this dolphin, and know how to find him. Let me go home this once, and I'll free him as soon as I can."

Laine squirmed, but kept his hand in place. "Emmalina."

"All or nothing, Laine. You might as well let me go. I'll just find another way."

Sighing with defeat, Laine completed the agreement. "We have a pact."

Laine guided Emma to the green iron gates, explaining how they appeared to stand free, but were pressed into place by a thick layer of ice. They rose above the hypnotic glowing passage that fed out to open sea, and Laine pointed out the curve of the ice, describing how, over time, a layer of thick silt had embedded itself, growing barnacles and vegetation, corals and thick, waving grasses. He took her higher still, to the edge of the barrier, where Emma saw that sunlight never reached them, because Atlantis lay buried beneath an ice cave.

"Has the ice ever melted? Can our city be breached?"

After glancing around to assure no other Mer lurked nearby, Laine took Emma's hand. "Come. There is a breach, though it is not yet large enough to concern the guards with threats of predators."

She left her hand tucked in his, and they picked up speed, covering a significant distance, until they'd circled behind the palace, past a corral of dolphins, and one of sea turtles. "These creatures belong to the Sea King as well," Laine explained. "But these are well cared for, and often assist the hunters in maneuvering prey. I do not understand why my friend was indentured, while these creatures are not, except that my dolphin was injured by those sharks, and of no use to our hunting parties."

*No wonder he needs me,* Emma though, taking in his unmistakable form. *He can't sneak around the palace the way I do.*

They continued beyond another field, this one flat and swaying with seagrass, and littered with beds of every size oyster imaginable, and came to a stop near the ice barrier, where vines of vibrant seaweed grew up and around the formations, creating the illusion of a spectacular garden wall. "Here." Laine poked at the thick layer, then pressed Emma's hand against the cool plants. "You see how this portion is spongy? Cold?"

Emma nodded, focusing on the movements of Laine's agile fingers as they pushed through the green with a squishy, suctioning sound. "You will notice that this section is warmer than the rest. The ice has melted here. For now, the breech remains small and hidden, but once it grows large enough for a predator to squeeze through, my guards must fill it with clay. Until then, the Sea King need not be informed of its existence."

Her heart pounded. The melted portion was tiny, narrow, but considering the amount of weight she'd lost lately, maybe she could successfully squeeze her slender body through. She pushed both arms in, up to her elbows, prepared to escape immediately, but Laine pulled her back. "Emmalina, wait. You must not go now. The hour is late, and you are expected at the palace before change of tide. If you do not wish to cause me harm, I must first return you to the palace for mealtime."

As if his words directed the water's movement, she felt the pulse, the shift of rhythm that indicated that the hour grew late. Laine was right. She knew he was right. And yet . . . "We have an arrangement. I will visit the surface today. That's the deal."

He whirled her to face him. "If we do not join your grandfather for the tide change feast, the alarm will sound, and you will be caught—we will both be imprisoned. You must wait until night tide, while the other Mer sleep. It will give you more time."

She studied their surroundings, making mental notes of exact formations that might help her find her way later. But the vine-covered wall stretched out for what must be miles. "What if I get lost? It could take me all night to find this spot again."

With two fingers, Laine plucked the abalone adornment from Emma's chest and drew it over her head. "We will leave a marker." He entwined the necklace with the vines, and Emma made note of how the iridescent disks gleamed in the dim blue light, giving off a soft glow.

"Yes. That works."

On the way back to the palace, Laine pointed out specifically shaped formations and uniquely situated plants in brilliant colors to help guide Emma's returning journey. A lone purple sea fan. A glowing turquoise sea anemone waving vivid yellow tips. A patch of white salt water lilies nestled in a heart-shaped stone. They could see the jagged palace spires from the oyster fields, and Emma took note of a mustard-colored sand dune not far from the animal enclosures. Laine swung Emma around, urging her to imprint their chosen markers in her mind before they entered the palace to attend the meal-time feast.

When her grandfather's guests had departed and the tide transformed, ushering with it the calming current of sleep, long after the palace Mer slumbered, nestled safely within their swinging hammock beds, Emma crept through the wooden door at the rear of the palace. She'd selected a thick gold chain from her stash of stolen treasures, along with a teardrop shaped pearl, and skulked along the barrier wall, surprised at how easily she found the breech again. She wriggled and fought, slicing off at least three scales, but managed to force her body through the child-sized opening, escaping into the freedom of the wide open sea.

# Chapter Nineteen

## James

**April 4**
*40 days gone*

JAMES SAT ON A CONCRETE wall outside the school, keeping his distance from the other lunching students. He'd stopped feeling like one of them weeks ago, and looked forward to finals, and then graduation—after which he'd never have to step foot on this campus again.

He slid the folded post-it out of his pocket, tapping his phone against his hip while he built a leaning tower of courage. Now, more than ever, he wished he could talk to Emma, ask her what he should do. But then he realized he didn't need to ask. He already knew.

*Make the call. Take the offer. Plan for our future.*

Fingers shaking, he dialed the number. The connection went straight to voicemail, and James let out a rare sigh of relief. Talking to recruiters usually required deep thoughts about major life choices, and after the week he'd had, his brain could explode at any moment. But despite the overwhelm, he left a message, requesting a meeting. Emma would be proud to know he'd kept his options open.

He checked his watch, anxious to leave school, get to work, and then to the shop for his last certifying open-water dive. The first dive turned out tougher than he'd expected. Tony took them to a safe location within the manmade reef, less than a mile from shore, and eons away from where James wanted to be. But he'd practiced every skill and allowed Tony to correct his mistakes, knowing that by the end of the week, he'd be free to dive wherever, and whenever he wanted.

With basketball season over, and finals rushing at them like a train without breaks, coach had turned their last period class into workout time—and even that was optional, as coach had stopped taking roll for the seniors. Usually, James skipped the class in favor of squeezing out an extra hour of work, but today he needed a distraction, desperately, and that distraction came in the form of heavy weights and fast, sweaty cardio. He plugged in his earbuds and cranked up the sound until his eardrums pounded with each beat.

Lyle and Mark were two of the six people in the weight room, and James refused to acknowledge them. Their predictions about his relationship with Emma had turned out to be extraordinarily accurate, even knowing less than a small fraction of the real story. Fortunately, since Emma's *disappearance*, both gave him a wide berth, as if they knew he would take out his frustration on them at the slightest provocation.

As he ran like a demon on the treadmill, James' back pocket vibrated. He braced one foot on either side of the machine's frame and withdrew his phone, heart doing a weird little dance as he accepted the call.

"James Phelps?"

"Yes, this is him." James hit the pause button on the treadmill, using his shirt to wipe the sweat from his forehead.

"My name is Barry Westover from Orange Coast College. I'd like to talk to you about your plans for next year, and what your interest level would be in potentially playing basketball for our program."

The moving tread had stopped, but somehow James stumbled anyway, dropping his phone on the ground, and then fumbling to pick it up again. "Have you even seen me play?"

Westover chuckled. "Wouldn't be calling otherwise. I received your play reel a couple of months ago. Came to some games at the end of your season, hoping to see you in action, but was told you'd been medically excused from the remainder of the playoffs. The real question is whether or not you'll be released to play before practice begins this fall."

James nearly choked on his tongue. Coach helped him start a play reel in the beginning of the season, adding to it as the team continued to win—but that felt like ages ago, and after skipping playoffs, he James hadn't finished it. And he certainly didn't send it to recruiters. But admitting that *he* hadn't applied for the college seemed like a bad idea. "Yes, I will. Or, I mean, I should be." He stumbled over the words, knowing he must sound like a complete idiot, and frustrated that he'd been caught off guard.

"Great. That's great news. What's your availability next week? Could you visit our campus for a meeting on, say, Tuesday afternoon?"

Zero. He had zero availability. Work. School. Finals. Emma. Emma. Emma. Diving to find Emma. But Orange Coast College—if they offered a scholarship, even a partial one—could provide a direction, a path for his, and maybe Emma's, potential future. "Tuesday's great."

"Fantastic." Papers shuffled on Westover's end. "Come prepared to talk about your field of study, housing and meal plans, and the other potential needs of an athlete. You're welcome to bring a parent. Your choice of school is a big decision, so helps to have a support system on board."

James ended the call and stared at his phone, brain throbbing like nothing more could possibly fit inside his cranium. A couple of weeks ago, he had no prospects for college, was on the verge of losing his construction job, and was facing potential homicide charges for his missing girlfriend. Then he'd gone to see Emma's Gran, and his world tilted right-side-up again.

He ducked into the locker room and stripped off his clothes, unable to wait any longer to get to Tony's shop. Maybe, just maybe this streak of luck would hold up during his dive.

Tony's boat sped away from the dock, past the reef that kept the bay waters mild. James pinned his gaze on the arch, and though they didn't veer toward it, neither did they steer away. Thirty minutes out, Tony cut the engine and faced the divers. "Okay. Now, I realize that none of you are familiar with this area yet, so it's important that you stay close enough that I can see you, just in case. This isn't another practice dive, so it's crucial that you follow my guidelines to avoid running out of air before we're ready to surface. We will not be skipping safety stops, under any circumstances, so be prepared to buddy-breathe if necessary. Do not leave your buddy behind. Remember that once you're forced to surface, the current will be stronger, and your swim more taxing. The idea is to return to the boat before we get to that point."

They reviewed the procedure for preparing their equipment, and then tested each tank to make sure the connections were air-tight. James was paired with a tiny woman named Kim, who asked question after question, never processing the given answers.

James suctioned his mask into place and bit down on the regulator, and one-by-one, the divers summersaulted backward off the boat. The cold-water shock threatened to steal precious air, seeping into every area where the cheap, used wetsuit had worn thin.

Tony gave the signal, and the divers sank below the surface. For a moment, his partner panicked, her eyes wide and afraid behind the plastic of her mask, bubbles streaming from her mouthpiece too rapid to be safe. James grabbed the front of her vest and signed for her to keep her eyes on him, instead of the underside of the boat. Soon, her breathing evened out as she calmed enough to enjoy the sensation of sinking.

When they reached their maximum depth, James and his partner headed in the direction Tony had mapped out for them. James held tight to his device, watching his air usage and depth reader closely. Rather than examining the ocean floor like his partner, he kept his head up, attention on the wide, bright sea spread out before him.

As the dive continued, James swam faster than he meant, drifting farther from the group until he and Kim had inadvertently left Tony and the others behind. His dive computer alerted, urging him to turn around and return to the boat before his air ran out. Kim tapped her tank with her nails, signaling that they should turn back, but James ignored both warnings, desperate to see something—anything that might be a clue. Kim stayed with him, as they'd been trained to do, until both computers lit up with low-air warnings. As much as it hurt to leave, getting that certification card was crucial. He couldn't rent equipment without it.

They glided hard and fast against the current, James expending extra effort to keep his breathing slow and even, despite the danger of his tank running out. But when a pocket of warm water sucked him backward, James whipped around, and from the corner of his eye, caught a bright flash that left his heart pounding. He hollered through the water, frustrated at the inability to speak. Kim grabbed his wrist, refusing to let go, and dragged him to the rope that would lead them up to the boat.

Once they'd boarded and offloaded their equipment, James leaned over the side, desperate for another glimpse. Emma was near, he'd felt it. He noted the coordinates in his dive log. This was the place where he and Emma's father would begin their search.

On the ride back to shore, James endured a stern lecture from Tony about the dangers of swimming off course, of separating beyond the line of his dive group's vision. He apologized to everyone, especially Kim—who had been giving him the evil eye since the moment her mask had come off. But Tony's words were lost on him. James had zeroed in on that one flash of hope that Emma might be out there.

Computer printed dive card in hand, he returned home and showered, feeling accomplished and hopeful. Since the police had taken Emma's clothes, he grabbed a T-shirt, an old pair of flip-flops, and the thickest, nicest towel he could find, shoving it all into a string backpack. As he had done so many times in the past, James headed for the cove—but this time, his only mode of transportation were the two feet he'd just used for swimming.

Paranoid about being followed or seen, James zigzagged through neighborhoods, avoiding the path he knew so well, and arriving to the cliff by staying in shadows and avoiding the warm puddles left by streetlights. He traversed the rocky footpath in such darkness that twice his foot caught on rocks and threatened to send him tumbling over the edge. As soon as he lost sight of the houses above, he used a flashlight app to illuminate the sharp, jagged terrain and avoid falling in tide pools.

Finding that the familiar cave hadn't been permanently damaged or changed by the police investigation brought him profound relief. He stood on the edge of the sand, hesitant to disturb the sacred place that had already been so violated. Evidence of the investigation lingered in the form of footprints embedded in the sand, and sweep marks spanning the walls and ledges. The nook where he'd stored Emma's clothes remained empty, but James swung the pack off his back and squeezed it tight. He didn't want to get in more trouble—but he couldn't stand to leave Emma with nothing, should she need clothes when she came back.

His eyes fell again to the footprints. How many officers had been here, and what had they taken, aside from her clothes? Most of the prints were left by large, boots with thick, specialty tread, but as his eyes adjusted, a smaller set of prints—damp, barefooted ones, became visible.

His joints stiffened as he kicked off his shoes and approached the ledge where he and Emma typically left tokens of communication. A shiny gold chain smiled up at him from the dark crevice. Shocked, James dropped his pack and picked up the chain, letting the smooth, cool metal shimmer over his fingers. Why would she leave him gold jewelry? And how? It didn't make sense.

"Where'd you get this, Emma?" he asked aloud, falling back into the habit of speaking to her through the bond of their common space. "And what do you want me to do with it?"

The wind howled, and a giant wave crashed against the rocks, veiling the cave in light mist. It reminded him of the night when Heather had followed him. Now that the cove had been compromised, he couldn't feel completely alone here—it left him on edge, whirling at the slightest noise, and paranoid that someone was watching, listening. The chain shimmered in the flashlight's beam, so he shoved it in his pocket, wishing she'd been able to leave him a note. What if someone else had been here?

He crammed the supplies into the nook, and as his hands scraped the ledge, a tiny stone tumbled out. No, not a stone. A purple-toned, teardrop pearl, the size of his pinky nail. James squeezed the treasure in his fist, barely resisting the urge to crow. The chain could have been left by anyone, but this pearl was Emma's signature. It's what she always left. Different colors and shapes, but always a pearl. She'd found a way back, for however short the visit, and this was all the proof he needed. She wasn't lost to him yet.

But he'd missed her.

And not by very long; her footprints were still damp. He should have walked faster, left sooner, taken the bus or driven the truck, instead of walking. He might have been here when she came, could have seen her, touched her, tasted her lips, her mouth, and then . . . Then what?

He wanted so badly to speak—to keep her updated on everything—but wasn't sure where to start. All the plans they'd made together, or that he'd made waiting for her, seemed paltry and selfish when he considered what Mona had told him about Caspian and Elise. Would making a life together cost them Emma's future? Her life?

Water lapped at the sand, and he extended a foot to reach it. The answers to life's questions wouldn't track him down and nail him on the head, and James couldn't predict when he'd be back to this sacred place. So, as he had done so many times before, he told the ocean everything, and by releasing the weight he'd carried for so many months, felt infinitely lighter.

# Chapter Twenty

## Emma

EMMA SLEPT FOR MOST OF the following day. It was the only way to combat the crushing depression that enveloped her after the momentary visit to land. She tried not to dwell on the condition of her cove, but it was hard. The minute she pulled herself out of the water, she'd seen signs of people—strangers—having been there, and they'd inspected every inch of her private, sacred place. Her clothes were gone, and the sand that wasn't covered in footprints was marked with lines from a sand comb. Even the walls and ledges appeared to have been wiped clean and streaked of some sort of chemical. The footprints, multiple sizes and treads, contended that more than one person had been there.

Her privacy had been invaded, and there was not a single thing left on the ledge from James. Something was wrong. She couldn't believe that James had betrayed her secret, that he would tell someone—anyone—about her change, or their private place, but why else would it be swept clean of all evidence that she existed?

Despite her uncertainties, she'd left the gift anyway, hoping that—whatever was happening—James might someday think of her, and come back to find that she hadn't given up on trying to come home. She'd returned to the palace moments before the wake tide, when the occupants would stir, and the galley maids would begin food preparations not far from the rear entry.

When Emma refused the first meal, Maia left her alone to sleep, but returned mid-day, baring—as she always seemed to be—more food, including another writhing octopus tentacle. *I really need to talk the cooks into finding me other options*, Emma thought.

Maia plopped the tray on Emma's reclined stomach with an unceremonious thud. "Emmalina, I am sorry you feel unwell, but you must eat. The Sea King has granted us permission to visit the chamber of palace history. We are free to go whenever you like."

Emma sat up, shaking off the gloom with the reminder of her mission. Her need to live on land was not *only* about the people she'd left behind, but also about her existence there, her plans for the future, her ability to overcome obstacles. "That sounds great. I'd love to get out of the palace."

Using the spear-like tool to slice open the tentacle skin, Maia tore out the gooey, slimy meat and shoved it at Emma, allowing drops of octopus blood to drip on her chest. "You must eat, first."

Shuddering with disgust, Emma shoved the food away, rising from her bed to peek into her reflecting glass. "I'm not a fan of octopus. I'll eat about anything else, though. Clams, crab, lobster, shrimp, and most kinds of fish—despite the lack of cooking. But octopus is tough and bland. And watching it move on my plate ruins my appetite every time."

Maia's face tightened with frustration. "But, Princess. The meat of an octopus is beneficial for you. It could . . . please taste it."

Emma whirled, pinning Maia with a glare. "Why does it matter to you what I eat or don't eat, as long as I consume enough to stay alive?"

Uneasy words tumbled from Maia's mouth. "I happened upon a sea witch in the market last tide. I do not converse with sea witches, but this one knew things. She offered me an octopus. Made claim that it will restore the Sea Princess' human lungs. I did not understand how she could know that I serve you, or that you wish to visit land again. I tried to purchase the octopus, but had not the coin she demanded, and when I returned with the price—the sea witch had gone. Disappeared."

Emma eyed the mushy, white meat, suspicion tapping on her skull. "An octopus? That's it? I find that hard to believe."

Blood dripped through Maia's fingers as she continued to hold the mangled essence. "No, Princess. Not just any octopus. A rare one, that exists only in the far away sea. I was not told the exact type—only that it must be alive when the venom is harvested."

Mouth puckering with distaste, Emma peered closer to peer at the contents of Maia's hand. "How much venom?"

"She only spoke of the octopus, not how much venom would be required. I hoped to bring a gift that would lift your spirits, but the only octopus available in the palace is that which the galley maids serve at meal time." Maia sighed, poking at the dripping mess. "Why would a sea witch tease me so?"

Emma took a turn poking the meat, forcing down a wave of bile that threatened to erupt. "It's probably best that you didn't purchase poison from a stranger. There is no guarantee of what you'd be getting."

"This is why we must go to the chamber of palace history." Maia shoved the destroyed octopus into

Emma's hands. "You should eat this anyway. To be certain."

"Fine." Emma closed her eyes and accepted the slimy, squishy mess, her stomach already revolting. "One bite. And then we go."

"Yes." Maia wiped her hands on the banana leaf the octopus had been served on, and then used sand off the ground to further remove the blood.

Emma brought the vile thing to her mouth, squeezing her eyes shut—unable to watch as she ripped a small chunk off with her teeth and chewed, and chewed, and chewed the tough, grainy meat. This wasn't the answer, and she'd known it before Maia brought it up. If restoring her lungs were this easy, all the Mer would be able to breathe on land.

But if eating a bite of octopus would satisfy Maia enough to help her do more reading, so be it. Something big was happening at home, maybe bigger than her being forced to join with Merrick. No matter how depression weighed her down, she had work to do. There would be no cavalry of police, or handsome strangers, or palace guards coming to rescue her from Atlantis. If she wanted to go home, Emma had to figure out how to save herself.

Emma dragged a heavy stack of tablets from a high shelf and delivered them to the table where Maia scrolled through page after page. Though she couldn't read the language, Emma continued to transport an endless supply of tablets and pages from the shelves. According to Maia, this room was where the most recently recorded histories were kept, but after what felt like hours, doubt set in, leaving her uncertain that the information they sought would be found here.

"Thank you." Maia waved at a stack of documents she'd finished. "You can put those away to make more room."

Emma hefted them off the table and returned them to the shelves, thinking what a strange role reversal, that Maia barked orders, while Emma did the work. But she enjoyed lifting and moving tablets. It gave her purpose, allowing her to feel productive, while her educated maid scrolled through page after page of writings that Emma could not read herself.

She retrieved another stack of tablets, pausing for a break while Maia studied the current ones, and pressing her fingers to the etched symbols. Some behaved as letters, others might be numbers, and still other markings could be considered drawings, but it was hard to tell. In a way, she wished she had time to learn the language, to understand the markings. This was a part of culture that fascinated Emma, any culture, all over the world. She guessed she'd absorbed this fascination from her human father.

Homesickness ached like a giant hole in her middle, a hole that throbbed, sucking away her energy, her very life blood. Her resilient family could move on, get past losing her—but she wasn't sure she could, and she would rather that they not have to either.

Finding no symbols that stood out to her untrained eyes, she slid the top tablet off the stack and set it near Maia's elbow, then blindly inspected the next one. She'd gone through four of the five tablets in her own stack, when one particular symbol stood out, glaring at her. She blinked, and then refocused her eyes to be sure. She tapped Maia's arm. "This. Right here. What does this mean?"

Maia regarded Emma. "You cannot read, Princess. I shall get to that page when I can."

More insistent, Emma gripped Maia's elbow and physically drew her closer. "Look. It's an octopus tentacle, hooked to a string of pearls."

Once again, Maia peered up from her tablet. "Princess, you are tired. Perhaps it is time to return to the palace?"

Frustrated, Emma picked up the tablet and slammed it on the table in front of Maia. "Look. At. This. Tell me what it says. If I'm wrong, you can go back to reading the other pages, but I'm not leaving here until we find something."

Startled by Emma's intensity, Maia focused on the page, her eyes widening. "And find it we have." She moved her finger to the top, working her way down until she arrived at the symbol that had first caught Emma's eye. "It seems the sea witch was correct. According to this, when Maui was granted rule over Oceania, each Mer was given the choice to come and go between earth and sea. Wishing to enable them to breathe, Maui asked a sea witch to create a token that could be worn when the Mer visited shore. She used a neck adornment of strung pearls, coated in the venom of a blue-ringed octopus. The adornment is said to have paralyzed their gills, forcing the mermaid or merman's human-like lungs to inflate, and require air for breathing."

"Blue ringed octopus," Emma repeated, her heart pounding into her throat. "Does it tell us how to find one? Or where?"

Maia continued her study. "Not here, but it does include grim warnings. It says that the venom from this creature is excessively potent. Used incorrectly or at an improper dosage, it could prove deadly, to Mer or human."

That would explain why it wasn't more common for Mer to visit land. Emma gulped, letting out a stream of bubbles. "Okay. We have to be cautious with the venom. Got it."

"Princess." Maia looked up from the page, her eyebrows folding together with worry. "There is more. I do not wish to tell you, but I also do not wish for you to die. The Sea King would see me dead, too, I am certain."

Distracted with daydreams of going home, Emma knocked into one of the rock shelves, bruising her elbow. Rubbing the wound, she returned to Maia's side. "I promise I'll be careful, but I can't do this right unless I know all the risks."

Maia drew the tablet into her chest, fear welling in her expressive eyes. "Princess, please. Could you not be happy in Atlantis? Laine would make a good mate."

It didn't escape Emma's notice that Maia made no mention of Merrick, but this was not the time to point it out—she needed Maia's ability to read, needed to know what else this tablet said. Years of experience in talking Keith out of irrational behavior had polished Emma's negotiating skills, which she now employed. "If I stayed long enough, made some friends and found a mate of my choosing—maybe Laine—I probably could be happy here."

Maia relaxed her rigid stance, but kept a tight hold on the tablet. Not that it would do Emma any good to take it from her.

Emma continued, "But if I was to stay, to rule the city, I must know about all dangers Atlantis could face. If this venom, this creature, is a threat, I must know about it. And I must know the cost of such a poison to the Mer."

"And if you choose not to stay?"

Emma pressed her hands to Maia's wrists, gently loosening her grip on the tablet. "Then I'll try the venom anyway, with or without the rest of the information."

"There is no promise with this venom," Maia reminded her. "Only risk."

Emma replaced the tablet on the table, jabbing her finger on the symbol. "Then explain it to me. Help me understand."

Maia read the next lines aloud. "The Mer of Oceania paid a great price for Maui's experiment. The venom-coated token only worked on the Mer who sustained a high percent of human blood, and whose human lungs remained undamaged from disuse. Those Mer not born of near-human descent had not developed working lungs, and not knowing this, traveled ashore expecting to take their first breath of air. When their lungs did not inflate, these Mer returned to the sea, but with their gills paralyzed, could no longer breathe in the water, either. As a result of Maui's experiment, Oceania lost hundreds of Mer to suffocation."

"See, that's not so bad." Hearing the words, in connection to the story Maia had just shared, she corrected herself. "I mean, it's horrible that so many died, but in my case, it's not so bad. I'm half human, and I know I have lungs, because that's how I breathed when I lived ashore."

Without comment, Maia returned to the page. "Hundreds of others reached the land and drew breath as though they were human, but upon leaving the salty protection of their home, the venom absorbed into their bodies, removing from them the ability to eat or drink, and eventually to move. They, too, died."

Emma blinked as the reality of the dangers soaked in.

"Princess," Maia whispered. "Thousands of Mer accepted the choice, but only four are known to have survived the effects of the venom."

Emma's chest tightened, heavy as if Maia had heaped bricks on it. "Scary odds."

"Yes." Maia stacked the tablets and began returning them to the shelves.

Emma set aside the tablet so she could put it where it could easily be found again. "My father was one of the survivors. And Merrick must be as well, because he spends lots of time on land." The puzzle shifted around in her brain, and another piece fell into place. "Merrick and my father are descended from Sea Kings, Maui and Tangaroa. I wonder if my grandfather and Maui, are the other two survivors? Just a theory, but if it's true, maybe I'll be the fifth."

Maia turned from organizing the shelf. "It is still a dangerous risk. Princess, do not forget that once you entered Atlantis, your human lungs shrank from the pressure, too damaged for you to return to land. There is a chance that they will no longer work once you return, venom or none."

Emma hadn't forgotten. That fact would have been impossible to ignore, even without the traumatic events surrounding it. But she had to try. Not only because she missed her family and James—though those were the most important reasons—and not just because she was desperate to fulfill her childhood hopes and dreams. If all those things were not issues—even if she decided to stay in Atlantis—she was now obligated to do this. For the Mer. Either she would prove once and for all that Mer could evolve to live as humans, or that the legends of Oceania were simply that: legends. Dangerous ones. Maybe once the Mer understood that it was not possible to go ashore, rebels and dreamers like herself could let go of the impossible and aim for other ideals. Maybe no more Mer would come ashore to create other Halfling children who would eventually be ripped from their families.

"The question now," she mused, carefully placing her chosen tablet on a corner shelf, where the surrounding tablets had already gathered silt, "is where do we find a blue ringed octopus?"

"We could attempt to find the sea witch." Maia joined Emma to cross the sculpture cavern, and then outside, aiming for the Palace.

"I don't trust that. What about the royal hunters? Would it be suspicious if we requested it as a delicacy? Or an ingredient for Paihana?"

"I am certain of it." Avoiding the market, Maia chose a path that took them around the city's edge, crossing near the field of oysters. "The Sea King must approve all recipes for Paihana. If any of the Mer knows the secret of this venom, the Sea King is that merman."

"So probably not for healing either, then?" Out here, the bright blue light that lit the city glowed like a bright blue sun, as if the Mer who settled the city knew they were missing something important, and attempted to replicate it.

"A risk. I do not believe the he would approve." Her wild green hair whipped from the speed and the current, tangling into a seaweed-like display. "He would know we did not study healing."

Realizing Maia was right, Emma determined to find a blue ringed octopus herself. "I wonder how far I'd have to go to find one?" They passed the netted corrals, reminding Emma of her promise to find and free Laine's injured friend. So much to do with the small amount of time she had left.

Maia paused before entering the palace. "Emmalina, you must not attempt to find this creature. There are many dangers for a mermaid in the open sea."

*There are many dangers inside the city, too.* Emma couldn't forget the conversation she'd overheard, the make-out scene she'd witnessed. No longer willing to argue, Emma opened the heavy door herself. "I'm no stranger to risk, or to the open sea. I've been swimming out there for years. I came here, by myself, to save my brother. I'm not afraid."

"The biggest risk will come when you are in contact with the venom. Your chance of survival is markedly low." Maia's tail swirled as they rounded the corner to Emma's room. "Have a sleep and think hard. Your death would mean the end of many customs in Atlantis, including the Sea King's legacy."

"I don't intend to die." But she did intend to leave, and had to shove away the guilt Maia's words piled on. Time was running short. If she didn't find a way out soon, she'd be forced to join with a *suitable merman*— most likely Merrick—on the day her grandfather had specified. And now, more than ever before, that was something she refused to accept.

# Chapter Twenty-One

## James

THOUGH IT WAS AFTER TEN o'clock, interior lights cast a cheery glow over the Harris' lawn as if not a single person inside intended to sleep. At least not anytime soon. James knocked, too wound up to keep his news until morning.

Russ answered, and waved James inside. "How did your final dive go?"

"Really well." He followed Russ into the kitchen, where Cindy had spread across the table several dusty, old books, stacks of loose papers, and a high-end laptop with no fewer than 25 open tabs. "I, um . . . want to tell you about it. If that's ok."

Cindy closed the laptop, and Russ sat next to her, clasping hands. "Of course," she said. "Please do."

James perched on the same stool where he'd once shared a carton of ice cream with Emma. "We dove near the arch, where Emma used to swim. Got a little farther from my group than I should have and ... thought I saw something."

Cindy fiddled with a pen, clicking it open and shut, rapidly. "I doubt it was Emma. From what I understand, she's not allowed to leave. Mona insists that our girl is captive in that place, same as Caspian. He had to escape, and so will she. I can't imagine her taking risks that will make life harder for her, until she's ready to come back and stay."

James recalled the flash of white and red, the moment of confusion when he was overwhelmingly dragged away from his group. "I know, but it felt so real."

Russ stood to lay a comforting hand on James' shoulder, squeezing in support. "I know, son. Cindy and I have experienced several sightings like you've described while diving—even when Emma was an infant, safe and warm, and at home in her crib."

The level of dedication Emma's parents displayed confounded James. He hadn't heard from his mother since she left, years ago, and his father only paid attention to his son when forced to do so. "The thing is, after the dive, I went to the cove."

Both parents gasped in alarm.

James held up a defensive hand. "It was late, and dark, and I avoided all streetlights and cameras. I haven't been there in ages, and I needed to feel her, be near to her. Anyway, I found these."

He withdrew the chain from his pocket and laid it on the table, followed by the newer pearl, which he deliberately placed in front of Cindy. "That first week after Emma left, she somehow came back and left me a pearl. It's lustrous white, slightly smaller than this one." He removed the original pearl from a credit-card slot in his wallet, and set it on the table next to the purple one.

Russ examined the chain with narrowed eyes. "We can't prove that these were left by Emma. Could be a plant from your accuser, or one of Emma's tormentors. Or that cave's now some criminal's new hideout. A lot of times, police tape is hard to resist."

As angry as James was over Heather's betrayal, he didn't believe she was the type of person to deliberately plant stolen goods, hoping to frame him. She may not trust him—for which he couldn't blame her—but she wasn't a liar. "Except that I found the white pearl long before Heather followed me to the cove. She couldn't have known to leave it back then."

Cindy retrieved a loupe from a drawer and scrutinized both pearls with an appraising eye. She rolled the white one around on her palm. "This is a good size. High quality. Natural, instead of tank-grown and color-dyed. Worth a little bit."

"I'm telling you, they're from Emma." James leaned back against the counter, staring at the ceiling. "Until Heather followed me, no one else knew about that place. No one other than Emma would think that I'd go there as much as I have. And I've left things too—they always disappear, eventually. Who else would take them if not Emma?"

Russ stroked the thick gold chain. "If Emma did leave this, I don't understand where it came from. Or why. Just seems so out of character—so random."

"I don't know." James rubbed his throbbing temples with his fingers, wishing his eye would stop twitching. "Maybe a shipwreck? Or sunken treasure? The point is, she's leaving messages. I'm not sure what they're supposed to mean, but I'm glad to know she still remembers me."

Russ scrubbed his hands over his face and into his hair. "I hate the idea of her coming back and finding no one there, but we can't be everywhere. If we want her back long-term, we've got to figure out how to keep her here."

"Agreed." Connie pressed the pearls into James' palm. "All we can do is to keep going back, until the day we find the answer."

Though it was late, he brought home a bag full of take-out tacos. Spending time with Emma's parents had caused him to reflect on the relationship between him and his father. He couldn't remember the last time the they'd eaten a meal together, nor could he remember whose turn it was to cook—thus the tacos.

He found his father sprawled in the same recliner where he spent the majority of his time, snoring, with the TV volume up loud. The man's stomach rose, pressing tight against the cotton of his work shirt, and then fell again, allowing very little relief to the thin, strained fabric.

Opting to shower before waking his father, James set the food on the kitchen counter and headed to the bathroom, where he stripped off his sandy clothes and let the steamy water soothe his tight muscles. He was so close to finding her, to reaching her. He could feel it. Taste it. Taste her.

He lathered the hair that had grown two inches since she'd last twisted it in her fingers, then held his head under the spray, refusing to believe that those fingers it wouldn't tangle in it again someday.

After less than ten minutes in the bathroom, his father pounded on the door. James turned off the water, irritated at being interrupted. "I left food on the counter for you." He flung the curtain aside and snatched his towel.

"Saw that," his father said through the door. "Thanks. But I need you to get dressed and come out. There's some cops here to talk to you."

A dry, coppery taste coated James' tongue, and his muscles went rigid. "About what?" Richard didn't respond, which told James all he needed to know. This was about Emma. Of course. "Be out in a minute." His fingers shook as he pulled on his basketball shorts and a T-shirt, and emerged rubbing his hair with a towel.

The house had filled with the scent of Mexican food, but the sight of two uniformed officers, standing like sentries near the door, banished all traces of his usual appetite. "Hey." James stuck out a hand to shake. "How're you doing?"

Officer Peters wasn't present, which only compounded James' anxiety. The officers—a small, dark-skinned female who barely reached her taller, broader partner's shoulder—would have made an ideal pair for a TV sitcom. If only James was an actor, and the scene unfolding in his living room scripted entertainment.

"Very well, thank you." The woman shook James's hand with a surprisingly strong grip, and introduced herself as Officer Caio, and her companion as Officer Fustamante, then instructed for James to, "Have a seat."

James forced his feet to take him there, then begged his knees to bend. "I guess this isn't a friendly visit to just check in?"

"Is it ever?" Fustamante's lips quirked, giving James the impression that the enormous blond man was the comic relief in this duo.

"Not lately." He'd reminded himself, numerous times, that the officers weren't trying to pick on him. They had a mystery to solve, and James was the last person to see Emma. He'd known her secret place, had possession of her clothes—or so it appeared from how they'd been found. "I didn't hurt my girlfriend. I couldn't do that, not ever. And I want to find her as bad as anyone, trust me."

The officers remained standing, towering over James until Fustamante crouched to eye level. "I'm not saying we don't believe you, okay? But all the evidence screams that you're hiding something. Something big."

*Of course I'm hiding something!* But he couldn't exactly tell the police what he knew. Not even to save himself from prison. His voice shook. "I know it looks that way. But like I told Detective Peters, she left on her own. It's hard to believe, and I get that, but Emma's alive, just gone away for a while."

And then Officer Caio confirmed his fear from earlier. "You keep returning to the scene, Son. After Peters told you not to. You've tampered with evidence."

James shot to his feet, fear and anger at war inside him. "I haven't tampered with anything. There's nothing left there to touch. I only went back because I miss her. Don't you get that?"

"Why do you miss her?" Fustamante asked, his deep baritone surprisingly gentle.

"Because she's gone!" James shouted. "And I love her."

During the conversation, Richard had hovered out of the way, listening, but now stepped to James' side. "Officers, my son has already signed a detailed statement about what happened the night that girl went missing. He's a good kid. Almost never been in trouble. Works hard for his uncle. Brought his old man dinner." Richard held up the bag of tacos. "Is there a reason you're here tonight? Because I'm starting to think we should get him a lawyer before he says another word."

Fustamante appeared unaffected by this turn of events, but Caio fumed with temper, her face so red, James half expected steam to jet out of her ears. "We found a backpack of clothing in the cave during our nightly check. Residential security footage shows James in the area, carrying the same backpack."

Richard took another step, positioning himself as a barrier between James and the officers. "It's not a crime to carry a change of clothes. Especially since he works construction."

The dark woman licked her lips, a nervous tick that betrayed her own nerves. "No. Not a crime. But he was instructed to avoid the scene until this case is closed, and he ignored those instructions." She peeked around Richard to catch James' attention. "We're going to have to take you in."

James coughed, grateful that he'd left the gold chain with Emma's parents. What if it was stolen? Merrick had been known to do things like that. "Am I under arrest?"

"I'm sorry son, but yes." Fustamante tapped his fingers on his huge, leather belt, a gleam of sympathy in his eyes. "I'm going to need you to step up and spread your hands on that wall."

He did as he was told, panic racing in his chest, while the giant of a man checked James for weapons, still talking to keep him at ease—though it didn't help much. "We don't have a body, so no homicide charge yet, but there's definite suspicion of foul play, and your fingerprints all over everything. Tonight, you're being charged with evidence tampering, but you're looking at far worse down the road." He turned his attention to Richard. "If I were you, I'd expedite that lawyer. He's going to need a good one."

James locked eyes with his father, the air being sucked from his lungs like the officers had hooked up a vacuum hose to his mouth.

He was going to jail.

But he had math and English finals tomorrow.

And work.

And then the Harris's were expecting him so they could plan the first search-for-Emma dive. "Can I . . . can I wait? Come tomorrow after school? Promise I won't run. I'll turn myself in." He knew the answer would be no, but every part of him revolted in denial of what was happening, the horrible timing of it.

Caio shook her head, reaching behind her for a pair of pink, metal handcuffs. "Sorry, kid. That's a no."

As if his heart had stopped pumping blood, his body numbed with shock. He loved Emma. Emma loved him. And he was about to go to prison for murdering a girl who was not only very much alive, but who might have a chance to come home. As the cold, hard cuffs clicked onto his wrists, he turned his face toward his father, wishing desperately that he'd opted to stay gone tonight. "Dad, will you to call Ryan?"

Richard already had his phone out. "Don't worry, son. We'll get through this. We'll find you a lawyer and get you out as fast as we can."

James nodded, throat too thick to speak as the officers led him out the door and down the driveway to the waiting patrol car.

# Chapter Twenty-Two

## Emma

EMMA PEERED AROUND THE HULL and watched dozens of enormous, majestic whales as they circled a school of translucent-orange krill. The pod had organized a complex dance, releasing air consistently enough to create a net of bubbles, in which they had trapped their prey.

She squeezed the edge of the sunken fiberglass boat, ducking further into the shadows of the sea grass into which the craft had settled, grinding her teeth with indecision. She'd been swimming this section of ocean for years, and had learned which sea creatures might act as predators, and which would not. Whales didn't usually prey on larger fish, especially not mammals. But in mid to late spring—the current season—hundreds, maybe even thousands of pods, passed this location as they returned from winters spent in warmer waters, where they'd enjoyed a robust mating season, giving little thought to food. That meant that these newly expectant mothers, and the mates they'd chosen for the season, were returning home extra hungry.

That alone was reason for Emma to be cautious, and when added to the sheer size of this particular pod—she'd counted no fewer than twenty-six— interrupting their meal in order to pass through felt slightly more than hazardous.

After returning to the palace with Maia, Emma had struggled for hours trying to sleep, but her mind kept landing back on the barren, foot-printed cave, replaying the experience in an endless loop until she'd decided that she had to go back again. Whatever happened in the cove didn't mean James and her family had given up on her. It could have been a storm surge. Maybe a stranger stumbled onto the hidden place. Maybe James or Keith or Gran had cleaned it for some reason unknown to her. There could be any number of explanations about why her things had disappeared.

Too conflicted to stay put, she'd crept to the deserted, hidden tunnel near the room with the jewelry, and squeezed through the narrow opening where the sun shone through, escaping the palace unseen. She crept along the barrier wall until she reached the breech. Determined to leave something that James was sure to find, she left a lovely, swirled shell.

She'd arrived at her cove in the dark of a moonless night, and though her vision had sharpened with the opening of her gills, still nearly missed her secret nook, where she found the Oceanside Pirates backpack filled with men's clothes. Suspecting that Merrick was up to his old antics, she dumped the bag and examined the contents. Immediately, she recognized the T-shirt as one James had worn on the day they'd first met. She wasn't sure why she remembered this, of all things. Maybe because it smelled like him, as did all the items, including the backpack. She'd buried her face in the shirt and inhaled, allowing the comfort of his scent envelop her while his arms could not.

When her gills pulled tight, desperate for the water, she'd hastily repacked the supplies and placed the shell on the ledge. She couldn't think why James would leave his clothes, unless someone had taken hers. She'd remembered the footprints, the feeling that her space had been compromised. Whatever had happened, James must have known her clothes were gone and brought her replacements.

Giddy relief had sent her swirling in circles on her way back to the city, inadvertently directing her into the path of these beautiful humpback whales. Now, as the city of Atlantis came back to life, Emma was stuck outside the perimeter, hiding in what was left of a decayed fishing boat.

If she didn't get to the palace soon, her grandfather would discover that she'd sneaked out, and then there would be hell to pay. But interrupting the lusty whales as they corralled their first meal in months would not go well, either. *I'm in deep trouble.*

Hours passed as the whales devoured more krill and other small fish than Emma could count. With each moment, the tide shifted, keeping her aware of the lateness of the hour. Eventually, the pod—filling the sea with waves and waves of musical song—moved on to find another school of fish, freeing Emma at last.

Panic pounded her chest as she swam, furious, through the empty corridors of the secret cavern, slowing only in the place where the hallways merged. Maia met Emma outside her room. "Oh, Princess. So glad you are here. We have been worried!"

A shiver raced down Emma's spine as she followed Maia into her room, retreating to speak in hushed tones. "Who is we?"

Maia blinked. "Everyone." Emma groaned as Maia continued, "I told the Sea King you weren't feeling well, but he sent Merrick to check on you, and I could not keep him from noticing your absence."

Emma sank into her hammock, exhausted from the swim, and from all the emotions knocking around inside her. "Lovely?"

"What could I tell him? I did not know where you went, and could not send him to catch you in the market purchasing a blue ringed octopus, or seeking a sea witch, or even visiting the surface." Her eyes asked the question her mouth refused to ask, and Emma nodded. "I could not tell him you were in the cavern of records, because Glan is also there, and he would have seen you."

Emma flung an exhausted arm over the edge of her hammock, trailing her fingers in the sand. "So what did you tell him?"

"That you have been visiting Laine for lessons at each waking tide." Maia twisted her hands together. "I am sorry. I did not know where you'd gone, but that seemed the safest truth."

Emma pulled water into her gills, and let it out again. Merrick had been exceptionally jealous over James—she hoped he wouldn't take out any new jealousy on Laine. She would feel horrible about it, especially given how much Laine had done for her—including teaching her about currents. "How did he react?"

"He left. I do not know if he reported to the Sea King, or went in search of you."

"Either way, this can't be good." Emma shifted, stretching full body and then curling into a ball. "Maia, do you know where the Paihana is kept? If you bring me a strong blend, I will drink it, and become ill before the Sea King summons me again. We will tell Merrick that I left my room in search of a healer."

Her eyebrows rose in surprise. "That is a good idea. I will bring you paihana right away." But instead of moving, Maia folded her arms across her bare stomach. "Emmalina, please warn me before you visit the surface again, so that I might be better prepared to conceal your whereabouts."

"I will, Maia," she lied. "I'm sorry I didn't this time, it's just that I couldn't sleep, and—"

"You visited the surface?" A deep voice jolted Emma's attention to find Merrick in the doorway, and behind him, Tangaroa.

"Grandfather," Emma squeaked, her hands flexing on the braided hammock edges. "I . . . I was only . . ."

"You were forbidden from leaving the city. There are many dangers in the wild sea, and you are a new maid here. The surface is no longer your home. You *will not* return."

"I'm sorry," she said, her voice shaking. "I wasn't trying to defy you, Grandfather."

The Sea King filled the space behind Merrick with shoulders as wide as the doorway, and a height that made him appear a mountain of a merman. "You will spend ten tides in the dungeon, to be freed only when the servants have prepared the palace for your joining to commence. You will no longer seek an alternative mate."

Her midsection constricted painfully. By the way his words had skewered her, she wouldn't need paihana to be sick—it was going to happen naturally. "Grandfather, please. I won't leave again, I promise. Please just give me a few more days."

Ignoring Emma's pleas, Tangaroa signaled for Merrick, whose eyes filled with regret as he took Emma's arm and dragged her out of her hammock. "Come, my mate. I will find you a comfortable place in captivity."

# Chapter Twenty-Three

## James

**April 10**
*46 days gone*

JAIL WAS A NEW EXPERIENCE for James. It wasn't a place he'd ever expected to find himself, but as a measure of distraction, he opted to keep his time here educational. As it turned out, real jail cells were nothing like what they showed on TV sitcoms. Rather than iron bars, concrete walls and floor, and a solid door with only a small, barred window that offered a great view of the cinderblock outer hall. Not how he'd anticipated to spend the night.

Officers Caio and Fustamante had brought him in by pulling the car into a private, double-sided garage bay, where James was removed from the vehicle and led up a single step into the building. No parading through the busy station or down more than the single, cold hallway that ended in a processing room. Fustamante took James' fingerprints on a digital machine, and his mugshot with an expensive high-tech camera, then he uploaded everything directly into a database. James answered a long list of personal questions, and was made to hand over every personal possession he'd brought with him, except his actual clothes. His wallet, cell phone, the pearls from Emma. They even took the string from his basketball shorts, and his shoes.

After being locked inside his private cell, he lay on the clinically padded concrete bench meant for sleeping, using a flat one-use pillow that reminded him of cheap airline disposables. He pulled the thin army-style blanket up to his shoulders, shivers wracking his body. Was this about to be his future?

For hours, James forced himself to lie still, counting the dots in the ceiling tiles, while the memory reel of his last few months played on an endless loop. How different would his life be if he'd listened to his teammates warnings about Emma? She hadn't deserved their cruelty and anger, but if James had listened, backed off and focused his attention elsewhere, he would have continued playing basketball. He would have applied to colleges, and might be dealing with sports recruiters—like the one who called the other day. He would be planning his future, on the cusp of leaving his father's house to begin a life of his own. He would be doing what he'd always planned, what he'd most wanted.

But all those things would all mean so much less, without the introduction of Emma into his life.

He felt as if fate was determined to make him regret loving her. But how could he regret experiencing the love he felt for Emma? And if he ended up wasting away in prison, how could he not?

Frustration cleaved his stomach, sharp scalpels threatening to rip him open, revealing all his most unlovable truths. Was this fate's intention all along?

No.

He sat up, pressing his hands to the cold concrete. No, it couldn't be. This wasn't how he and Emma would end. This was not how his life was going to continue to go, or hers. He refused to stop fighting and allow himself to sink. It took him only three steps to reach the door, where he yelled out the window. "Hey! Hey! Shouldn't I get a phone call or something? I never made a phone call, and it's been hours. Is anyone listening? Can anyone hear me?"

He gripped the barred window and shook, rattling the metal door and causing a ruckus of noise. Maybe no one was out there right now, but he knew that someone, somewhere in the building watched him. He waved up at the camera in the corner opposite the door, miming that he wanted to make a phone call, and hoping that whoever watched would respond.

Minutes later, a heavy door squealed, and Officer Caio strode down the hall, shaking her head as James' rattling echoed off the concrete surfaces. "Son, I'm going to need you to settle down so I can hear. What's the problem?"

He dropped his hands from the bars. "Don't I get a phone call?"

Caio's lips quirked in surprise—or amusement. James hoped it was surprise, since his situation wasn't a laughing matter. "You have that right, yes. I didn't think you'd need to make any calls, since your father has spent the last two hours in our lobby. He even threatened to call the mayor, if we don't let him bail you out immediately."

Surprised, James blinked, backing a step from the door. "He is? He did?"

"Let's just say the man's raising enough hell that we've considered waking the judge with a phone call, just to get you both out of here. Problem is, we've got to convince the judge that you're not a flight risk." The woman's dark skin glowed copper beneath the florescent lights, and high on her left cheek bone, makeup had smeared in a streak of black. Bags swelled under her eyes, indicating that she was due to go home soon, or maybe that she never truly slept.

"What time is it?"

Her eyes grazed the utilitarian watch that dwarfed her bony wrist. "After four a.m." Then, she clarified—as if she could read his mind. "You've been here just under six hours."

Exhausted as he was, James figured the math in his head, his compassionate side peeking out. "Shouldn't you have gone home by now? How long are your usual shifts?"

Her lips turned up, but it wasn't a smile, so much as fatigue. "I should have been off at one. Fustamante, too. But by bringing you in, we've stirred a pot of . . . well, something. Graveyard shift is shorthanded, so we're stuck here until the judge approves a bond for you."

James wasn't sure if they were more concerned with cutting him loose, or getting rid of his father. Pride swelled in his chest, and a knot of emotion climbed into his throat. He couldn't remember the last time Richard fought a battle on his behalf. In this, the darkest moment of life, his father showed up, was here with him, for him.

"I'm not a flight risk. Got no money, and nowhere to go, and on top of that, I'm not guilty." He rubbed at a spot of peeling paint on the edge of the barred window. "Officer, how long before the judge comes to work?"

She shifted her weight and rolled her shoulders, evidence of a deep level of exhaustion. "Should be in chambers by eight. Maybe earlier. He doesn't love being woken in the night." Now she did smile. "The man has seven daughters. Can you believe that? Needs his sleep."

"I imagine so." James scrutinized the pathetic concrete bed, deciding that he'd hate to stay here long term, but that he could survive a few more hours. "I don't suppose you can give me a pen and a piece of paper?"

She shook her head. "Sorry, no."

"Okay, well would you do me a favor and take down a note for my father? His health isn't the best, and I don't want him giving himself a heart attack or something."

Caio withdrew a mini notebook and a pen from her breast pocket. "Last thing we need tonight. Why do you think Fustamante is out there babysitting him?"

"You should probably go to bed. Both of you." James grabbed the bars again, leaning heavily on the door as the day caught up to him, as well.

She squeezed the bridge of her nose as if to keep her eyelids open. "I agree. I'm happy to take a note to your father if it will make a difference." She flipped to a blank page and clicked the pen open. "Go ahead."

"Okay, write this, please. Dear Dad, I'm okay. I'm alone in a cell, and have everything I need to sleep. I can survive until morning, so please go get some rest. Thank you for being here—it means everything—but there's nothing you can do to help me until I see the judge. Tomorrow is going to be an exhausting day, and we'll both need our wits." He hesitated, wanting to say the words, but unsure if his father would believe that they came from him. Theirs was not the type of family who got sentimental in person, let alone on paper. But maybe it was time to start. If not now, when? "I love you, Dad. And thank you for being here."

The officer finished transcribing, then ripped out the paper and held it up so James could see that she'd taken it down word for word. "Not sure that's going to do the trick, but thanks for trying."

"I'm going to try to sleep." James trudged to the bed and sat on the vinyl cushion, thinking that it was so thin it might as well not even be there. "I assume that the morning shift will let me know when we make any progress?"

Caio tapped on the door with her pen. "Yep. And they'll bring you a delicious, nutritious microwave breakfast, too."

As disgusting as it sounded, the thought of food— any food—had his stomach grumbling. He couldn't remember the last time he'd eaten an actual meal. "Sounds like paradise."

Caio must have stood on her toes, because half of her face peeked through the bars. "You still want that phone call?"

If he had to wait for a judge, calling Emma's parents wasn't going to change anything. Might as well let them sleep. "Not tonight."

Caio patted the bars that James had so recently rattled. "Goodnight, kid. I hope things work out for you."

"Me too." He laid his head on the pillow and dragged the thin blanket over him once more. "Me too."

Partly because of his age, and since investigators didn't have a body, the Judge set a high bail amount and allowed him to bond out—which meant that if he did run, Ryan would lose his business, since he was the one who signed the bond note.

It was after ten by the time they sprung him loose. James accepted the plastic bag with his possessions inside, grateful to find the pearls rolling around in the bottom. Without them, he hadn't felt whole. His father and uncle waited in the lobby, both red-eyed, in rumpled clothing, with their hair standing on end, as if neither had slept a wink. James was greeted with a squishy three-way hug. "Son, I'm so sorry." Sympathy oozing through Richard's voice. "We tried to get you out sooner, but—"

Ryan interrupted. "I rounded up money and got in touch with a bondsman as soon as your dad called. But they insisted on talking to a judge first. Sent us both home."

"I know." James squeezed both men again. "I know it's not your fault. Either of you. And look, I survived." He broke from the embrace and turned in a circle to prove it. "See? Still alive." As true exhaustion set in, James pressed a hand to his uncle's shoulder. "Okay if I skip work today? I know I owe you my life at this point, but I'm just not sure I'll be any good on the job, as tired as I am."

"That's an excellent idea." They pushed through the glass doors to outside, where the bright sun temporarily blinded James. Ryan stumbled, shading his eyes. "I'm taking the morning off to get a couple hours of sleep, then I'll get back to your house so we can discuss what comes next. We need to make a plan, James."

When his eyed adjusted, James scanned the lot for his father's car, but only found Ryan's personal truck. "I know." The way things had gone down left James wondering if he should tell Ryan and his dad the whole truth—everything. They deserved it.

Sandwiched between the men who had raised him, he understood that some problems are bigger than one person. Bigger than two or three people, even. He'd sworn to keep Emma's secret, and everything in him rebelled against betraying that promise, but with each passing minute, his future became infinitely darker. Without help, neither he nor Emma would survive the dangerous rapids into which they'd been so violently hurled.

He hoped she would someday forgive him.

Ryan dropped him off at school, still dressed in the clothes he'd meant to sleep in. Though he hadn't slept at all, lying in jail had given James plenty of time to think about the future. Though he intended to give it his all, there wasn't a lot he could do to bring Emma back, or to avoid going on trial for her disappearance. The hurricane of his life had twisted out of control, and there wasn't much he could do to contain the aftermath. But school, grades, and finals all remained within his control, and even if he was looking at life in prison, he'd always know that at least he'd finished this one big thing.

The empty halls echoed as he fumbled with his locker combination and retrieved the notebook and pencils he'd been instructed to bring for his math and English finals. His head throbbed from lack of sleep, and the frozen breakfast sandwich he'd been given in the cell sat like a rock on his gut, but fate took pity. Although he was fifteen minutes late to math class, he arrived before testing began.

He reached in his pocket and rubbed the pearls together, thanking Poseidon for small miracles. It was about time something went his way.

Three hours later, James collapsed onto his rumpled bed, thinking that genuine mattresses were the best invention ever. He punched his pillow, fluffing it just right, and drifting into slumber without bothering to take off his jail-soiled clothes. Ten minutes later, he jerked awake, fumbling for his phone. He set an alarm, and had to force his eyes to stay open long enough to send a group text to his dad and Ryan. Neither had gone far—Ryan was currently dead-to-the-world on James' living room couch—but James intended to keep them in the loop from now on. He typed:

*Important meeting at six o'clock. Love to have you come.*

Ryan replied first:

*Setting alarm for five. Got to call lawyers first. Happy to attend your meeting.*

Then his father:

*I'll be there. Wake me up if I sleep through alarm.*

That afternoon, James fell asleep feeling more supported, more at peace with his family relationships than he had since his mother left. As he slid into oblivion, he pictured a giant canyon towering over a gushing river. James stood alone on one cliff, his father opposite him, and Ryan on yet another, all separated by the gulf. James looked down and found a pile of wood, and a hammer at his feet, and when he looked again at the other two, he noticed that they were already hard at work puzzling the planks together. James picked up his hammer and a plank of his own, collaborating with the efforts to build a bridge.

# Chapter Twenty-Four

## James

NERVES DANCED LIKE NAPOLEON DYNAMITE in his stomach as he rang the bell at the big, expensive house. Behind him, Richard shuffled his feet, and Ryan fidgeted with the zipper on his leather jacket. None of them spoke a word, though James knew they were confused, wondering why they'd been brought to the home of the missing girl. There was no easy explanation, but he hoped that Emma's parents could help him to give his family a clear, and at least somewhat believable, rundown of reality.

The front door flew open. "James! My best friend." Keith wrapped his arms around James' middle and squeezed with all his might. Whatever Keith's parents told him had clearly made a difference. "I'm sorry I was mean to you."

Though his arms were trapped beneath Keith's, James patted the boy's back as best he could. "It's okay, buddy. That night Emma left was scary for both of us. But I'm happy you're not mad at me anymore—I've missed you."

"Missed you, too." Keith squeezed again, and then abruptly let go, hollering for his parents.

Cindy arrived at the top of the stairs, wearing the same wrinkled clothing as yesterday, puffy circles beneath her eyes. She glanced past James to the men on her stoop. "Oh dear. Something's happened." She stumbled down the stairs, attempting to smooth her hair, and shook hands with Richard and Ryan. "I'm Cindy Harris. Come on in; have a seat." She directed the men to the family room. "Just let me collect my husband."

James settled his father on the wide recliner, then chose a spot for himself on the couch, between Ryan and Keith. When Cindy returned, with Russ in tow, James noted that Emma's father didn't appear to have gotten any more sleep than his wife. "Hello. I'm Russ Harris, and this is my wife Cindy. Looks like you've met Keith."

"They did, Dad." Keith bounced with excitement. "I let them in because of James is going to help us bring Emma home."

Cindy's shoulders slumped as she sank into the chair opposite Richard. "Yes, Keith. James is going to help us look, but remember that Emma might not be able to come home for a long time."

Keith folded his arms, scowling at his mother. "No, James is going to bring her home fast, aren't you, James? Because I miss my sister, right? And you miss her, too."

He stood, patting Keith's knee. "I hope so, buddy. Bringing her home soon would save me a lot of grief." James hugged Emma's parents, and introduced his guests.

"What's happened?" Cindy chewed on her lip as though added stress was more than she could take, a feeling for which James had the ultimate sympathy. "Tell us everything."

Richard straightened in his chair. "I'll tell you what's happened. My son was arrested last night, on charges having to do with the disappearance of your daughter." He jabbed a thumb in Ryan's direction. "We don't have much money, so this guy put up his business for collateral. To be honest, bonding James out of the slammer was the easiest part of what he's facing."

The color drained from Russ's face. He positioned a supportive hand on James' shoulder. "I'm so sorry. It was naïve of me to believe that we could stay ahead of this part."

Richard cleared his throat, glaring at Russ's hand. "My brother-in-law and I are here to be let in on whatever big secret you're all so hell-bent on keeping. We're going to need everything we can find that will help us land a reliable attorney."

Russ perched on the edge of the end table next to his wife, dropping the professor tone and switching to his fatherly one. "I absolutely agree that James' defense is a priority. Cindy and I are prepared to help however we can." His eyes flashed to James. "Why don't you tell us what's happened since you were here last night."

And so he did. In front of everyone, all the people who mattered most to James, except Emma. With Russ and Cindy's help, and some input from Keith, James relayed the impossibly improbable story, beginning to end, including the details Mona had shared about Caspian. He concluded by shoving a hand inside his pocket and withdrawing the pearls. "In the days since Emma left, these have been left in our secret place. That's why I keep going back, searching for her, even after the police banned me from it. I have to catch Emma, because she's the only one who can help me clear my name."

Ryan stood to inspect the pearls, swearing under his breath. "I . . . I don't know what to say. I knew you had strong feelings for this girl, and that she disappeared under weird circumstances, but I had no idea that you know what really happened to her. That you were there." His face twisted in pained thought. "I don't believe in mermaids—never have. But even I can admit that your story explains a lot. Like why you'd sell your bike and buy a boat, and your sudden determination to give up basketball and certify in scuba."

Richard scrubbed a hand over the back of his neck, wiping the residual sweat on the front of his shirt. "I do. I believe in them. Sometimes I've even convinced myself that your mother was a siren, that she left because she had no choice."

"Dad . . . " James inched closer to Richard, longing to hug him, but still unable to cross that chasm, despite their recent progress.

"Don't worry." Richard chuckled, a genuine, foreign sound that James remembered from his childhood. He hadn't heard that laugh in years. "I know it's not true. Therapist calls it a coping mechanism. I'm sure he's right. But you—you've seen the evidence. And your story explains a lot. More than just your newfound extracurricular interests." He adjusted in the recliner, groaning. "James, mermaids have siren powers that can trick a man into falling for them, even unwillingly. She's probably ensnared you so that you'll never concentrate on anyone else again."

James rubbed the pearls together, shaking his head in denial. "No. Dad, I need you to trust me. I haven't been ensnared. I mean, yes, Emma emits pheromones, but we all do. Hers are just slightly stronger than normal, and pheromones had nothing to do with me falling for her. She never pursued me, not once. In fact, she tried her damndest to warn me off, to push me away. Emma has been through some horrible things in the past, and she considers herself poison. She didn't want to drag me into any of it—and I knew about all of this *before* I found out she's a mermaid—which she told me, voluntarily. I think even that was a sort of warning. Emma never tricked me, she never lied to me, and she never came after me. *I* pursued her, *I* was the one who wouldn't leave her alone. It was *me* who decided to do anything I could to keep her safe. I love her because she's strong and smart and the most beautiful woman on the planet—she just happens to be a mermaid, too."

"James." Ryan stood from his seat, joining James' nervous pacing. "You have to admit that you've been exceptionally obsessed. I can't think of anything in the world that would have prompted you to sell your prized possession to buy a beat-up, old boat. Nothing. It's just not like you."

"But it is." James let his memories tumble back to the moments he'd spent holding Emma in his arms, feeling her lips yield beneath his. "You've never seen me fall in love before. This is exactly how I behave after I've found the love of my life. I'm going after her. Tomorrow. Two weeks ago, I expected to be doing all of this—everything—on my own. And if every person in this room were to back out, I'd still go. In this family, we protect what and who we love with everything we've got. That's all I'm doing, Ryan. Protecting her. And bringing her home."

Ryan scrubbed his hands over his face, reminding James of where he'd inherited the habit. "Do you even hear yourself? You just told us that this girl was forced out to sea because she couldn't breathe on land anymore. Let's say that by some miracle, you do find her. Let's say the timing is right and you and she are there at the same time, and you try to bring her back. How do you intend to keep her alive once you get her here?"

Russ, who had allowed James to work through the shock with his family, laced his fingers through Cindy's. "I've been working on that since Emma was an infant. We know that there's a way. Venom from a poisonous sea creature can be used to re-inflate her lungs. We're just not certain which creature, or how to get our hands on one."

Cindy pulled her husband's arm around her waist, keeping her fingers in his. "We refuse to rest until we figure out which creature, and either purchase or harvest this magical venom. I doubt we'll find one in the ocean, so as a backup plan, I've emailed every aquarium within a hundred-mile radius, and a few further than that."

"Oh, I see." Losing patience, Richard turned up his snark to full power. "Because aquariums regularly sell venom to random strangers, just because they've requested it. That's not suspicious at all."

Russ's lips quirked. "Luckily, I'm *not* a random stranger. I'm a professor of science. Trust me, I can get my hands on almost anything we need *in the name of science.*"

"Are you going to get those things now? Today?" Ryan gripped the back of Richard's chair, leaning heavily on it. "Because James is looking at more charges by the weekend, and he's lost access to the only place where he can leave communications with Emma. Seems to me like you're expecting the impossible, from yourselves, and from my nephew."

Before Russ or Cindy could respond, James jumped to their defense. "*They've* never asked me to do anything. Until last week, I've avoided even *talking* to Emma's family—including Keith, who attends school with me. Mostly because the detectives ordered me to stay away. I got scuba certified on my own, sold my bike on my own, bought the boat on my own, and have been visiting the cove to leave messages for Emma— also on my own. Like I said, I've been prepared to do this without help, but I'm more relieved than I ever imagined, to know that I don't have to."

Richard pushed himself out of the chair and lumbered to his son, bracing one hand on either of

James' shoulders. "As a father, I have to tell you that this—all of it—worries me. What we're discussing right now is craziness, and I'm struggling to process that it's real. I wish you'd stay out of it and let these fine people find their daughter themselves. That said, as a man who has known the agony of losing a woman he loves, I recognize that I can't keep you from this, even if I tried. So please be careful, or jail might not be the worst thing in your future." When no one immediately responded, he squeezed James' shoulders, glancing at Ryan. "Why don't you and I get this boy to give us a tour of his boat? Maybe we can tinker with the engine, help him make sure it's not going to quit on him in the middle of nowhere."

Ryan shook his head in disbelief. "This might be the weirdest conversation I've ever had, but my nephew's future is at stake. If you're going to ride a race, you do it planning to win. I'm in." His hand joined Richard's meaty one on James' shoulder. "Tell me how to help."

## Chapter Twenty-Five

### Emma

EMMA PACED IN THE DARK, claustrophobic cavern. The subdued dungeon lighting was a mercy, a trickle of the glowing blue that lit the palace and crept through tiny natural crevices in the rock ceiling. Without it, the hollow would be nothing more than a blackened void, bubbles from her breath the only audible sound. Unlike her bedroom, this cell had a door. Most likely salvaged from the wreckage of a sunken ship, unusually small, with an arched top carved with elaborate designs.

On the day she first arrived, her grandfather ordered the guards to take her to the servant's grotto, which she'd later learned was a slightly improved version of the dungeons. After she'd freed her brother and been forced to return to Atlantis, he'd had her locked in this very same dungeon, for what felt like days, but now that her body had learned the rhythm of the tides, she understood that it was probably only a few hours. Still, she'd hated being locked up then, every bit as badly as she did today. The difference was that she now had a better understanding of the culture. It helped, somehow, knowing that her grandfather truly believed that he was doing what was best for her. That her life mattered to him, regardless of his peculiar way of showing it.

She absolutely disagreed with the Sea King on where her future was headed, but she'd come to know that his decisions weren't about power or authority. His main goal was to establish a line of succession that would promise peace and abundance to the citizens of Atlantis. In doing so, he hoped to secure Emma with a solid, bright future, a family with someone who he believed would take care of her and her offspring.

Knowing this caused a painful amount of guilt, and Emma spent a good deal of her prison time trying to convince herself that she could stay, that she'd make a good Sea Queen.

Unfortunately, even if she were to find a merman she liked who was not Merrick—a merman like Laine—and if she were to decide that she wanted to stay in Atlantis forever, there was still only a fifty-fifty chance that she'd produce offspring in the way of the Mer. In that area, she had every reason to believe that her reproductive organs were of the human variety, since she'd begun having cycles at the age of fourteen. Her inability to produce a line of succession would not be what the Mer expected, or wanted, and one way or another, Merrick, being the last royal descendant who was able to reproduce, would have to resort to other measures to produce an heir. What would that would do to her grandfather? How would it change the culture?

On the other hand, Merrick was a sure thing. He already loved Atlantis, even having been raised in Oceania. He could be the ambassador who would bring peace to the two cities, perhaps rebuilding the bridge between Maui and Tangaroa, who had been at odds with each other for centuries. If Tangaroa hadn't known of Emma's birth, if she didn't exist, he'd have named Merrick, his only living blood relative, as heir. Merrick would be joined with a mermaid who understood him far better than Emma, and the city would thrive, because Merrick loved it the way Tangaroa had, the way Emma never could.

The pull of the water altered, current swirling in warning. Change of tide was near, and with it, a guard would bring her meal. She hovered near the sandy ground, feeling around for a rock or shell—anything she could use as a weapon, or other means of escape, but found nothing. Frustrated, she curled into the hammock and let the movement lull her into a state of calm, needing to think her way out of her current mess. While she swung, she thought, and while she thought, she picked at a thread of seagrass that had broken free from the woven fibers. She gave it a tug, and it grew in her hand. She wound the thread in her fingers and pulled again until she had a long, brittle piece of grass that had been braided so tightly that it resembled string. Only stronger, like floss.

Interested, she pulled another one, working hard to loosen it from the tightly strung pattern. When she was unsuccessful at breaking more, an idea formed, and along with it, hope. The hammocks in Atlantis weren't made with string. They weren't stretchy, and had no give, but the seagrass held strong. Perhaps a weapon was not what she needed to escape. Maybe her most important tool would be the use of a fisherman's net.

With quick and nimble fingers, she freed the intricate knots from the iron rings that held the hammock aloft. She checked the door hinges to predict which way it would swing—in or out—and then secured a corner of the hammock to the ring nearest to the entrance, and another corner to the bottom hinge, praying it would hold long enough for her to do what was necessary. She then gathered the bulk of the hammock into her arms and pulled the weight of it across the doorway, so that when a guard swam in from the light hallway, he would swim directly into the hammock, allowing her to subdue him.

When the guard brought her tray, Emma was prepared. Her muscles ached with the effort of keeping herself aloft, despite the heavy bundle weighing her down, but the minute the door swung opened, she darted around, heart racing with each subtle twist and swing. Before the guard could realize he was caught, Emma had him wrapped like a burrito in the remains of the hammock, lying on the floor inside the dark, soundless cell while she jetted into the hallway.

Knowing she wouldn't have much time to escape, she veered up, into the shadows of the tall coral walls, avoiding the more populated caverns and tunnels as she made her way to her room. Thankfully, Maia was nowhere to be seen, nor was Merrick. *Probably hiding out together*, she thought, for once grateful to them both for the duplicitous lifestyle. Seizing the banana leaf from her fashion-craft supplies, she laid it on the ground and dumped her treasures in a pile on top, including her sizable collection of pearls, and folded the ends into a tight bundle. Anxious to get moving, she ripped two long strands of woven sea grass from the privacy curtain, and tied the heavy package to her lower back, pulling the rope tight.

A last, over-the-shoulder glance at her personal space stung more than she'd realized it could as she snagged an eating tool and crept stealthily into the hall.

Though she knew her time was limited, Emma couldn't leave without keeping her word.

She hid in the tunnel that led to the treasure room for what felt like hours. When captive the dolphin to swam by with his cargo, Emma followed. Soothing him with a hand on his flank, she used the tool to pry open one link in the heavy chains. Without that link, the rest fell apart. Laine's dolphin was free.

She led him down the servant's hall and to the outer door, careful to stay as quiet as possible as she opened it and let the dolphin swim away. She hoped it knew where to find Laine.

Uneasy about leaving the palace through the much-used door, she escaped in the opposite direction, and squeezed through the narrow crevice near the treasure room. Getting through the breech in the barrier took more work than usual, but with some work, she managed to squeeze through with her package intact. She jutted into the open sea, picking up speed as the alarm sounded.

# Chapter Twenty-Six

## James

**April 11**
*47 days gone*

As THE SALESMAN HAD PROMISED when he demonstrated the motor at the dealership, the boat started, just not on the first try, or the second. James and Ryan had the engine compartment open and were staring at it, puzzled about the cause of the issue, when a man passed them as he strode to the end of the dock. "Engine trouble?"

"Yep." James turned his attention from the motor to the man, surprised to discover that he looked a lot like Tony, only slightly more wrinkled, with threads of gray winding through his hair. "You must be Tony's brother."

"Graham." He extended his hand to help James from the boat to the dock, ending with a shake. "Assuming you're my brother's favorite scuba student. James, right?"

"Yes." Embarrassment warmed James' neck. "I doubt I'm his favorite. More like the most demanding. Thanks so much for letting me dock here. I can't tell you what a lifesaver this has been."

Graham waved a hand like the gesture had been no big deal, watching as Ryan fiddled with battery connections. "I sold my boat hoping to upgrade, but haven't gotten around to buying a new one yet. Figured at least someone should use the slip."

"Well thank you. I hope you'll let me pay you, when I can."

Graham grinned, his jolly eyes finding James' and holding. "Nope. Don't need money. Just enjoy this boat, and pay it forward, someday." His gazed flicked to the engine. "Mind if I take a look?" With James' invitation, Graham stepped into the boat and introduced himself to Ryan, then took a single glance at the open engine compartment, before continuing to the helm. "No offense intended, but you must be new boat owners."

"Yeah," James admitted, not embarrassed in the least. "Other than Tony's dive boat, I haven't ridden on one for years. Never drove one, ether, so this will be a new experience for me."

"Well, the good news is that your engine's probably fine. The kill switch is off." Graham flipped a silver lever next to the throttle and dropped his hand on the wheel. "Mind if I give it a shot?"

James signaled for him to go ahead. Graham turned on another switch and a low-pitched hum sang out beneath them. "First, you want to run the blower, get the air out of the lines." He turned that off, then pushed a neutral button on the throttle and threw it forward. "Then you want to give it a little gas in advance to avoid a start delay. Give it just a few seconds before you turn the key." He did just that, and the engine roared to life, rumbling like a dependable vintage car that was likely to rust into bits before the engine burned out. Graham pulled the throttle out of neutral and back into park. "You're all set."

Ryan closed the open engine compartment and brushed off his hands. "Well, now I feel stupid. I've been around boats for a while, but never owned one. Had no idea there was a kill switch."

Graham let out a good-natured laugh. "It won't take either of you long to get the hang of this. Driving a boat is a learned art. Just remember that unlike a car, your water craft is controlled by propeller. That means you can try and coast to the dock, but the second you put that throttle in park, you're going to drift whichever way the water's moving." He patted the wheel. "You're steering up here, but all the power comes from behind you, so, keep that in mind. Also, try to avoid hitting waves head on. That can be like smashing into a brick wall if you're going fast, and even when you're not, you can do serious damage to the boat, and to your body. What else?" He tapped his fingers on his head as if accessing a memory. "When you take her out to dive, always find somewhere to drop anchor, or tie off. Even if you drag a rope down with you and secure it in the sand wherever you're diving. Make sure it holds, too, because in the time you spend below, the current will carry this vessel a long way. Maybe miles. You want to keep her in place. My preference is to leave someone aboard to man the boat while you dive, because drifting happens, even when you've tied off, and if you surface to no boat, you're likely to drown trying to get to shore."

James pressed his hands on the warm, now closed, engine compartment, the motor rumbling in time with the beat of his blood. "Thanks a lot for your help. I really appreciate it."

"No problem." Graham hopped out, continuing to the end of the dock, where two thick ropes dragged tight at something below the water. "Just be careful. I prefer not to get called out on a rescue and have to pull you from the merciless sea. I'd feel responsible."

"Nice to meet you," Ryan called.

"You as well." Graham reached the end of the dock and hauled one rope until he brought up a cage in which he'd caught four lobsters and two small crabs. He dumped his haul into a white bucket, then towed up the second.

Ryan checked the sides of the boat, humming with approval as they bobbed over a wave and the craft adjusted with the movement. He indicated Graham and the cages. "That looks fun. How about once things settle down, you and I get your dad and the new toy out for a bit of family bonding-slash-fishing?"

James laughed, remembering how his father had been gung-ho to see the boat, until he realized it was already in the water, at which point he'd held back and watched from the shoreline—refusing to even set foot on the pier. "Uncle, if you can get my father into this boat, you're absolutely on. Even if you can't. I'd love to go fishing with you. Bet I catch the biggest fish."

Ryan guffawed, laughing heartily at James' reference to Richard's water phobia. "You wish. I'm going to teach you technique. I'll be the one bringing in a whale."

The banter continued while they untied and spun cautiously away from the dock, into open waters, where James gunned the engine until the wind buffeted their bodies, and the salty air glazed their teeth.

For this first ride, both remained standing, holding tight to the towering bars and the windshield frame as the wind lashed at their clothes, and James' hair ripped free from the elastic he'd used to tie it back. "You know," Ryan shouted. "I could get used to this. I enjoyed riding your motorcycle a lot, but this—I don't think anything compares to flying over the open sea."

"I agree," James shouted back. "It's exhilarating. I'm glad I did this."

Ryan gripped the windshield tighter as James—following Graham's advice—turned out of a wave to avoid hitting head-on. "I just hope we can find your girl so you can be free to enjoy this feeling for a long time."

The half hour spent buzzing around the bay was the freest and most at peace that James had felt in longer than he could remember. An extensive, rough battle loomed ahead of him. Sooner than later he'd have to face the authorities, maybe a court battle. Everything in his bleak future hinged on his ability to find a single sliver of glass hidden deep beneath a mountain of sand.

But for the trivial window of time, while he and Ryan cut through the waves, he found himself smiling. Because the sun warmed his cheeks, his hair tangled into a matted mess, and the air carried the distinct brine unique to this section of ocean.

Ryan tapped his watch, indicating that it was time. James curved around, slicing a path back to the dock, where Russ waited with a wagon-load of equipment and supplies. He managed to glide right up to the dock, and with Ryan's help, tied off.

"Nice job." Russ brought aboard the first of four tanks. "For a first-timer, that was impressive docking."

"Beginner's luck." James bounded onto the pier and passed the remaining cargo over the stern, where Ryan stacked it all in a pile. Russ had brought four full tanks, a cooler packed with snacks and water bottles, wetsuits, BCDs, his personal mask, snorkel, and flippers, and a stack of dry towels.

Ryan whistled at the complexity of the provisions. "How long have you been diving, Russ? You're almost over-prepared."

"Since before we had Emma. And a diver can never be over-prepared. Scuba's a risky sport." Russ found a ski rope in a compartment beneath a bench and used it to secure the tanks upright against the inside of the boat. "Originally, I got certified hoping to better understand my brother, where he'd come from, what he'd given up. When he died and left us Emma, Cindy got certified too. We knew the day would come when our daughter might be called back to the sea, and we felt the need to prepare to help her through it, or rescue her from it, depending on what she wanted."

James left the empty wagon on the dock, boarding with the others. "Why didn't you ever talk to Emma about it? She would have been relieved that you knew."

Russ strapped down the last of the tanks. "Because we weren't positive she'd experience the change, and we didn't want to scare her. School, alone, was a turbulent surge of hurricanes for her. Not just high school, but every year since kindergarten. She struggled to identify with other kids, and they struggled with her, and we didn't ever want her to feel like *we* considered her different, even if she thought of herself that way." He tied the final knot and stood, arching to stretch his back. "Cindy and I have spent every day of the last seventeen years waiting for Emma to come to us with questions about her birthparents, or about unusual changes in her body, but she never did. And it was easier to let her be, while we worked at a frenzied pace searching for a way to keep her."

James and Ryan each untied a rope and dragged the bumpers aboard, shoving off from the pier, a second time. James started the engine, grinning at the beautiful purr as he offered the wheel to his uncle. "Mona knew. Emma never came to you, because her Gran told her not to."

"I know." Russ released a breath of annoyance, waving at the distant arch. "Emma's Gran kept a lot of secrets. I'm certain there are plenty more where we found these ones. But this—" His eyes found James', held there. "I should have pushed for Emma to talk to us, I know that. I should have tried harder to pay attention to how often she went swimming. I've been so busy looking for a solution, that I almost missed the problem that took her from us. Does that make me a bad father?"

James rested his hand on Russ's forearm. "No. It makes you human. I can't imagine how hard it was to keep a secret that big from your family."

Russ patted James' hand and drew away. He planted himself on a seat opposite James as Ryan leaned on the throttle, and the boat lurched toward the open sea. Minutes later, they approached the infamous arch. The giant rock jutted out from the water with very little to hold it in place, except tiny islands of eroding sand. Below the water level, the limestone formation sheered straight down into the deep, unfathomable blue—far below where they could safely dive.

Between the two islands, the eroded limestone created a glorious work of natural art, a sculpture that towered hundreds of feet above, leaving James feeling small, an insignificant grain.

Ryan killed the engine, whistling in awe. "Spectacular from this angle."

"It's better from below." Russ tossed James a tiny camera encased in hard plastic. "Battery won't last the whole time, so don't hit record until we're down twenty or thirty feet."

James fiddled with the camera, hit by the magnitude of what he was facing.

Russ had one foot his wetsuit already, and directed James to suit up as well. "Nervous?"

"I'm okay, I think." He'd studied harder for his scuba class than for his school finals, including watching each of the online videos at least twice. He'd practiced, been praised by his instructor, as well as other students, and during his open-water dives, never once wondered if he was brave enough to continue.

Maybe it was the way the sun stretched below the water, emphasizing the depth of their location, or maybe the exhilaration of driving the boat had restored his fear of dying. Whatever caused the shift, recognition slammed into James like a wall: scuba wasn't even a little bit like basketball. In basketball, if you miscalculated a shot, you might lose the game, but not your life.

He was about to put on weights and plunge so deep that if he ran out of air, he wouldn't make it back to the surface. This, alone, tied his stomach into thick, hard knots. When added to the thought of seeing Emma again, nervous nausea bubbled, sending him to the edge of the boat, where he clung, praying for the feeling to pass so they could get underway.

Ryan patted his back, sprinkling water from a bottle over his neck. "Breathe, James. Just breathe. It works the same way in the boat as it will under water."

James gasped, accepting the bottle and gulping huge, refreshing mouthfuls.

Russ zipped the wetsuit to his neck and moved to prepare the tanks. "Listen, Son. I've been diving for eighteen years. Never opened a shop, or taught others how it's done, but I could. I know what I'm doing, and no matter how far we go from the boat, the two of us will never be separated by more than a few feet. I've got your back, okay?"

"Yes, okay." James drained the bottle into his mouth, steeling himself for what he was about to do. "I just hope I remember everything."

"You will. I know there'll be a lot of multi-tasking happening down there, but you're sharp, athletic, and motivated. You and your brain can handle this. And if you forget something, I'll be right there with you, and I'll help you through it. We're going to be okay. We're going to find our Emma."

Gritting his teeth, James shimmied into his wetsuit, and strapped the camera to his wrist. Russ attached the hoses to the tanks, checked the air pressure, and helped James adjust the straps on his BCD vest. They secured their flippers and suctioned their masks, perching on the edge of the boat. James took a practice breath, then popped the regulator out of his mouth. "Hey, Ryan, don't let the boat drift too far away."

Ryan had his phone on camera mode, already snapping pictures. "Don't worry. I've got it. I'll remember my job—you just remember yours, and be careful."

James absorbed a last encouraging look from his uncle and replaced the regulator in his mouth. Not wanting to overthink the process, he rolled off the edge of the boat, backward. Russ followed close behind, and once the two had given Ryan the signal that their equipment was working, they began the slow descent. At first, they remained vertical, descending slowly while James remembered how to equalize.

As they sank lower, James could feel his body becoming heavier, less buoyant, and by the time they reached the maximum depth of sixty feet, gravity threatened to drag him below the threshold. He gave the inflate button a quick shot, sending a puff of air into his BCD, and having reached neutral buoyancy, clicked his camera to on, signaling to Russ that he was ready to begin. They skimmed along, eyes trained on the dark sand below, but when he rolled over, James could also see the surface. They had reached the ideal between.

Despite how dark the water appeared when looking down from the boat, his eyes adjusted well, giving him clear visibility thanks to the sun's strong rays. Vivid colors spread across Emma's underwater world, revealing more life and activity than James ever imagined. Red and yellow corals, bright purples and greens and neon blue. He couldn't name the shapes or formations, but he recognized a stingray flapping in the sand below, concealing itself for a hunt. A school of bright orange clownfish darted between the divers, disappearing into a crop of neon green seagrass.

When they reached the limestone pillars, James was disappointed to discover that the ocean floor dropped, and the stone stretched below what they could see, much further than they could safely dive. Appearing unconcerned, Russ circled the thick, strong stone, reaching out to touch a section where the algae and plant growth had been rubbed low, and then nodding as if this was something he'd expected to find.

James signaled, pointing down to indicate that he was sure the city lay much further below, but Russ shook his head, curt and firm, clarifying that they would not go that deep. Once they'd inspected both pillars, Russ pulled a bright cloth from up his sleeve, and tied it to a thick cluster of brown sea kelp, then waved for James to follow as he continued on. When the size of the pillars shrank with the distance they'd traveled, Russ circled around, creating a radius, with the arch in the middle.

This was not a technique James had learned in class, but he recognized that the scientific approach worked similarly to how the police canvased Emma's neighborhood on the night the stranger broke her window with a brick. Logically, step by step. But there were a lot more than two cops looking for that suspect.

They continued with this method until their air ran dangerously low, Russ continuing to tie strips of cloth to mark odd growth patterns along the way—things that, James assumed, he considered clues. Without having seen any sign of Emma, they returned to the arch to begin the ascension process, allowing for the necessary safety stops. By the time they surfaced, each breath James took required more work than he had energy—his tank had run out.

Ryan helped them into the boat, equipment first, then divers, and though they hadn't found a single sign of Emma or Atlantis, both men emerged grinning.

"Well." Russ gulped from a water bottle. "What did you think?"

James nibbled on some grapes as gas bubbled in his chest, leaving him light-headed, and somehow refreshed. "I can't believe how beautiful it is down there. How colorful and light."

"That part never gets old." Russ took apart the plastic cover on the camera and switched out the battery. "I used to worry that Emma would want to stay in Atlantis because it's so gorgeous, but where she's been leaving you presents in the cave, I'm betting that *her* heart lies ashore, as much as *yours* lies at sea."

The second dive went very much like the first, only they widened the circle, which required them to cover more distance, using less air. Occasionally, Russ stopped to tie another cloth to some plant or another, and then they would continue the search, widening the perimeter.

For five days, the three men met after school and returned to the private dock, armed with fresh supplies. After James proved himself a proficient diver on the first day, Russ increased their number of tanks to allow for a third hour of bottom time, and when James finished the last of his finals, he skipped class on Friday and they upped the goal to four dives on both Friday and Saturday, with a plan to get some solid rest on Sunday, allowing their bodies to offload the excess of nitrox.

Other than exotic sea-life and fascinating plants, James found nothing of real interest. A couple of turtles, a dolphin from a distance, and a colony of tiny clear seahorses that appeared to be in breeding mode—which didn't help his mood any—but nothing that would bring them closer to Emma.

He knew they needed a new plan that included riskier, deeper dives, and Saturday evening as they tied down the tanks, James composed a dialogue in his head, intending to deliver it to Russ the following day after they'd rested and could both think with clear minds. He stripped off his wetsuit and retrieved his phone from the glove box, intending to make a few notes. Instead, he found his phone inundated with frantic texts from his father. Alarm collapsed him into the nearest seat, blood draining from his face.

Ryan dropped the towels he'd gathered to stow, rushing to his nephew's side. "What's wrong?"

James stared at his phone, voice already strained from dry-throat—a side effect of the amount of diving they'd done—and re-read the messages again. "The police came to pick me up again," he told the others.

"They didn't have a search warrant for the house, but they'll be back with one tonight. Dad told them I've moved out. They want me to surrender peacefully, turn myself in."

Russ stood, groaning from the ache of over-used muscles. "Turn yourself in?"

James' eyes blurred with anger. "I guess. How can they have enough evidence to arrest me again? I haven't gone anywhere near the cove!"

Ryan pried the phone out of James' hand so he could read the texts, shaking his head in disgust. "You can't catch a break, can you?"

"Nope." He felt hollowed out, spent. Despite Russ's newfound excitement, the hope that had been driving James whittled away, sliver by sliver, until almost none remained.

Russ took a turn with the phone, and when he finished reading, dropped the device on the seat. "What do you want to do?"

The scalpels from before ripped at his insides all over again. He had to find Emma, soon. Now. "I want to keep looking."

Ryan tapped his fingers on the steering wheel, but didn't start the engine. "How do you feel about sleeping on the boat? Cops don't know you bought it yet, do they?"

James stared at the water, his brain having reached max capacity. "I don't think so, but it's possible."

"Even if they do, it'll take some time to figure out where you're moored." Ryan started the engine. "If nothing else, it gives us a few more days."

James had officially become that guy who lives in his car—except in this case, his car was a beat-up old fishing boat. But at least it had plenty of room for sleeping.

# Chapter Twenty-Seven

## Emma

ONCE SHE WAS FREE OF the barrier, Emma kept low and did her best to conceal herself among the terrain and any sea structures she could find. The alarm had sounded, so by now, the guards knew she'd escaped from the dungeon. It was only a matter of time before they realized she'd left the city, and broadened their search. And that time would only be allowed if Laine gave away the secret of the breach.

Either way, she hoped that her history, and her known inclination for sneaking out to visit the cove, would cause the guards to focus on the open water between Atlantis and the shore, since she had no intention of going that way.

Instinct begged for her to take the risk, to put herself back in the familiar place she loved, but if she were to do that, she might as well swim right back through the tunnel and present herself to her grandfather, would then force her to be joined with Merrick. She'd known Merrick long enough to understand that if he believed that Emma might escape, he would keep her captive however he could, and he was far better at deception than her grandfather.

Since heading to shore wasn't a risk she could take, she veered in the opposite direction, out to sea, and even farther from land. She swam for hours, and though paranoia kept her alert, her inhuman ability for speed took her far enough from the coast that the water warmed gradually, and her muscles grew fatigued. When the tide changed, indicating that night had fallen on land, the moon risen, she came upon the remains of a sunken ship and took shelter there, pleased to discover a slew of useful, human trappings. Fishing nets, rope, a small, decaying treasure chest, clay pottery, and best of all, a large knife with a sharp, silver blade.

Further exploration of the broken hull uncovered a shredded painting of the sky, a green clock that might have been brass or copper, clay pots and ceramic plates and crystal glasses—she would have treasured displaying these items in her room at the palace. But while each artifact withdrew from her a wistful sigh, she could think of no practical purpose for any of it, and so she left each item where she'd found it.

There was a cabin toward the back of the broken ship, windowless, and though at first the heavy wooden door wouldn't budge, she exhausted what was left of her strength and managed to close it far enough to prop the chest against the slanted bottom and give herself an illusion of safety. Desperate for rest, she strung the fishing net between decaying wood pillars to create a make-shift hammock, and then fell into it, exhausted.

A jet of bubbles streamed from her gills, trapped by the ceiling, so she counted them to lull her over-taxed brain into rest-mode. From what she knew of geography, and if her sense of direction still worked, she figured she was somewhere between Mexico's coast and the Pacific Islands. If she continued traveling west for a few more days, she could, in theory, find her way to Oceania.

She hoped her cousin Maui would grant her the same choice he'd given Caspian.

Emma woke with the tide change. Before leaving the ship, she again took stock of the items she'd admired the night before, saddened that she couldn't salvage them. On her way out, a hint of light glinted off the knife's blade. Such a weapon would come in handy, so she wrapped the blade in a cloth napkin from the galley, and jammed it into the ties holding the package against her back.

She allowed the current to lead her, grateful for the ocean science class she'd taken in high school, where she'd learned about the North Pacific Current and how it flowed south along the California coast, turning west just past Baja. According to the teacher, ships continued to utilize this current for travel between California and Hawaii, even with high tech equipment and gas-powered engines. She decided if sailors could depend on the current to direct them, so could she.

This far from shore, the sun's rays stretched deeper, reaching unusual depths, warming the water and creating light where none existed before. Relaxed by the tropical climate, Emma let her mind drift to memories of James.

He'd pursued her through thick and thin, even when she'd pushed, shoved, shot him away as a means of survival, he'd come back to her. He'd kissed her softly in the moonlight—holding her as if she were a fragile sculpture of glass—and roughly in the sunlight—arms and hands and body desperate to touch, to reach every part of her. She'd begged him not to wait for her, even as she swore to herself that she'd never love another the way she'd loved him. And he'd vowed to wait anyway.

She hoped he wouldn't have to wait much longer before she came back to him, the way he'd always come back to her. When her muscles grew weary, she drifted, and the current dragged her along while she daydreamed about the potential reunion. Lost in thought, she got careless, noticing far too late that the current had dragged her directly into the path of a giant pacific octopus.

Startled, and more frightened than she'd been when facing the whales a few tides ago, Emma dropped into an underground river, curling into a ball beneath a coral overhang. She'd interrupted the beastly creature as it feasted on lobster and clams from a nest in the sand, but she'd gained its attention, and its long, slimy tentacles slithered toward the place where she'd disappeared from view.

The whales she'd encountered last week weren't usually interested in flesh and blood Mer, but octopus weren't picky about what they ate. At least eighteen feet long, and three hundred pounds, its tentacles and teeth would be deadly if the creature managed to reach her. She'd never come face-to-face with something so large, or armed with long, super-glue-like tentacles.

Shaking like she hadn't in years, she withdrew the knife, gripping the hilt so tightly that her hands ached as she peeked up and over the coral. The octopus moved closer, one tentacle reaching for Emma, while another scooped more oysters from the nest, its attention divided.

Desperate to escape before the clams were gone, Emma slithered along the riverbed, careful not to make large movements that might draw more attention. She managed to creep far enough so the creature's tentacles couldn't reach her, and then she picked up speed, afraid to look back, and too aware not to.

When she gathered the courage check, fear rippled up her scales. The octopus had left the burgeoning nest behind, in favor of following Emma, clearly the larger, more interesting prey. The knife's hilt bit into her palm as she gathered her strength and mustered a burst of speed, remembering a specific ocean science lesson. They'd watched a video of octopi, escaping from unimaginable places, playing hide-and-seek, and winning. On top of being ridiculously smart, those things moved fast.

She jutted away to avoid a seeking tentacle, and then another, her breathing labored, mind spinning as she searched for somewhere to hide. An hour or two ago, she'd journeyed along underwater hills and valleys, grassy fields and colorful coral forests, but she'd left those behind for a flat, sandy bottom, dotted with reedy, barren growth, and broken from monotony by an occasional dune. Hiding here would be next to impossible.

A smooth, sticky tentacle brushed Emma's pack, sending her swaying as gummy panic welled in her throat. As fast as she'd always been, Emma struggled to stay ahead, forced backward by the draw of the octopus suckers. She curved left, then right, zig-zagging so fast that the ties holding the package in place burned lines across her scaly stomach. Still, she continued, too terrified to slow down.

When the octopus caught up, it wrapped first one, then two, then three extended tentacles around her body, suctioning to her with such a strong draw that Emma worried her skin might pop, furthering fuel the creature's bloodlust. The tentacles squeezed, carrying her toward the creature's mouth.

With an inhuman, very mermaid-like scream, Emma violently stabbed the tentacles that held her trapped. Adrenaline fueled her strength, as she sawed and jabbed and sliced until the tentacles detached. One strong kick from her webbed feet pushed her away from the squealing, thrashing predator, but the tentacles stuck fast to Emma's tender skin, continuing to wriggle and tighten, and threatening to cut off her ability to move, or even to breathe.

Covered in octopus blood, Emma made her escape, persistent with her use of the knife to free herself from both tentacles and suckers. But no matter how many times she stabbed, or where she cut, the offending appendages stuck tighter than if she'd superglued them to her body.

The creature screeched an unnatural yowl and skittered behind her, angrier than ever after having lost three of its tentacles. Emma cut to one side, allowing fear and adrenaline to propel her, then swiveled, preparing to zig-zag again. From the corner of her eye, a slow, steady movement had her whipping around, but she found only shadows. Moving shadows. A section of tentacle finally peeled free, so she darted at the sandy ground to slough it off, then started up again, but stopped, cold. Hovering feet above, glaring down at her with hungry eyes, swam a two-ton tiger shark big enough to swallow an entire school bus without chewing. It would chew on her, though, especially as she was covered in blood that attracted sharks the same way syrup attracted flies.

# Chapter Twenty-Eight

## James

**April 19**
*55 days gone*

AFRAID TO GO HOME, AND unwilling to put anyone he loved at risk of being charged with harboring him, James gave up on everything else and camped on his boat. Each morning, Ryan came, armed with supplies like food, water, blankets and clean towels. Russ came too, supplying tanks filled with the magic combination of nitrogen and oxygen that would allow them to dive, and gas cans, to ensure that the boat wouldn't run out.

Four more days passed, with no sign of Emma or Merrick, and no indication as to where the city entrance was located, despite the risks they'd been taking by diving below the threshold of safety. Every night while he slept, desperation clawed at James until he shot up in a cold sweat, knowing that he was already on borrowed time, and what he had left of that was about up.

Thursday morning, Ryan woke James from his restless sleep, offering him a hot cup of coffee and a fast food breakfast platter, which James devoured in minutes. Fugitive living took a lot out of him. "Russ should be along shortly." Ryan watched as James stood and attempted to tame his salt-stiff hair using the reflection in the window glass. When his dollar-store brush got caught and snapped, James growled at it, then tossed it overboard.

"Maybe you should cut it."

"What, my hair?" James glanced at himself again, agreeing that short hair would be easier to care for if he had to go on the lam—like he was now.

"Yeah. I mean, I know the longer style is your thing, but might not hurt to change your look for a while." Ryan tossed James freshly laundered swim trunks, and then turned his back to dump the melted ice from the cooler and refill it with a new bag he'd brought. While James changed, Ryan loaded a case of water bottles and a bag of fruit into the cooler. "Police brought that warrant to your house last night. Searched the whole damn place. Richard told them—again—that you don't live there anymore, but they didn't believe him. I'm half surprised they haven't come to the shop yet."

Now that Ryan mentioned it, James was surprised, too. Odd that they wanted him bad enough to search his father's house, but not enough to check his work or at the homes of the other people in his life. Unless they already knew where he was, and were biding their time. A shiver of unease shot across his shoulders. "I'm sure they'll be there, soon enough."

Ryan helped James shove his laundry into a garbage bag, then hauled it onto the deck so he could load it in his truck. "That lawyer finally called back. Wants a truckload of money, but I'll find it. Says he won't talk to you until you have formal charges, so he knows what he's getting into."

Swallowing his distaste for what that meant, James focused on the outlet that would send them back to the arch. Always the arch. "Thank you. I'm really sorry you have to deal with this."

Ryan didn't move to take the laundry, instead watching James grieve. "You can't look for her forever. At some point, we need to come up with a plan B, just in case. I'd love to see you find her, for a plethora of reasons, but we might have to come to terms with the possibility that maybe she's not findable. At least, not now. If that's the case, we need to know what comes next."

James watched his uncle hurry down the pier, knowing that Ryan was right, but unable to think past today, this moment. He'd known that finding Emma was a long shot, but in the days and weeks since he'd discovered scuba, he'd allowed himself to hope. Now, though, discouragement settled in, forcing him to face the harsh reality that they might not find her. Not here, and not now.

It *was* time to consider his next steps. Should he turn himself in and see how he'd fare in a trial? Run to Mexico and start a new life? Maybe Emma's parents could keep him updated on the search. Should he change his name and his looks and stick around for a while, trying to stay a step ahead of the cops? The guy who'd returned Ryan's call was the first of four attorneys to respond. Maybe he could find a good one who could truly help.

While he mused about possibilities for his future, James opened a water bottle and used it to brush his teeth, then spit the excess overboard, as movement in the parking lot caught his attention. Ryan and Russ were running, tanks in their arms and wetsuits over their shoulders as a police car, red and blue lights spinning, squealed to a stop at the edge of the lot. An officer jumped out, yelling words none of them could hear, and bounding after the running men, followed by a second officer.

James jumped to action. He started the engine and untied the front cleat, then loosened the back one, holding the craft in place long enough for the guys to jump in. The moment they had, James flung the rope over the cleat and tossed it on the floor, hitting the throttle, and departing from the dock at a speed considered illegal in the wakeless bay.

Shouting and yelling reached out from the pier, and James laughed. Neither officer brought a bull horn, and even if they had, they couldn't be heard over the wind. Russ caught his breath, standing to squeeze James' shoulder, as he'd done so many times before. "Good job, Son."

James thanked Russ for the praise, but his stomach was buried under a barrel of rocks. The future was now. If they didn't find Emma today, he'd be forced to take the next step—whatever that was supposed to be— whether he was ready or not.

# Chapter Twenty-Nine

## Emma

THE SHARK CIRCLED, FOLLOWING THE path of the blood, jaw open and showing off rows of enormous, razor-sharp teeth, and one . . . two . . . three . . . four . . . five gills she would pass on her way down its puckered, white throat.

It shot toward her, swallowing gallons of blood-tainted water and enjoying every drop. Stunned immobile and terrified beyond belief, Emma closed her eyes and waited to be eaten. Between the octopus and the shark, she had no chance.

She wished she'd had the opportunity to see her family once more, to see James once more.

Would he feel betrayed when she never came back? Or would he find a way to let her go and move on? She hoped he would, and that he would find happiness and success. She hoped her parents never found out how she died, and was grateful to know there was little chance of that. Even her family in Atlantis would never know what happened to her. Perhaps they would assume she made it to Oceania, or back to land.

The impact came swiftly, and though she tried to remain still and not spend her last living moments fighting the inevitable, the water swirled and churned, bubbling as if a great battle had ensued. She waited for the pain, waited for the bladed teeth to split open her skin and crunch her bones to oblivion—but other than the sting from the tentacles already stuck to her, she didn't feel a thing. She opened her eyes, confused to find herself in the center of a cyclone of silt, the water still churning.

When the silt cleared and the struggle calmed, she located the octopus, its remaining tentacles wrapped around the lower half of the shark, the upper half having disappeared inside the octopus's over-stretched mouth.

With both predators occupied, Emma sped away, terrified and confused about what had just happened. She'd never realized that any predator was tougher, more devious than a tiger shark. It all reminded her how little she knew of the underwater world.

She picked up speed gradually, grateful for every second of distance between herself and what was left of the predators. When the tide changed, she continued swimming, unwilling to stop and sleep, no matter how exhausted she was, or how much harder she had to swim against the current, rather than with it.

Eventually, her muscles shook from exhaustion, the weight of the tentacles too heavy to bear. She stopped to rest, digging up clams to eat straight from the shell, and wrapping the beautiful, thick pearls into her pack with the rest. When a tiny, blue crab scuttled by, she smacked it over the head with the butt of her knife, and then she ate that, too.

With her belly full, her skin burned like fire everywhere the suckers held onto her scales. Lying on her back, Emma scrubbed them with sand, wishing for paihana, to help dull the pain. When sand didn't work, she got brave and pried each sucker off with the tip of the knife, taking some of her scales with them. Once the suckers were gone, puss oozed from open wounds all over her battered body, and bruises swelled where blood vessels had popped beneath her skin. Not wanting to attract another shark—or any predator, really—she dressed the worst of her wounds with seaweed, relieved when it brought immediate relief.

Feeling slightly better, she re-wrapped her knife, tightening the strings and adjusting her pack. Still too nervous to sleep, Emma continued, determined to reach Oceania before resting again. She pushed through the night, more exhausted than she'd ever been, but by early wake tide, faint lights flickered in the distance. With a last burst of speed, Emma made her way to the city gates, elated and relieved to finally arrive.

# Chapter Thirty

## James

"I THINK THAT WAS MY fault." Russ stumbled to the bough, belatedly tying down the tanks so they wouldn't roll around and lose precious air. "Last night after I left, I had that eerie feeling of being watched, but there was no one around, so I chalked it up to decompression. But this morning, when I left my house, a dark blue car followed me. I know I wasn't imagining that. I tried to lose them before coming here, which is why I was so late. Obviously, they found me again. I suspect that they've been watching me for days."

"Why would they be watching you?" Ryan claimed the helm so James could squeeze into his freshly cleaned wetsuit. "You were out of the country when your daughter disappeared."

"I was. But the last time Emma was seen, Cindy and I were on a plane to home. We literally missed our daughter by hours. Without a body, or much evidence, I'm sure the police are uncomfortable with the amount of time that passed between the two. It's a gray area for them." Russ finished his task and then settled next to James on the bench they'd designated for donning equipment. "At least the focus isn't *all* on you."

James stood to zip his wetsuit. "You're not a suspect. If you were, they wouldn't be about to arrest me."

Russ tugged a mask and snorkel set onto his head. "They don't know what to think. The story doesn't add up, no matter how they look at it, because they don't have all the facts. A teenage girl is missing, and they have every reason to suspect foul play. If I were a cop, I'd investigate everyone involved in her life until I figured it out."

"What if they never figure it out?" Taking his cue from Russ, James positioned his mask and snorkel as well.

"Then they'll go with the most logical theory and make an arrest based on the evidence they do have. At least, that's what I would do."

James knew exactly what that meant. "Me. The evidence is against me."

Russ tossed James his BCD. "Don't worry. They might keep you for a month or two, but they don't have enough to get a conviction. There's still no body."

James busied himself connecting the tubes to his tank, and then let out a puff of air to test the connection. "They have her clothes. And her cell phone. And my fingerprints, and Keith's statement."

Russ slid on his vest and jammed his feet into his flippers as the boat slowed. "Keith will give them another statement. One that's not so damning. And *of course* your fingerprints are on her things. She's your girlfriend. They have to assume that means you've touched her."

"If I were them," James muttered, "I'd suspect me too. Especially after Tom. Any girl who's dated one abuser is twice as likely to date another." Merrick's face popped into his mind, amplifying in James an urge to punch something.

Russ stood, tank and all, forcing James to look him in the eye. "You're not an abuser. Abusers are obsessive and mean and controlling. The fact that you're here, that you bought this boat and learned to dive before ever meeting my wife and me, that has nothing to do with obsession, and everything to do with love."

Uncomfortable though the conversation had turned, James refused to look away from Russ's steady gaze. How observant that Russ could already see his level of dedication, before they'd even brought Emma back. "Yes, it does. I do love her."

"And that's how I know we're going to find her." Russ urged James to the equipment bench as Ryan cut the motor.

"I hope you're right." James pulled on his flippers, blinking back frustration so he could concentrate on the task at hand. "I really, really hope you're right."

They expanded the perimeter again, making a circle too wide to cover in one dive. Once they'd completed the second round of bottom time, all three men had lost faith, discouraged that their luck today had been no better than all the previous days, all the previous dives. With only one tank each remaining, and no new plan for where to search, time had become the enemy.

James stood on the deck, wetsuit unzipped to his waist, guzzling a bottle of water. Ryan handed him a sandwich. "Eat. You need the strength. And while you eat, let's talk. All of us."

They lounged on the padded seats, each having claimed enough space to spread out, relax. Ryan started the conversation. "We have a colossal problem, and before we turn back to the dock, we need to make a plan. The police know where to find you now, and frankly, I don't see how we can go back without them meeting us at the dock and taking you away."

James swallowed the bite he'd taken, his appetite rapidly disappearing. All day, he'd avoided thinking about the end result, but his uncle was right. "If they take me to jail, do you think I can bail out again?"

Ryan pressed his fingers to his eyes. "I doubt it. No bondsman will touch you twice in one week, and your dad and I are going to have to retain that lawyer—has to be priority for the long-term results."

"What if the police aren't waiting when we get back? Maybe I can leave the boat and hide out somewhere."

Russ laughed, unamused. "Oh, they're not waiting. I'm betting harbor patrol is stationed at every American territory border. Only reason they haven't found us is because we're into international waters. The minute this craft passes that invisible line, they'll be all over us."

James set the sandwich aside, unable to finish. They weren't going to find Emma today, and he was not going home. He wouldn't even spend another night on the boat, a place where he'd felt unexpectedly comfortable. He was going to jail, and there was no telling for how long. He wouldn't even be able to leave Emma a message. If he did, the cops would just steal it again, anyway. "I wish she had a phone."

Ryan tapped his fingers on the bench. "Weren't you communicating before? Leaving things for each other?"

"Yeah, but she hasn't been back for weeks. I'm worried that she's trapped." James zipped his wetsuit, overly warm in the bright, afternoon sun, and anxious to get back in the water.

"She might be, but you might as well try, anyway" Ryan said. "At this point, you have nothing to lose."

Numb all the way to his fingers, James shrugged. "Just the rest of my life. No biggie."

Russ guzzled the last of a water bottle and reached into the cooler for another. "We're not going to let that happen. Cindy and I have already discussed it, and along with Keith, we plan to fight the courts on your behalf. You won't be alone through any of it."

Gratitude, shadowed by grief, crashed into James' chest and clogged his throat. "Thank you."

Ryan tossed James a bag of chips, still urging him to eat. "It's going to be okay. We'll figure something out, I promise. Let's leave Emma one last message tonight before we turn you in. She'll have to get it eventually."

James wasn't sure of that. He wasn't sure of anything anymore. But at least he had people on his side, and despite his bleak outlook, other than Emma, he hadn't had a lot of support—ever. Having it now provided some comfort. At least the people who were most important to him believed he was innocent.

At least that was something.

THE FIRST THING SHE NOTICED about Oceania was the lack of a barrier wall and guards. The absence of authority made it easy for her to float into the city without raising an alarm or drawing unwanted attention, which was good, but after living under strict Atlantian rules, felt strange. Though the tide had turned hours ago, the city streets bustled with activity.

She passed a structure made of rocks and colorful coral that appeared to be a dignified place, except for the inebriated Mer spilling out through the open doorway. Raucous laughter roared from inside, competing with music and voices and the noise of a robust social scene. A couple burst out the door, swimming sideways in a drunken stupor. *It's a bar.* Emma thought. *They must be serving paihana.*

She peeked inside. Other than the prohibited party she'd attended in the servants' wing of the palace, Emma had never witnessed such joyous revelry in Atlantis. While she hadn't experienced the public bars in Atlantis after the change of tide, vast culture differences between the two cities stood out to her.

Even fashion was different from city to city. Here, many of the mermaids wore tops that appeared to have been inspired by human swimwear. Cloth, woven from kelp or seaweed, and decorated with lovely, colorful shells, coral shavings, and pearls. Neckwear didn't seem quite the rage in Oceania as it was in Atlantis. Rather than piling on as many neck adornments as a mermaid could carry around on her shoulders, most wore only one or two strands, leaving the fashionable tops exposed—an adornment all their own.

Emma left the bar behind and continued deeper into the city, marveling at how the swim-paths had little rhyme or reason, turning and curving in arbitrary directions, but never, ever straight. Dwellings cropped up haphazardly, some attached townhome style, others standing alone. She passed through what she assumed to be the market place, but since the tide had changed, the shops and free-market stands had been secured and deserted, and that was fine with her. She only intended to stay long enough to get in touch with Maui and ask about the blue-ringed octopus.

With no directing light, no hypnotic mermaid song dragging her toward the center of everything, Emma had no idea where to find the palace. She turned a corner and reached a dead end, then backed out and swam around, only to reach another dead end. She did this again and again, perplexed about the layout of the city. After swimming path after path that ended without warning, she encountered a young merman. He'd propped himself against the corner between two dwellings and sipped from a funnel-shaped shell.

"Excuse me, could you tell me where I might find the palace?"

The merman's lavender hair flowed long and wild around his face, nearly as long as his arms when he extended them. "Palace? There is no palace here."

If not for the safety of the water, Emma would have stumbled. "Oh. What about your Sea King, Maui? Where can I find him?"

The merman looked her up and down, his gaze lingering on her disconnected feet. "Sea King? There is no longer a Sea King in Oceania."

Nervous about the way he looked at her, Emma distanced herself from the stranger. "Okay. Who's in charge, then?"

"In charge?"

Emma's human side manifested, giving her the urge to tell him *take me to your leader*, even though she knew that no merman could understand a reference to the pop culture she'd known in her youth. Instead, she chose old-school wording. "Who rules this land?"

The merman inched closer, not bothering with subtleties. "Pimoe, god of fishes."

Her discomfort grew by the second, as the steely-eyed merman somehow managed to keep her within arms-length. "Where can I find him?"

The merman seized her elbow and dragged her along, bubbles surrounding them both. "Pimoe cannot be found. He must find you."

The nearby lights flickered, giving Emma an idea of how dark the paths would be once the illuminations were extinguished for the night. "Find me? But . . . I don't actually live in this city."

The merman continued to tug her along by the elbow. "I will locate you a dwelling in which to rest. If Pimoe wishes to grant you an audience, he will arrive before the next lunar cycle."

"The next lunar cycle?" Emma stopped, yanking her arm out of the merman's grip as she blinked away heat from behind her eyes. That could be a month away. "I can't wait that long."

The merman skewered her with his gaze. "If you wish to speak with Pimoe, this is the only way."

"No. I'm sorry, I shouldn't have come here." Emma turned to leave. "Thank you for your help." She couldn't imagine lodging in a dwelling with strangers, waiting to find out if this guy she'd never heard of, who wasn't even a Sea King, found her worthy of a conversation.

The merman snatched her arm again. "You must wait."

Her fight-or-flight instinct bloomed as she wrenched her elbow again, and when it didn't come free, she balled her hands into fists. She would not become this merman's prize, or his captive. "I will not." For the first time since she'd been dragged to Atlantis and forced to stay, Emma straightened, affecting the title her grandfather had insisted that she accept. "I am Emmalina, Princess of Atlantis, daughter of Caspian, and granddaughter of Tangaroa, Sea King of Atlantis, and you will take your hand off me, or face the wrath of my grandfather."

Unfazed, the merman tugged harder. "Princess of Atlantis, I am to take you to the dungeon and await the edict of Pimoe."

The scuffle drew a crowd of late-tide Mer. All the training she'd done with Laine, while it had been frustrating, came to her in a rush, instilling confidence that she had the ability to uncover, and use, her current. She yanked her arm again, sending a jolt through them both as her bony human wrist slid through the merman's webbed fingers. "If Pimoe wants to talk, he can find me in Atlantis."

She took off, swimming at the same speed she'd achieved while escaping the octopus. Unsure if the merman would follow, Emma shot up, away from the dwellings and the Mer who had gathered. "Pimoe will not be pleased by this behavior," the merman shouted. "You have come to seek favor, and if you do not wait for him, you will not have it."

Emma refused to look back as she approached the outskirts, keeping her speed, even as exhaustion threatened to send her spinning. After passing through the city border, she skirted an underwater land mass covered in growth for what must have been several miles. She rounded the tip, discovering a small, narrow cave, and stopped to peek inside.

She met a school of clownfish and some grouper, and sent a family of crabs scuttling out, but the hollow wasn't deep—barely big enough for her to curl into, an ideal place to get some rest. She ran her hand over the soft grass, checking for sharp or poisonous things, and then curled up on the cool, uneven stone.

She had no time left, and she'd wasted what little her grandfather had allowed, studying Maui and Oceania as if they were the key. Emotion burned in her eyes, throbbed in her throat as she lay in the cold, dark space aching for the comfort of her mother's arms.

She missed the way her father smiled and called her Princess, and the way her scatterbrained mother lost her keys, and phone, and planner, all while combing the house for her shoes. She missed her brother, and the way he'd always been happy to keep her company, and how his love for her was so pure, so certain, that she'd never, for a single moment, questioned it. Not since the day he was born.

A chill worked into her toes, causing her to shiver for the first time since she'd come to live in the sea. Either the cave's location was deeper than that of the city, or a storm brewed on the surface, stirring the water and dredging up the cold from farther below.

On the night when Keith disappeared, James had held her while she slept, keeping her calm. She wished he was near enough to soothe her shivering now.

Reality slammed into her. Maui was no longer in Oceania, and from what she'd learned, hadn't returned after his visit to meet her father in Atlantis. She guessed that meant he had also gone to live ashore, taking with him the secret to fixing her lungs.

She'd sworn not to cry after that first night in Atlantis when she'd been forced to leave everyone behind, and there were days when she'd suffered true darkness, but she'd kept that promise to herself. Now, having allowed herself to hope, she could no longer control the storm bursting from her chest. She let it free, sobbing tears that left gummy tracks on her skin.

She couldn't go home. Not if she wanted to survive. Oceania was not the Utopia she expected, and if she returned to Atlantis, she would live as Merrick's prisoner for the rest of her life. If the journey across the sea had taught her anything, it was that a lone mermaid wandering the ocean was not the safest or wisest plan, nor did it appeal to her any more than her alternative options.

Rubbing the sludge off her cheeks, she shifted on her package, and felt a sharp poke. She drew out the knife, covered in blood and octopus goo, and rubbed the blade against the grassy rock, trying to clean it, but no matter what she did, the sucker glue remained. Frustrated, she set the knife aside, convincing herself that a little octopus jelly wouldn't hurt her. Not unless the octopus was poisonous.

"Why couldn't you have been the octopus I need?"

She had one chance, and only one. Find the blue-ringed octopus and harvest its venom. She peeked out through the mouth of the cave, her hope deflating. The ocean was a very large place, much bigger than any continent of land, or even all of them smashed together, and she didn't have a clue how or where to begin looking. From what she and Maia had read, few of the rare creatures remained living. She tugged a long, glittering necklace from her pack, thinking how much money it would be worth on the surface. "Why can't I just buy the damn thing?"

Oceania had a market. Surely one of the older Mer there would remember Maui and his experiments. Maybe the venom was for sale or trade, or even the full octopus. Jewels and money weren't such a big deal in Atlantis, but after watching the Mer at the bar, she felt certain that she could somehow work the Oceanian culture to her advantage.

By the time the waking tide arrived, Emma had a plan. She'd used some of her jewels to decorate her top, in the way she'd seen done in Oceania the day before, only more sparkly. She removed her neck adornments, leaving only a long, shimmery strand of multi-colored pearls, then she unfolded the napkin and used it to create a pouch, in which she tucked a sparkling diamond bracelet, and a heavy, gold hair pin. She cut off a short length of the seagrass string and tied the bundle together, winding it around her wrist, like a purse, then tucked the knife and the remaining treasures into the pack, and re-secured it to her back.

"Once," she told herself, stomach jumping with nerves. "I'm only going back once. If no one has the venom, I'll find my own."

Oceania's market wasn't outrageously different from the one in Atlantis, or even some at home in Oceanside, and Emma had always excelled at shopping. She scoured every vendor and shop, lifting each item and every vial that could potentially hold such a precious substance as octopus venom.

Hours passed, and nerves skipped up her spine with each swell of current that told her the tide would change soon. A prickling sensation rose on her neck, as if someone secretly watched her every move. She kept her head down, not wanting to attract unwanted attention—a feat made easier by the diversity of the Mer in Oceania. She wasn't even the only mermaid with separated legs. This similarity pleased her more than she'd imagined it could. Though she didn't feel safe, she fit in here much better than in Atlantis. It was a comfort, however small.

Yet, no matter where she turned or how she lurked behind wares and walls and other Mer, the sensation grew to overwhelming. Someone stalked her, remaining beyond view. After Tom, she'd gotten good at following her gut, at staying aware of the sights and sounds and scents surrounding her.

When she approached the doorway of a drab-stone dwelling, a very distinct odor grabbed her attention, reminiscent of the dusty paper aroma experienced in used bookstores. It seemed such an odd thing in the underwater world, and drew her into the dwelling for a closer look. Thick stone shelves lined the walls, and stood upon the sandy sea floor, reaching the tip-top of the ceiling. Every available surface boasted beakers and glasses and shells and bottles of multi-colored substances.

An elderly mermaid, wrinkled and gray, lounged from a sitting-hammock in the corner, her dark eyes piercing Emma with suspicion. "You lost, little maid?"

The fine hairs between her developing scales stood erect at the way the woman's voice grated. Emma gulped a breath, gathering the courage to swim closer. "No, ma'am. I'm looking for venom."

The mermaid twitched. "Any particular type?"

"The blue-ringed octopus." Emma twisted her hands together as though doing so would release a hidden supply of bravery.

The mermaid's eyes widened, and she shot out of her seat, slicing her hand through the water between them as if to stop Emma from saying the words. "Do not speak of this venom here."

Emma blinked, confused as she took in the shelves of concoctions. "Why? Are you out of it?"

The mermaid shushed Emma again, grabbing her wrist and dragging her through a doorway shielded by a curtain of sea grass. "The venom of the blue-ring was outlawed after Maui disappeared. You will not find such a potion in Oceania."

All hope deflated in Emma's chest. "Nowhere? Can you tell me where to find the creature?"

The mermaid's eyes crinkled. With a curt nod, she led Emma through the back and down a tunnel. The hidden room housed cages and enclosures of captive sea creatures—enough to leave Emma feeling ill. The mermaid swam to the top of one stack and brought out a solid chest. She opened the top to give Emma a view of the yellow-orange, cone-shaped octopus, and the bright blue circles up and down its body. The creature didn't move, indicating that it was as dead as the many octopus parts on which it sat inside the chest.

"Is that . . . ?"

She reached out, but the woman snapped the lid shut. "The blue ringed octopus? Yes."

"Then you *do* have venom." Confused, Emma glared at the mermaid. "I can pay." She untied the pouch from her wrist and removed the hair pin, hoping to tempt the woman with the shiny gold. "Very rare, just like the octopus."

The mermaid's hands twitched with the desire to touch. "Such beauty." She tore her eyes away from the pin and skewered Emma with her gaze instead. "Human made?"

Emma nodded, pinching it between thumb and finger so the woman could see the intricate details. "Valuable on land, too."

The mermaid scowled. "What else?"

Emma blinked, confused. "I . . . you want more? This is very valuable. A one of a kind."

Unfazed, the mermaid folded her arms across her ample bosom. "You do not want this venom badly enough."

Afraid to offend the mermaid and lose her only chance, Emma extracted the bracelet. "The value of this piece is immeasurable. See how the stones sparkle?"

This time, a wrinkled hand snatched the trinket, and the old maid cackled with delight. "This will do as well, but it is still not enough."

Emma dropped the napkin, proving that it was empty. "I have nothing else."

The mermaid slid a finger between Emma's skin and the long strand of pearls. "Nothing at all?"

Sighing in defeat, Emma drew the strand over her head and passed it to the mermaid, who clapped her hands hard enough to ripple the water around them both. "Very well. It is a bargain price, but I will accept this payment in exchange for one tentacle. I cannot guarantee the potency of the venom."

Emma frowned, closing the golden pin, her last bargaining chip, in her fist. "I don't want a tentacle. I only need venom."

The mermaid cackled. "Blue ringed venom is dangerous to harvest, even for a sea witch. And venom is forbidden in Oceania." She gestured at Emma's closed hand. "This is not payment enough for such risk."

Emma held her ground. "How do I know the tentacle has any venom at all?"

"The Sea Witch cannot lie." She opened the chest and used a long, sharp tool to pick out a tentacle, which she sliced with a knife and slid into Emma's napkin pouch. "You will find the most potent liquid in the suckers."

The situation didn't feel right, though Emma couldn't figure out why. "Can you at least prove that it has venom?"

The Sea Witch jabbed another tentacle with the tool and gestured for Emma to watch as she snatched an empty coconut shell and dropped the tentacle inside it. She then used the same tool to probe one of the suckers until it had latched onto the tool's tip, coating it with an orange, gooey substance. The Sea Witch glared at Emma and set the tool aside, holding out the pouch in one fisted hand, the other open in wait for the hair pin.

Desperate to complete the transaction and be on her way, Emma accepted the pouch and handed over the valuable treasure. The moment the exchange was made, the witch shoved her through the tunnel and into the shop, brushing off her hands as if disgusted, the Sea Witch returned to her seat. "Go now. And speak of this to no one, lest the guards find you in your sleep and strangle you with that tentacle."

Emma left the shop gladly, feeling dirty, and not entirely satisfied that what she'd paid for was the thing she needed. But after the Sea Witch's warning, she didn't dare ask other Mer about the venom. Instead, she continued to browse the market, hoping that if she found something else, another *right thing*, she would somehow just know.

Not long after she'd left the Sea Witch's shop, the impression of being stalked returned, hitting her so hard and so strong that she whipped around in the middle of a busy square and dropped the pouch that held the precious tentacle. She took stock of her surroundings, but no one paid any attention to the thin, red-haired mermaid who was apparently afraid of her own shadow. She bent to pick up the tentacle, and noticed that the bottom of the pouch had turned bright blue. Worried that she was losing the substance that could save her, Emma opened the pouch, dismayed to discover that some of the rings had rubbed off from the bottom of the tentacle, and beneath some sort of paint or dye, the tentacle was actually gray.

Tears gathered again as she realized that she'd been swindled.

With her attention focused on the leaking pouch, Emma didn't see the merman from yesterday approach until he had grabbed her from behind. "You must stay in a shelter. Pimoe will find you and speak to you there."

Emma's blood pressure spiked, she wiggled and slashed, determined to break free from the merman's grip. "Let go of me. I don't want to talk to Pimoe anymore."

"He will speak with you," the merman insisted. "You have done business with the Sea Witch—he will know why."

Emma searched again for the spark inside her that could shock another Mer, and when she found it, anger helped her funnel that spark into her fingers. She stunned her captor hard enough to loosen his grip, and then slipped free, swimming away. The merman chased her this time, joined by two others, who fast enough that Emma wasn't sure she could escape them—not all three—on her own. Instead, she opted to evade. She rounded a corner at the end of the market path and ducked into the next dwelling, which happened to be the bar that had been so busy the night before.

Now, though, Emma was the only visitor. The dark-skinned bartender hovered behind a sleek counter made from lovely, pitted wood. "Help you, maid?"

It took time for Emma to remember how to breathe, and she ducked behind a wide pillar as her merman pursuers hurtled past the entry. She blinked, afraid to speak until they were long gone, and when they were, asked. "Is it okay if I hide in here?"

The merman nodded, squinting at her now profusely leaking pouch. "Been to see the Sea Witch?"

Frustrated and annoyed, Emma dropped the pouch on the wooden bar. "Yep."

The merman opened the bag, laughing when he pulled out the now-entirely gray tentacle. "Blue-ringed octopus?"

She nodded. "How did you know?"

The bartender dropped the tentacle into a round tub, pouch and all. "Happens a lot since Maui disappeared. Pimoe has outlawed surface living, and that witch can *smell* surface hunger on a Mer."

Emma leaned on the bar, burying her face in her hands. "I don't know what to do. I really, really need that venom."

The bartender set a deep, thin shell in front of Emma, then selected a container of Paihana from the wall. "Perhaps a drink would help."

She knew she should refuse, expecting that she'd have a journey ahead once she left this place, but with her frustration level at its peak, a bit of liquid courage couldn't hurt. "Thank you." She didn't bother to look before downing the contents of the shell.

Unlike the Paihana she'd tried in Atlantis, this vile concoction sent a burning line of fire all the way down her throat. Emma coughed in a way that she hadn't known possible since she'd been changed—through the gills in her throat, as well as behind her ears. The sting hit her stomach quickly, stealing her breath and pounding on her gag reflex. Luckily, she hadn't eaten much on her journey, which left nothing in her stomach to come out.

Cool, strong hands steadied her shoulders as she heaved. "There, now, maid. You must calm yourself."

After several long minutes, Emma managed to breathe again, though her chest felt inexplicably tight. "That tastes horrible. What was it?"

"Paihana made from fire coral. Very strong for someone your size."

*You think?* She fought the instinct to roll her eyes and get sarcastic, reminding herself that Mer didn't do sarcasm. "Why did you pour it for me then?"

The bartender, seeming satisfied with her recovery, returned to his post behind the bar. "You are wanting the venom of a blue ringed octopus. It's a dangerous thing to seek, and even more dangerous to drink."

Right now, what she wanted was to beat her head against the bar with frustration, but she refrained. "Yes, I understand that."

"But you did not die from fire coral Paihana, nor did you become paralyzed. You are descended of royal blood."

Uncomfortable admitting such things to a stranger, Emma responded with a noncommittal shrug. But the bartender's gaze dug into her soul, pulling out truths her mouth would not, could not speak.

"You are of the bloodline of Poseidon. I have been waiting for you since the time of Maui." He set a tiny, sealed clamshell in front of her.

"What is this?" Emma asked, afraid to touch it after the fire coral paihana.

"A gift." He reached for Emma's hand and set the clam inside it, then closed her fingers around it. "You must not open this clam until you reach land. Once you swallow its contents, you can never return to the sea. You must be certain. Very certain."

Emma's heart skipped. "Is this . . . is it what I think it is?"

The bartender covered her hand with his, attention darting to the door, ensuring that no one eavesdropped. "Maui lives. He left the sea to live ashore, and has charged me with guarding the last supply of the venom that will restore royal Mer to methods of human breathing. Be aware, this change is forever, and the risk is great."

Emma squeezed the shell in her hand, nerves battling in her stomach as she tried to figure out why she should trust a bartender any more than she trusted the Sea Witch. Her gaze fell again on the discarded gray tentacle. She'd paid a high price for the fake. "How do I know it's real?"

The bartender's eyes lit with a fire Emma hadn't seen in a Mer, perhaps ever. "You do not know. You must try it for yourself. I cannot test this potion, as I am not of royal blood. If I was, I would not be running a tavern in Oceania. I would have gone ashore with Maui, long ago."

Emma opened her fist and pushed the shell around her palm with the tip of her webbed finger. "What's your price?"

His eyes glazed over, focusing on dreams that eyes couldn't see. "If only once, I wish to touch the wide, bright sky."

Emma floated, surprised. "You don't need my help for that. You can swim for the surface any time."

The bartender selected a different Paihana, filling a shell for both Emma and himself. "Pimoe, god of fishes, has forbidden it. Citizens of Oceania who swim for the surface are forever banished. Pimoe is not a strong leader."

After the last round of Paihana, Emma lifted the shell with caution and stuck her tongue in the liquid before sipping. Luckily, this one had a fruity, sweet taste. "So, you want to swim for the surface with me, even though you'll never be allowed to come home?"

The bartender knocked back his serving in three gulps. "I wish to make a life in Atlantis, where the Sea King protects his people, rather than punishing them."

"Are you prepared to depart immediately? Once I exit this tavern, I must leave Oceania and never return. I'm not going to Atlantis, but I will pass by, and can show you the way." Emma thought of Merrick, how he loved guarding the gateway, and visited land often, with her grandfather's blessing. "My grandfather, the Sea King, will soon be looking for a new guardian for the gateway between land and sea."

The bartender's eyes lit with fire as he withdrew a cloth sack from behind the bar. "We must wait for the tide, when the market slows."

Emma held out her hand, sensing the buds of a mutually beneficial friendship. "My name is Emma—short for Emmalina."

"I am Tuck. Only Tuck." He accepted her hand, holding on, but clearly confused about what to do with it. Emma taught him to shake, the way a human would greet him.

"Nice to meet you, Tuck. I'll be happy to guide you on your journey to touch the sky."

# Chapter Thirty-Two

## James

As PREDICTED, THE FINAL DIVE ended the same as the rest. With a big fat zero to show for it. They'd widened the perimeter, left markers, and even broken lots of diver safety rules. Desperation drove them to recklessness, but even their reckless risks had been fruitless. The only thing different was that they'd managed to creep into darker, scarier waters where predators surely lurked.

When his tank ran low, James turned his air valve down, forcing himself to breathe slower, shallower. He'd about reached the point of distress by the time Russ sent up the inflatable marker, signaling to Ryan that they were ready, and supplying a visual location where he could pick them up. Once the boat arrived, James tossed his flippers in and handed up his BCD so he could climb the ladder. He couldn't remember a time when he'd been more frustrated, more miserable—even when his mother left, at least he'd been able to find a silver lining—knowing that he still had his father and uncle, and that between the three of them they'd make it through.

Russ joined him aboard, and for the first time since they'd met, even Russ seemed at a loss. Their tanks were empty, and they simply couldn't drift in international waters forever. Still, none of them made a move, or even suggested that they should start back, despite the sun's low position in the sky.

James picked at the sandwich he'd set aside earlier, wishing he had an appetite, and Ryan stood to open the cooler, from which he withdrew a thick, square bottle. "Under any other circumstances, I would never consider offering you alcohol. As the one stable adult in your life, I feel obligated to point that out. But I can't let this opportunity pass, not knowing what tomorrow—or even tonight—will bring. So." He popped the cork out of the top and poured a small amount into three disposable cups, offering one each to James and Russ, and keeping one for himself.

James accepted, wanting to assure his uncle that under normal circumstances, he wouldn't accept such an offer. His mother's penchant for drink had forever destroyed any desire he might otherwise have developed for such things. But he couldn't speak, so he sniffed the contents, pleased when the scent alone sent searing heat up his nostrils. "What is it?"

"Tequila. The good stuff."

James put the cup to his lips, only to have Ryan stop him with a hand on his arm. "Whoa. Not yet. We need to toast to something. It's tradition."

"Who's tradition?" Russ asked.

Ryan's gaze focused far in the distance. "My sister's and mine."

The fondness in his voice reminded James of so many good moments with his mother. Times when they'd spent all day and half the night doing cartwheels on the beach, when she'd drained their grocery account to rent a convertible so they could see how fast it would go. He had so many vivid memories of her cliff-jumping and tree-climbing and sprinting up mountains just to feel the wind. Maybe his mother wasn't the type of person who could stand to be tied down. She'd spent years longing for freedom; sacrificed her youth to raise him. He'd accepted that he might never know her story, and it hurt like hell to not know *her* anymore. He hoped that his mother had managed to escape the ties that held her down, and in doing so, found the happiness she'd always longed for.

He stood. "A toast then. To family, love, and freedom. May we find all three someday."

He didn't wait to see if the others drank, or if they wanted to say anything more. He knocked back the liquor and let the fire burn his mouth, throat, and then his stomach, until the tightness in his chest began to ease. Once it had, Ryan refilled the cups, and they knocked back two more shots before recorking the bottle. Still in no hurry to turn James in, each found a comfortable spot to lounge in silence while they drifted, watching the waves curl up and crash against themselves.

An hour passed, then two. James' mind spun. He decided not to fight the inevitable, to go willingly and in peace, if for no other reason than to prove that he truly had nothing to hide—except his own fear.

Fear brought out the worst in people, the cynicism and anger. It caused individuals with loving, generous hearts to turn those hearts away, to harden their soft inner cores and become someone entirely different from their normal, everyday persona. No. He wouldn't let fear rule his life. When the authorities arrived to take him away, he would hold out his hands and obey. He would go quietly, not because there was no longer a reason to fight, but because if he had to fight, he needed to save his energy and use his focus to fight the right sources, the hardest battles—the court. Jail was inevitable. The question now was how long his stay there would last.

A large swell rocked the boat, splashing cool water on the feet James had hung over the edge, and out of the blue, Ryan belted out a tune James remembered from his youth—a song his mother had played over and over throughout his childhood, specifically before she left them for good. James sang along too.

*Fly, fly away,*

*The dream is not so far.*

*The moon calls your name, calls you home, no matter where you are.*

*Love is fleeting, youth fades fast like falling stars.*

*Love big, love strong, love true—there will never be another you.*

*When the moment comes, find someone who will love you too.*

*Even if that someone is only you.*

Russ blue-toothed his phone to the stereo, and the beloved song blared through the silence, triggering more memories. James cranked the volume, shouting the lyrics through the emotion rising in his chest. Hot tears burned his eyes, and for the first time since Emma left, he let them fall. Luckily, he didn't have to cry alone. His beloved uncle—and best friend—wrapped his arms around James, holding him the way he'd always wished his father would, the same way his mother had when he was young and hurt or scared. Through his uncle, he made peace with the mother he would never see again, and because he still had Ryan, was finally able to forgive the woman who gave him life.

The minute Ryan let go of James, Russ stepped in, encircling James in a new variety of comfort.

Secure in Russ's fatherly embrace, James understood that even while he was in jail, the search for Emma would not end. There was an entire team of people who loved her, and him, and who would do everything they could to protect them both. He didn't have to go through this hard thing all alone—not this time, or ever again.

He wiped his eyes and broke free, searching his bone-weary soul for valor, or at least courage, as the sun touched the water, threatening to steal what was left of the daylight. "I think I'm ready. I'm going to be okay. I can face this, and survive."

Ryan wiped moisture from his eyes and started the boat. James sat next to Russ, absorbing strength from the large, mountain of a man as they putted toward shore with the speed of a swimming turtle—toward the next hurdle in James' future.

Tuck closed his tavern before the tide change to prevent the late crowd from gathering, and as the market slowed and settled, he guided Emma through less populated paths that would take them past the edge of the city and the tiny cave where she'd camped the night before.

They'd gone far enough for Emma's nerves to ease, believing that they were about to leave the city without incident, when the merman from yesterday called out. "Princess Emmalina, Pimoe would like an audience with you. I shall bring you to the palace, now."

Emma froze. The command didn't sound like an invitation, and after learning more about him, she knew that Pimoe would be more likely to imprison her, than to help her. Tuck grabbed Emma's wrist and erupted with a burst of speed. Emma sped as well, hoping that together they could swim fast enough to discourage her pursuer, but this time, he was accompanied by at least a dozen mermen of varying degrees of intimidating muscle and speed—soldier variety.

With their pursuers close behind, Tuck dragged Emma toward the bottom, concealing them within a thick, waving crop of sea grass and kelp. Unwilling to slow their pace, they cut through the field, continually moving. Emma prayed that they were masked well enough to confuse the merman guards, who would eventually give up and go back to Oceania, until one seized her foot and dragged her into his arms. "Pimoe will see you now."

Emma's attention darted to Tuck and the mermen who also held him captive, refusing to go quietly. She kicked, punched, clawed, struggling to wriggle free. But her captor held firm, and the guards dragged the two of them back to the city. Emma's chest thundered, constricting as instinct begged her to breathe through her mouth rather than her gills. Something was happening. Something big enough to squeeze her chest and throat at once, as though a window of time was sliding closed. If she wanted to go home, she couldn't afford to waste another minute.

Energy sapped from lack of food and rest, she dug into her deepest places, heart and lungs and soul, the parts of her that still belonged to James, and to her family, and managed to unearth a single spark. She pulled it into her fingers, begging it to come alive. Light flashed, jolting both her and her captor with a current fierce enough to leave them both stunned. Emma slid from his grasp, tempted to leave Tuck behind and swim for shore before it was too late. But Tuck's eyes begged for help, and she'd forever regret deserting the merman who had willfully and generously given her the one thing she wanted most in all the sea—especially if it worked.

Tuck struggled with his own captors, already bloody and swollen from a battle well-fought. Determined to free Tuck, Emma pressed her electrified hand to her guard's back, the resulting jolt enough to smoke the tips of his long, black hair like they were on fire. She whirled on the remaining guards, prepared to strike them as well, but after seeing what she'd done to the first two, they released Tuck and whirled away, eyes wide with terror. Emma grabbed Tuck's wrist and bolted—again—out of the city and across the stretch of rocky terrain.

"What was that witchcraft?" Tuck glanced back at the city one last time.

"Not witchcraft." Emma didn't need to look back. From here on, her attention pointed forward—always forward. "It's the sting of Mer current. We're all capable of it. One of the Atlantian guards taught me to use mine. Does no one in Oceania do this?"

Tuck rolled so he could focus on Emma, continuing to swim at their present speed. "I have never seen a Mer with the power of fire."

"What do you know of fire?"

"Only that it is a cause of pain and destruction."

"And warmth." Soon, she would feel the sun on her skin again, and excitement had her grinning. "The sky is filled with fire. Did you know that? It's the source of all light."

"Fire in the sky," he murmured, rolling again to avoid hitting a reef. "I have heard such stories. This is something I long to see. To feel."

Emma lifted her face toward the surface, knowing that this would likely be her last swim—and she intended to make it count. "Stick with me, Tuck. Maybe we'll both get a shot at what we want."

They didn't stop to sleep, or even rest. Days had passed since she'd last eaten, leaving Emma running on salt water and adrenaline. Fatigue weighed her down, but with each passing breath, a noose of time closed more tightly around her neck. Though she knew nothing about what caused it, the sensation was not something she could ignore, so they persisted toward the arch. Emma planned to leave Tuck at the guardian post, where Merrick would eventually find him, and then continue to her cove. If the serum worked, she would have access to clothes she could wear until she got home. If it didn't work—if the damage in her lungs was too extensive, and she died—the cove was where she knew someone would find her.

Unfortunately, as with everything in Emma's life, those plans would have been too easy. A mile from the arch, and two miles above the tunnel to Atlantis, Emma and Tuck came face-to-face with representatives from Tangaroa's army.

Merrick called out. "Emmalina, you must return to the palace. We will be joined this night, and you will no longer have a need, or the means to flee. A mermaid cannot wander the sea alone forever."

*Of course he led the charge.* Wasn't he always the one to thwart her plans? "I'm not going back. Tell my grandfather I'm sorry. And Maia. Thank them for me, and let them know that I've found a way to return to shore, and I'm going to take it. I'm sorry to leave you this way."

Darts of electricity shot from Merrick's hands, hitting random targets—innocent fish and coral and plants. "You will not reach the surface, and you will not return to land. If you do not come peacefully, I will be forced to lock you in the dungeon until you bring forth a youngling."

Her stomach dropped. He had never threatened to imprison and then impregnate her. This was the dark side of Merrick that she knew existed, but hadn't seen for quite a while. "I said no, Merrick. You and your army can try to stop me, and you might succeed, but I won't let you keep me there."

She dug her hand into the fold of her pack, feeling around for the clam, and when she found it, closed it inside her fist. Tuck's eyebrows raised in question, and she nodded. "I still intend to fight, but I don't want you to pay the price for my choice. Let them take me. When I'm in distress, tell them about the serum, and then find a way to bring me to the surface."

"Where is the surface?" Tuck twisted one way, then the other as if he might find the surface the way he would find a plant.

Emma pointed upward. "There."

"But the tide—"

She shook her head, continuing to point up. "Always there. No tide or current will change the location of the sky. Up. Always up. You will be able to see the shore once we reach the air."

He seemed skeptical, but agreed, reluctantly. "I will do as you ask, because this is your wish, as it was Maui's, and I will honor you as I did him. Besides, I wish to touch the sky, see the fire as payment for the serum."

The current shifted, reminding Emma how quickly the time passed. "The fire is dying. We must be quick."

As the army circled, Merrick shouted again. "Emmalina, you cannot return to land and live. If you go with me to the palace now, I will ask the Sea King to be lenient in his punishment, and perhaps you will be allowed visitors in the dungeon."

Oh joy. Like any Mer in the city would even *want* to visit her. "I'm sorry," she shouted. "I can't." With that, Emma bolted up, up, up, swimming for shore like a car on a racetrack, desperate to pass the finish line ahead of ten others. Tuck followed, slower than he'd proven capable of, so that the mermen reached him first. They jerked him into submission and stunned him immobile, then continued after Emma. Merrick, always the fastest of the fast, caught her first, pinning her ankles as she fought to be free. Another merman joined Merrick, then another. They held her arms and feet and waist, and when she had no fight left, she went limp. "Merrick." She allowed her broken heart to bleed through her voice. "Please let me go. Please. I'll die if you force me to stay."

Merrick didn't loosen his hold. "A Sea King must have a mate."

Emma only needed the guards to free one of her arms enough so she could swallow the serum. "Maia loves you, and I know you feel for her, too. You should court her, Merrick. Join with her. A union between you would bring you both happiness."

"I am not betrothed to Maia." Merrick dragged her to face him, releasing her ankles so another guard could take over. "I am betrothed to you. We will not play this game anymore."

"It's not a game. Merrick, don't you see? Maia wants to stay in Atlantis, and she wants to be with you. The two of you make a great match. And you share the royal bloodline of Poseidon, so whether I stay or leave, you still inherit the throne. I don't want to be here, and I don't want to be with you. Don't you see that this is the only way we can both be happy?"

A murmur of confusion traveled among Emma's captors, and one loosened his hold, allowing Emma to slip her hand free and open the clam, releasing a deep purple gel into her mouth. The gel scorched down her throat and into her chest, causing her insides to shift. Cold seeped into her skin, her bones, wracking her with violent shivers, while the saltwater burned her eyes like fire.

At their current depth, pressure squeezed tight, intensifying until her bones threatened to break, the pain so great that Emma shrieked from the torture.

Merrick caught her as she flailed, eyes wild with fear. "What is happening?"

She tried to respond, to speak, but her voice didn't work, and no water would filter into her gills. With every second, the weight on Emma's chest multiplied. She had to get to the surface soon enough to breathe air, or this experiment would be for nothing.

Tuck yelled to Merrick, "She is drowning. We must get her to the surface."

Merrick's grip on Emma tightened. "Emmalina is not permitted to visit the surface. As ordered by the Sea King."

Through the spots blinking in her vision, and the hazy film of the water, Emma managed to find Tuck. He'd been released and, as promised, urged Merrick to listen to reason. "If we do not bring her to air, she will die. Emmalina has swallowed the venom of a blue-ringed octopus, which will close her gills and repair her human lungs. She does not have much time."

Still, Merrick held on, refusing to let go of his prize. "Who are you?"

"I am Tuck," he said. "Servant and friend to Maui, the young Sea King of Oceania."

The water stirred, flowing past her skin as if she were swimming, though Emma had lost control of her body. Even her senses dulled, leaving the ocean dark, quiet, and confusing.

"Maui no longer rules Oceania." Merrick's voice sounded distant and tinny. "He has left the Mer, and Oceania, to live ashore as a human."

"Correct." Tuck agreed. "And Emmalina shall follow in the same manner." A gentle hand grasped her elbow, and the flow of water passing her skin became a torrent as they rose toward the surface. Pops of air snapped in her ears, sending jolts of pain through her head and into her feet. Emma screeched again, her brain muddled as memories of her life—both in Oceanside and in Atlantis—flipped through her mind like a death reel.

"This is not possible," Merrick said, his voice resigned with sadness. "Tangaroa destroyed the venom harvested by Maui. It is forbidden in both cities."

Tuck laughed, creating a storm of bubbles. "Tangaroa destroyed Paihana made from the venom. He did not destroy the serum of He'e, of which I have been the guardian since before Maui left Oceania."

With Tuck's words, everything made sense. Maui wasn't just a progressive. He was a scientist, who used himself as a guinea pig. This last version of the serum must have worked, because Maui had left the sea and never returned. The numbness in her throat and gills spread until even her brain felt stuck. Her vision dimmed. They weren't going to make it. She tried to squeeze Merrick's hand, then Tuck's, but couldn't feel or move her fingers, even to offer a form of thanks as she lost consciousness.

# Chapter Thirty-Four

## James

THE WIND BUFFETED JAMES' FACE as he stood at the bow of his beloved boat. Ryan had engaged the throttle, but only enough to push them toward the distant shoreline at the pace of a snail. Russ's playlist continued to sing through the speakers; a small comfort.

Russ offered James the discarded sandwich from earlier. "You should eat this. And drink as much water as you can. It won't help for you to show up drunk when they come to take us all away."

James accepted the sandwich, but didn't eat. "All of us? You think they'll take you and Ryan, too?"

"Harboring a fugitive. Won't last long, but tonight, I'm certain we'll all end up in the pokey."

Russ's joking tone did nothing to console James, whose mood darkened with every minute that brought him closer to the inevitable. Sick with dread, James turned his back to the shoreline. "I'm sorry. I didn't mean to drag you into this. I should have left your family alone."

The hand Russ had left on James' shoulder squeezed in comfort. "Don't apologize. We're all glad we got to know you. Even if our support complicates things, my family is invested in your defense. We're here for you, and I'm glad to be able to tell you that."

"Thank you. That means a lot to me." Still too queasy to eat, James turned to toss the sandwich into the water, freezing in place when a distant shimmer caught his eye. He dropped the sandwich at his feet, squinting at a white spot in the blue, blue water, more than a football field away. When the spot moved, but didn't disappear, James' shoulders tightened. "Stop the boat. Ryan, can you stop for a minute? Stop the boat."

Ryan slowed, but didn't stop. "We're running out of daylight. Can't put this off forever."

Ignoring his uncle, James dug into Russ's supply box for the binoculars he'd seen a few days earlier. "I'm serious. Stop the boat. Just stop."

By the time Ryan cut the engine, Russ had joined James, watching the moving spot in disbelief. "There's something out there."

"It's not her." James told himself, but his hands shook as he twisted the focus, trying to get a better view. "It's probably not her." He adjusted the eye pieces, but his hands shook, vision blurry with nerves and tequila. He passed the binoculars to Russ. "These are broken."

Russ held them to his eyes, muttering as he adjusted the focus and attempted to locate the right place. "To be honest, I've never seen my daughter swim in the ocean. How would we know the difference between a mermaid and, say, a dolphin?"

"Silver, white, and blue." James had seen Emma swim, and Merrick, too. He even had a vivid memory of the army that had taken her away. "Like a fish, except for the red hair. Emma has the most unusual hair. Lighter than red coral, deeper than the cherry red paint on her car." Maybe she wasn't the same as he remembered. Maybe Atlantis had changed her, but no matter how she'd transformed, he would know her, and love her every bit as much as he had when she left.

Russ let the binoculars fall to his side and appropriated the water bottle out of James' hand, draining it in one gulp. He tossed the bottle on the floor and raised the binoculars to his eyes again. "Don't get your hopes up," he said, a hint of excitement in his voice. "But whatever we're looking at doesn't have a dorsal fin. It's not a shark or dolphin, and it's too small to be a whale, even a calf. It kind of moves like an octopus, only . . . not. We should get closer."

Ryan had joined them at the starboard side, squinting at the white patch before he cast his gaze to the sky and the full moon, rising as quickly as the sun was setting. "We haven't tested the lights on this craft, but I did see a couple of flashlights in the emergency kit. We might be able to make it."

For once, James felt confident in calling the shots. "Do it. I have nothing to lose." He continued to study the splotch, surrounded with deep, deep blue, his pulse pounding. "If we don't go, I'll always wonder."

They kept the speed slow and cut the music, none of them willing to scare the creature—whatever it was—it was into dipping below again. As they approached, James' pulse roared with a last, thin thread of hope. And then he saw it. A tangled mass of three, and though it was darker, slicked down, and hard to see—Emma's red, red hair.

"Holy shit. It's her." He seized a life jacket—not for himself, but because for some reason, the jumble of people appeared to be struggling—and dove into the water, before Ryan had time to cut the engine. "Emma," he yelled. "Emma, I'm here. Emma!"

Every ounce of strength he'd built in years of playing basketball, in the hours spent hauling tile and grout, in the days spent swimming for miles and miles against current and tides and rough seas, searching for his love, now went into crossing that last stretch of space between them. Merrick and the other merman pushed her along, carrying her to him, which made no sense. It took everything he had to not seize with panic. Something was wrong.

"Emma," he croaked, but she didn't open her eyes, didn't stir. He pinned Merrick with a sharp stare. "What's wrong with her? What's happened?"

Merrick held tight to Emma's waist. "She has swallowed the venom of the blue-ringed octopus. Her gills are sealed and she cannot breathe until her human lungs inflate."

"Venom? Isn't that dangerous?" James handed the life vest to the second merman, who seemed obsessed with watching the sun complete its descent. "Put this on her. It will help keep her afloat."

The merman accepted the vest, but appeared more confused by it than anything, so he handed it off to Merrick, who slid Emma's arms into each of the holes, and snapped it across her chest. "Many Mer have attempted to make a transformation in this way. Most died before reaching shore."

Gaining another reason to fear, James opened his arms, urging Merrick to let him take her. "I'll make sure she gets there. Has she breathed at all?"

Regret etched in every line on his face, Merrick floated Emma into James' arms. "Not much. The venom has paralyzed her. She needs a healer—a human one. Quickly."

"I'll get her there." Once he had her in his grip, James refused to let go, aiming for his boat at record speeds—even for him.

"Human," Merrick called. "She must not return to the sea. Not in the way of the Mer."

"Got it," James didn't stop, towing, swimming with everything he had.

Ryan started the boat and cut the distance faster than James could swim, and Russ reached over the edge to lift Emma into the craft. Once Emma was safely aboard with her father, James climbed the ladder, stopping halfway up to. "Merrick? Thank you. I know you planned to marry her. This must have been hard to do. I promise I'll take care of her."

Merrick whooshed closer, reminding James how incredibly fast mermen could move. "We were never joined. Emmalina was not meant to be confined within walls, especially those of Atlantis. I understand this now."

James climbed aboard, knowing they needed to get Emma to a hospital immediately. "I know I can never repay you for bringing her home, but if you ever need anything—you know, like clothes—" They both laughed. "Leave word at the cove. I'm sure we'll visit from time to time."

"I will not return." Merrick stared at the sun as if he might never see it again. "I must learn to rule. It is time for a new Guardian of the Gate."

Russ stripped off Emma's life jacket and started CPR, and Ryan thrust the throttle forward. James sent one last wave to the mermen who'd brought his Emma back, and then fell to his knees on the floor of the boat, taking over the mouth-to-mouth, while Russ handled chest compressions. When he was finally able to feel a shallow, barely perceptible breath, he continued his task, but allowed a joyful tear to fall. Whatever else came next, he had Emma in his arms again, and that was worth everything that came before. Everything.

# Chapter Thirty-Five

## Emma

**April 19**
*Found*

THE WORLD SPUN IN CRAZY, fast circles as Emma opened her eyes to a view of the gray sky, dotted with blinking stars. Her breath hitched, shallow and almost worthless in her chest—almost. Spasms of pain rocked her body from even the slightest movement, including the effort required to pull air into her repairing lungs. She wasn't aware that she'd whimpered, but the arms around her tightened as the world shifted and moved.

Air, dry and stinging, assaulted her skin, leaving it parched and raw, and while water drained from both of her ears, she could only hear out of one, all sound either amplified or muted, depending on the source and pitch. Stars whizzed by in a blur of white light, and then a face, familiar and beloved, entered her line of vision. She recognized that face, those eyes, the strong jaw and the tiny scar near his hairline. "James," she croaked, though the sound came out weak and otherworldly.

James stroked her cheek, cradling her on his lap. "Shh. Don't try to talk. You're going to be okay. We're almost to shore, and we'll get you to a hospital." The arms around her squeezed tighter. Every part of her tingled—she still couldn't feel her fingers or her toes, and several other random sections of skin. It was as if she'd been cryogenically frozen, and was in the process of thawing out. They'd covered her with something—a towel or blanket—but it didn't help the chill that came from deep inside her. "So cold."

She wanted to return his loving embrace, to kiss him and tell him everything she'd done to come back to him, but the only thing she could manage was a violent shiver. James exchanged words with someone else, and her father appeared, arms full of towels and emergency blankets, which he piled on and tucked around Emma's freezing, exposed skin. She wanted to talk to him, thank him, tell him how badly she'd missed him and her mother and Keith and Gran—but she could only manage an inhuman croak, reminiscent of the call of a whale, or the chatter of a pod of dolphins. None of this made sense, so she closed her eyes and relaxed into James, relieved that at least she'd succeeded in seeing these two most important people in her life.

At least if the venom killed her, she would have these last moments with them. They would be the last faces she saw.

Since she couldn't speak, James filled the silence with words that seemed—to Emma—distant, and shy in a way he'd never been before. "Are you comfortable? Can I get you anything? I'm sorry you hurt so bad. I promise the worst will be over soon, and then you'll get to see the rest of your family."

She had no way to respond, but found she could move her pinky, so she hooked it with his. From the look on his face, it was enough. Eventually, the boat slowed to a wakeless pace, which meant they had entered the harbor and were near docking. The stars faded, blocked by bright lights—red, blue, white. She closed her eyes, dreading the part where they had to deal with people. Aside from seeing her loved ones, the thing she wanted most was a soft bed to sleep in and some cooked food.

As the motor's roar dulled to a hum, radios and voices exploded, a cacophony of noise that assaulted her sensitive working ear, and caused her deaf one to throb with the pain of water pushing against her ear drum. Overwhelmed after living so long in the quiet of water, she burrowed into James, who stood, carrying her in his arms.

The moment they stepped onto solid ground, the world fell still with the absence of current and tide, the constant flow of water against her skin. For a sad moment, she mourned the loss of the life she'd given up. As badly as she'd wanted to return to this, she would miss her connection with the sea something fierce.

James tucked her face into his neck, and she smelled the remains of the oh-so-familiar cologne clinging to his skin, mingling with salt water, remembering that she'd come home. She nestled in until hands grabbed at her, asking questions, demanding answers, angry, angry voices. Drained, she croaked, "Please stop."

More murmuring, shouting and movement, but James held on, and she snuggled into her safe space, refusing to let go. He moved with her, sliding into the back of a police car, and settling her on his lap. "I'm so sorry, baby. I can't take you home yet, because you need to see a doctor. We have to go to the hospital, okay?"

She'd never been to a hospital before, and that was a lucky thing, because any tests they ran would likely come back abnormal and potentially cause problems for her mermaid self. She gripped a handful of James' shirt and steeled herself for the inevitable. At least they couldn't force her to demonstrate her skills, the way she had for James. As far as she knew, she was no longer a mermaid.

At the hospital, James laid her on a gurney, but she held tight to his hand, refusing to let go. Her father flanked her other side, and she clutched his hand, too. These men were everything to her, and she had no intention of letting either go, ever again.

# Chapter Thirty-Six

## James

THE POLICE HAD LOAD OF questions. Where had Emma been all this time, and how did they find her? Was she a victim of kidnapping—or worse? And most puzzling—to them—how had she managed to survive, alone in the sea for so long? James had no answers, and because the staff rushed her directly to the ICU, it was easy to tell them that he wouldn't know anything until she could speak again.

The doctors put her on oxygen, filled her with IV antibiotics, and covered her in warming blankets to treat her for hypothermia and a severe case of pneumonia. Then they determined that she'd been stung by a poisonous creature, and treated her for that as well.

Ryan had stayed behind to tie off and clean up the boat, and James hoped his uncle got rid of any alcohol bottles or remains, because he was certain that the police would search the craft as soon as they got a warrant. Bringing Emma back wouldn't clear his name completely—but he was no longer a suspect in a murder investigation, and now that she was here, he had nothing left to hide. Or, at least, nothing serious that anyone could prove. He doubted that anyone was accuse his girlfriend of being a mermaid—life wasn't like the movies.

He couldn't take his eyes off her.

While she was gone, he'd felt like a hole had broken open in his soul, and now that hole filled again, expanding with happiness. Refusing to leave her side, James kept vigil from the recliner next to her bed, watching her sleep and sending up prayers of thanks to the gods who had allowed her to come home.

Emma continued to improve by the hour, and once she was released to go home, James predicted that the two of them might get their happy ending after all.

Emma gave a statement to police, and she kept it so simple that James decided she was genius. Four officers camped in folding chairs around the foot of her bed, and Emma, white-blue skin and purple-tipped hair, frail, sick, coughing, croaky Emma, relayed a story that, while mysterious, made perfect sense to all.

"I went swimming to save my brother," she croaked, and James handed her a cup of water. "Just as I got him to shore, a current carried me out again, and I wasn't strong enough to swim back. I tried. I gave it everything, but I just kept going further and further out to sea. A driftwood log popped up next to me, so I grabbed onto it to stay afloat, and then I passed out. The next thing I remember is waking up on the boat with James and my father."

Once the news scouts got their hands on the police report, journalists swarmed the hospital, setting up equipment in the lobby, and then the parking lot, after security kicked them out. The story of the missing girl who survived two months in the sea ran during prime-time, making national headlines. It seemed like half the state of California stopped in to visit, but the ICU kept tight security, for which everyone was grateful—especially the hospital staff. They did allow Russ, Cindy, Keith, and Mona to visit. The whole family cried happy tears, and between them and James, they worked out a schedule so that no matter what day or time, or how long she had to stay, Emma would never be alone in this strange, sterile place.

Emma's room filled with flowers, balloons and get well cards—many of them from people she'd never met. Apparently, this type of survival story garnered a lot more sympathy than the one about her and Tom. James spent his shifts—which were lengthier and more often than anyone else's—catching her up on everything that had happened since she left. He couldn't stop touching her, holding her hand, kissing her arms, her wrists, her neck. On her sixth day in the hospital, with an oxygen tube in her nose, Emma finally found the breath and the will to talk about what happened to her.

She told James about Maia, and Laine, finding the room filled with treasure, and how she was locked in the dungeon. She told him about freeing the captive dolphin, and escaping to Oceania, where she'd been swindled by a sea witch, and then met Tuck, who gave her the serum for the price of seeing fire. "I could have paid him. I had treasure in my pack . . ." She paused, memory hitting her. "I had treasure. Did you take a pack off my back when you brought me into the boat?"

James froze, stunned. "Your dad might have. I was busy giving you mouth-to-mouth, so I wasn't paying attention to that part."

"It had jewelry in it—expensive stuff."

He fought a momentary bout of panic. "I hope the police didn't find it. That's all I need." He took out his phone and called Ryan.

His uncle told him, "Oh, yeah. There's a gooey bundle stuck to the life jacket. I brought it home to clean it, but haven't gotten to it yet."

James relayed the message to Emma, and then instructed Ryan to hide that jacket somewhere safe until Emma was released—and then they made plans to open the bundle together.

Lastly, she explained about Merrick. "I didn't marry him. But I would have been forced to if I hadn't found the venom. This was the only way."

James put a finger to her lips, partly to silence her explanation, and partly because he'd been dying to touch them for months. "It wouldn't matter to me if you had. You're here now, and my world is right again. Everything about everything is a hundred times better than it was a week ago."

She coughed—something doctors warned her might linger for quite some time—and, grinning, grabbed the front of his shirt dragging him toward her. "Then why haven't you kissed me yet?"

"I have." He pressed a kiss to the back of her hand. "I've kissed you here," and her wrist, "and here," her inner elbow, "and here." Then he moved to her neck and kissed along her collarbone. "And all over here."

"You haven't kissed my mouth," she reminded him. "And I really, really need you to."

He scooted onto the edge of her bed and took her in his arms, touching his lips to hers with gentle sweetness, trying so hard to be careful, until she hooked her arm around his neck and pulled him across her body, taking the kiss deeper, and proving to him how very much she'd missed him. When she let up to fight for breath, he kept his eyes locked on hers. If he were to die in an hour, his life would have been full and rich, all because he loved Emma. And then she brought him to her again, her lips and hands and body demanding things he'd dreamed about, longed for, been desperate to have in the time that she'd been gone.

James ended the kiss, eager to catch a breath of his own. "Emma, I love you so much. While you were gone, my life was empty. I was about to lose everything. Having you back now—it's a miracle. I keep expecting to wake up and discover that this whole thing was a dream."

She pressed a kiss behind his ear, causing him to shudder as other parts of him reacted in all the right ways. She intoxicated him, through and through. "It's no dream," she murmured. "I'm here, and I'm staying for good."

He relaxed against the raised mattress and pulled her into his arms, kissing the top of her head, determined to slow things down—she was still on oxygen, after all. "Guess that means it's time to plan what comes next, huh?"

She nuzzled his neck. "Yes. I'm anxious to move on, as long as it's with you."

He sighed, closing his eyes in contentment. "Baby, like I told you that night in the cove. I'm not going anywhere. I'm in this for the long haul."

She draped her arm across his chest, reminding him of the first time they'd spent the night together, and reinforcing the relief of knowing that the worst of all the things he'd dreaded were now over.

"Good," she said, her voice sleepy and soft. "Because you're stuck with me. I'm never letting you go again."

He kissed the tip of her ear, the bone on her cheek, her temple, her hair. "Neither am I, my mermaid Princess. Neither am I."

# Epilogue

Emma watched from the stands while James shot his fourth free-throw of the night. Every time he did something good, she surveyed the coaches' reactions. If all went well today, James would be looking at a scholarship for at least one of the colleges on his preferred list—possibly more.

It had been a shot in the dark for him to approach these coaches after graduation, especially since most of them had already recruited their teams, but a few had heard of the Oceanside Pirates star player who had missed the playoffs due to an unexplained illness, and they'd come to see what he could do.

She fiddled with her shiny gold ring, pressing her finger against the pearls she'd once left for James, and the two small diamonds he'd added, insisting that her engagement ring had to be as unique as her. With *this* engagement, she had no fear, no questions—only excitement for what lay ahead for the two of them.

Keith joined her in the stands, fumbling with the drinks she'd sent him to get from the vending machine. "Is James winning?" he asked. "I hope he wins."

She popped the top of the can, relishing the sugary taste, and the way the liquid bubbled as it ran down her throat. "Me too. We want to stay close to you, but even if we're a few hours away, we'll come visit all the time, okay?"

"Yeah, okay." Keith sipped his own drink, and Emma was grateful to see that the haunted look that plagued him in her first few weeks home had now faded. "When you and James get married, can I come live with you?"

Emma draped her arm around her brother's shoulders, surprised—once again—at how much he'd grown during her short time away. "Maybe someday. And always when Mom and Dad have to go out of town."

"I want my own room," he said. "Or I could share with James, because we're both boys."

Emma suppressed a giggle. Her brother was so innocent. "I'm pretty sure James is going to keep sharing my room, even when we move. But we'll see about getting one for you, okay?"

"Yeah, okay I guess. Don't know why he would want to share with a girl."

She patted his arm, hugging her brother closer. "I don't know either, buddy. Maybe it's because he likes me."

He turned to face her, his expression a mask of seriousness. "He loves you, Emma. That's why he saved you."

"I know." Her eyes traveled to her fiancé as he outplayed the majority of the established teams—both of them. "And I'm the luckiest girl in the world, because of it."

## *About Nichole Giles*

NICHOLE GILES, author of the *Descendant* trilogy, and the *Water So Deep* series, has lived in Nevada, Arizona, Utah, and Texas. She is a fan of all things paranormal and magical, and her dreams include raising a garden full of fairies, riding a unicorn, and taming the pet dragon she adopted at a recent local ComicCon. She loves to spend time with her husband and four grown children, travel to tropical and exotic destinations, drive with her convertible top down—even when it rains— and play music at full volume so she can sing along.

# *Acknowledgements*

I can't believe this series is complete. It's been almost a decade since I first started writing *Water So Deep*, and I had no idea the journey this story would lead me on. It's been a fantastic adventure!

As with all adventures, I've been lucky to have some very important people holding my hand. My husband, Gary, has stuck by and supported me on all the days and nights (and more days and more nights) that I was sure this book would break my brain. This was by far my hardest project to date, and he was incredibly patient, and even offered me some serious incentives to push through. I couldn't ask for a better accountability partner. My children, Brayden, Brittany (Trey), Madison (Richie), have cheered me on in the best possible way, and Mckay, who still lives at home, and has gone on countless drink runs, grocery store trips, and a whole lot of other errands that needed doing so that I could finish this book. I couldn't have done it without these seven incredible people in my life.

My parents Deanne and Steve, Joe and Pam, and all my crazy awesome siblings, Ryan, Matt (Nichole), James, Jodi (Nick), Chandi, Zack, Cameron, Justin, Daeton, and Troy (Anna). Can't forget to mention my in-law siblings, Craig (Keeley), Jalayne (Mike), Jennifer

(Rick), and JoAnna, as well as the late Kay and Carol Giles, who we all miss terribly. This has been a year when I really needed all of you, and you all came through. Thank you so much for being mine.

As if the lists above aren't enough, I also have some incredible support from people who are not related to me. Michelle Argyle has pulled through in so many ways to help me out this year. I seriously couldn't have gotten through it without her support on all levels. Heather Justesen is always willing to lend a hand, and then teach me how to do things myself. Tristi Pinkston has taught me more about editing than I could have learned on my own. Jaclyn Weist has offered marketing support, silly ComicCon pictures, and all around friendship, and the late Keith Fisher has continued to cheer me on from his place in heaven. Erin Summerill has always been a light during dark times, as has Brekke Felt, a flag of friendship, flying high and silent, and who also has mad graphic art skills. Elana Johnson has been a huge support and is in large part a reason for my success, as is Jenn Johansson, who brings brightness and color everywhere she goes. Julia McCracken has a ridiculous knowledge of—well everything—but especially marketing and food. Thanks for making sure I always eat well, wherever I am in the world!

I haven't mentioned them before, but my friends of the BWB are always good for comic relief, for rallying when I have a panel or reading, and for just the most incredible sense of belonging in a crowd of crazy intelligent nerds. I adore you all! My friends at Authors Incognito (now renamed Storymakers Tribe) and the LDStorymakers—what can I say? You've been there since day one, the very earliest stages of my writing journey, and you're still here for me now. I am so crazy lucky to have been a part of something so special. Shout out to all my Blue-Line Sisters, wherever you are in the world, but especially in the city of Orem. You are all tough as nails, strong as leather, and soft as bamboo. I'm lucky to be one of you.

Readers, this series would not exist if not for you. Thank you for your loyalty, support, and friendship. I love you all!